# Good Guys Finish Last

## By
## Laurence F. Cook

Copyright © 2008 by Laurence F. Cook

ISBN 0-7414-4574-3

*Published by:*

**INFIN(∞)ITY**
PUBLISHING.COM

*1094 New DeHaven Street, Suite 100*
*West Conshohocken, PA 19428-2713*
*Info@buybooksontheweb.com*
*www.buybooksontheweb.com*
*Toll-free (877) BUY BOOK*
*Local Phone (610) 941-9999*
*Fax (610) 941-9959*

*Printed in the United States of America*

*Printed on Recycled Paper*

*Published December 2008*

# Table of Chapters

# Chapter 1

## *In Passing*

"It's time for a change in life, don't you think?" asked Simone.

Rodney responds, "Sure it's time for change, but change to what?" Is something happening you haven't told me?"

"No," Simone replies. "Just thinking of these internal feelings and how they battle with the now and what should have been."

"Simone, you are going through a challenging time and I wish you would make up your mind on what it is you want. I find myself always taking sides to your 'what if or the now' just to keep you happy with who you are."

Just a few years earlier, Simone landed a great job, finished her graduate studies, and relocated to her home city. Her thoughts were quite content with recent accomplishments. Her fascination with Rodney began years earlier as they met in a swank art store, debating over an art piece that may become one to own, and agreed to disagree. Simone was dressed in the office casual style, gallantly done with simplest treasures. The black pants suit loosely fitted her body hiding the true curves. Her hair was styled to project the professional image flowing downward towards her shoulders. Her bangs curled to the left, barely covering her eye. Simone wore her, as she calls, lucky perfume. It was just enough to give a refreshing odor to a passer by. She has this energy about her that lifts every room once entered. It was as if a whiff of confidence preceded her entry into every chamber. Just a glimpse of her brought many smiles of envy or comfort. She could work a room just with her eyes, smiles, and conversation. Her walk was simple and elegant, as if she took ballet lessons for most of her life.

Rodney saw her enter the gallery. His first glimpse sparked an immediate "oooh my" expression and he mouthed such words. He stood across the store and observed every move of Simone. Smiling with implicit thoughts of meeting her, Rodney maneuvered into the gallery to position himself for a quick interaction. It's a good thing he came into the gallery after work to avoid traffic. Amazingly, he'd rather wait the rush than to take part of it. This day he broke his normal routine and attended the gym during the morning hours. He'd go to the gym during rush hour; it's a better use of time instead of fighting the stress of traffic. No plans for the evening, so there was time to enjoy anything he wanted to do. This day, Rodney wore his casual business attire, quite the classy guy, always dressed for appearance sakes. He stayed abreast of latest fashions without going over board. This day he wore a shirt jacket, a crew neck nylon/silk shirt, with pleated slacks. His shoes were immaculate, stylish, and clean, but not the real expensive type, just quite nice looking, especially matching the outfit he wore. You could tell he took great care in himself. He is a clean-cut type of guy, well manicured, and takes great care in his manly appearance.

The gallery is an old brown stone building used as side store in the middle of a city block, located in the center of the town's revitalization. Since it's on the first block of revitalization, there isn't much support for crowds, parking, or traffic for that matter. Once entering the gallery, the paintings starts from the immediate right and flows from eye level to the open ceiling with pictures of all sizes and shapes. Every picture was hung with such light, accenting the vision of the viewers. The gallery staff was the exceptional. No quarrels about delivery, quite responsive to customer inquiry, and always offered a positive and enjoyable environment. Their focus was a true reflection of the owner.

Rodney stepped lightly as he wandered throughout the gallery. He would periodically glance up to see if Simone would move in his direction. Simone unknowingly did the same without acknowledging her intent to meet Rodney. Simone moved to her left while observing a particular painting, finding herself standing next to Rodney.

"The painting is so colorful and full of life. It's as if the artist wanted us to change our moods from dreary to excitement, said Simone in a soft undertone."

It was as if she spoke loud enough for Rodney to hear as he moved closer to the painting. "Yes, it is quite colorful and full of energy. It's like a bright moon on a dark night giving life to whatever the light touches," he responded.

Simone takes a quick breath as she starts blushing; happy for his response even though it wasn't intended for him to hear, she quickly thinks of another point to make. She glanced to her side and took a good look at Rodney. "My, he is absolutely a handsome man," she utters in thought. "He is better looking close up than in a distance. Oh and he smells great. I love that cologne he's wearing."

"Oh, did you hear me? I didn't think I was talking that loud." Admitted Simone

"Hi, allow me to introduce myself in case I hear something more" said Rodney. He smiles and extends his right hand as a proper custom of introduction. She extends her right hand and smiles as he takes it.

"I am Rodney Witherspoon and it's my pleasure to meet such a lovely art connoisseur."

"Thank you kindly for the compliment, but I wouldn't say I am a connoisseur of art. I enjoy interpreting what the artist had in mind for us. I'm Simone and its nice meeting you" said Simone."

"Well at least you're here for enjoyment, do you come here often?" He inquires "That sounds like a horrible pick up line" he acknowledges and laughs.

"No, not often, I come from in time-to-time and see if there's something eye catching and maybe gasp at some of the prices she comments with a giggle. And it helps me relax after a day at the office. It helps me escape fighting traffic."

"Oh yes, you too. Traffic is terrible during this time of day. Like you this is somewhat a cycled event. Its funny we haven't met earlier during the year."

"I come in but not that often. So I understand how we would miss one another."

Simone starts moving left looking at other paintings and sculptures. She slowly steps away and subconsciously waits for Rodney's movement. Inviting as she wants to be, but reserved to quick encouragement, she turns to him and says, "Well, its nice meeting you Rodney" as she walks to the next painting.

Rodney replies, "Again, the pleasure is mine and I hope we see each other again really soon." "Did I say this out of being polite or am I serious?" he wonders to himself. "Man I hope we do run into each other. It would be nice to see her again. She is fine and I bet just as intelligent. There's nothing greater than having dinner and wine with a woman who can hold her own. She seems to be the perfect candidate, unlike some of the others I seem to run into. Should I move in for a number so I can follow up? It would be a nice gesture to ask her out."

"Well, didn't you say your name is Simone?"

"Yes I did."

"Simone, again it's lovely to meet you and I do hope we run into each other again."

"So do I Rodney."

"Great, then please take my card and feel free to contact me." With a gentlemanly bow he presents his card and excuses himself; he walks away from her to another section of the store, signals her to call him and waves with a smile.

Simone turns to another painting near the ceiling. The colors weren't as vivid, but with the right lighting, she sees something that has promise for her office. Looking for the custodian, she glances about the room and capture's Rodney's stance. For a second time she sees the physical attributes of this man. "How well dressed and in such great shape. I suppose he is dedicated to being self-centered. The last guy I dated with a great shape and good taste in attire was so into himself that he didn't have room for me. I guess that's a sign to not call him."

At the art gallery, Simone makes a purchase spending quite more than expected. "The painting is great and I hope this helps my office aura: it's so stuffy and needs something. I hope this picture serves as a focal piece for all who enter, and encourage some type of reaction. Hell, I need the painting for myself to spark another venture for the business." Simone takes the painting to the car and struggles to place it in the trunk. She maneuvers things and eventually finds success.

Walking to his car, Rodney sees Simone struggling with a package trying to place it in her trunk. Just as he walks her direction, she closes the trunk, enters the car, starts the engine, and drives off. Rodney observes her leaving the parking lot. He exclaims to himself, "what a nice car, a really nice car. Man this woman seems to be classy or high maintenance." He turns back to his original path and finds his vehicle. After starting the engine, he thinks of her driving away. "What a nice woman she is and how fortunate I am meeting her today."

Simone driving with thoughts over and over again, wondering if Rodney is worth seeing another time, "I know he seems like the type of man I would like in my life. I wish we'd have an opportunity to interact, especially a date. Maybe I should call him later...No, it would be too aggressive or way too soon. Maybe he would think I'm over confident or just too modern."

Three hours pass for Rodney and multiple thoughts of Simone runs rampant. For some reason, he cannot get her off of his mind. "I guess her impression has me at wits end. I have never been so intrigued with such little interaction. I didn't get her number or get any means of contacting her. If our paths should ever cross again or maybe I get a call from her, I'll be ready to grasp the rollercoaster of change," he admits to himself.

"Another morning from an interesting night, there's nothing like heading out for a morning run. It's the middle of spring and the weather embraces you with a comfort of cool warmth. This day is a perfect gift from God. He has blessed us with another beautiful day. Thank you lord," prays Rodney.

Rodney ties his shoelace and heads for the door. He looks left into the mirror and psyches himself before walking down stairs. It's a routine he does before running three miles. "It's going to be an easy run. I'm going to feel great." Opening the door, he notices how the street is silent. He looks at his watch and realizes he's out quite early. Stepping down the stairs, he looks ahead to his routine course, starts his warm-up, stretching the muscles, and feels slight pain. "I am not getting younger and need this for my health. The last thing I need is an injury. I have to make it all the way." he admits.

Running on the street he observes the awakening population. Every step on the course, he notices something different. From trees to the animals, from cars to planes, and then the people coming out of their homes, he notices the increase in movement. He occasionally speaks to passers by while maintaining his pace. He passes one street, which seems so dead, for some reason he stops and looks down the street. He notices a person laying on the walkway. Probably some homeless person, but I better check it out.

Running to the body, he sees the person dressed quite well, at least a lot warmer than for the weather. "It must be a homeless person for sure" he thought. Closer he realizes it's an older woman, about in her late 70's or early 80's. He stops and bend over to check see if she's ok. He touches her lightly. No response. He pushes a little harder and still no response. He then checks to see if she's breathing. Yes, there is breath going into her lungs. He can see her chest rise, not by much, but its air going into her lungs. He tries to find a pulse. He finds a faint pulse and then tries to wake her. No response, he immediately runs to the house in front of him and knocks on the door. A man answers the door:

"Yes, what can I do for you?" asked the man.

"I need you to call 911 please."

"Why, what's the problem?"

"A lady is on the sidewalk; she has a faint pulse, and seems to be in some sort of coma or passed out. I'm no doctor, but she is alive. She is breathing but won't respond. It's important to call 911. Please hurry."

"Right, I'll get my phone and meet you outside."

"Thanks "

Returning back to the older woman, Rodney again tries to get her response. He checks her pulse and sees if she stopped breathing, and finds her the same as before. "It seems like she's in a deep sleep, won't respond or maybe she's deaf. Either way, she shouldn't be on the street."

The man arrives talking to the emergency dispatcher. "The address is 793 Dover Place. It's a lady in her...oh my God, it's Mrs. Blaine! Please hurry she is laying here and there is no telling how long she's been here.

Dispatcher, "What's your name sir? "

"Dan Slocum," he answers in frustration "What does this matter? Can you get me an ambulance?"

"I have to tell the EMT who to talk to. Does she have any noticeable injuries?"

"No not than I can see. Hey, do you see any other injuries?" talking to Rodney.

"No," Rodney replies.

"She is still breathing so far. How long will the ambulance arrive?"

Dispatcher replies, "It's on the way and will be there shortly. Do you know of her medical history? Is there anyone who knows of her condition? Does she live with someone? Is there anything you can tell me about her that I may pass to the medical technicians?"

"No, there isn't anything that I can help with. Wait, I hear sirens. I guess this is the ambulance."
The dispatcher tells "Dan it couldn't be there so fast. A different team was dispatched. Your ambulance should be there within the next five minutes."

A few seconds later, Dan hears another siren. Dan tells the dispatch that it's pretty close in proximity. Meanwhile, the dispatcher is trying to find out more of Mrs. Blaine's condition. "Has her condition changed since you've called, asked the Dispatcher."

"No, not at all, replied Dan. She is still breathing on her own and isn't responsive to calls. She hasn't moved since I've been here."

Rodney, who is still attending to Mrs. Blaine, noticed track marks on her arm when he pushed her coat sleeve while trying to get a better pulse. "Hey guy, he shouts, do you know if Mrs. Blaine is a diabetic?"

Dan shrugs his shoulders answering he didn't know. "Your guess is as good as mine."

The ambulance finally arrives, after what felt like a long wait, and the EMT team is asking multiple questions. The same vital information the dispatcher inquired to earlier. Right off they started an IV, checked all vital signs, and tried to wake Mrs. Blaine for more information. Mrs. Blaine opened an eye and moved her head from side to side. Not realizing anything happening at all. She understands that there is a lot of pain all over her body. It's as if a large truck struck her while she crossed the street. She recognized the EMT uniform and fell back into a deep sleep. The EMT team transferred her to a gurney and then to the ambulance. One team member asked if there is anyone who knows this lady. Dan jumps in and says I do. The driver instructs him to come to the hospital with them and tell them as much as possible. Dan points a finger to Rodney and tells the EMT tech that he found her and stayed by her side the entire time.

You did a good thing with the patient, said the EMT Tech to Rodney. We can take it from here.

"Ok, glad to help," said Rodney.

"What hospital are you transporting Mrs. Blaine to?"

"East Medical Center."

"Thanks."

The ambulance pulled away and Rodney started back on his run. He looked at his watch and concluded its time to return home. He cut his run short but knew he'd make it up later in the evening.

Its morning for Sabrina and she moves slowly in her routine. After a dressing, the phone rang.

"Hello?"

"Hello, May I speak with Sabrina Willingham?"

"Yes, this is she. May I as whose calling?"

"This is East Medical Center. You were listed as the emergency contact for Mrs. Blaine. A Marge Blaine."

"Yes, that's my aunt."

"Well we have her here and need you to come in. She is in intensive care at the moment but stable. She is…"

"Oh my God, I will be right there"…cutting the clerk off ending the phone call. She quickly finished dressing, called her job, and left for the hospital. She thinks, "I just saw her yesterday and she was doing great. We did our usual weekend errands and all was fine. The last time I saw her we were in the living room having tea. I reminded her to take her medicine and to call me before she went to bed. She called me and I don't understand how she is now in the hospital. I wonder how and why she is there. I need to call my sister. I'll do that after I find out what's happening with her."

Meanwhile across town, driving on the way to the office and in a great mood, Simone sipped her morning coffee and after parking her car, stepped lively to the bagel shop. She spoke to the counter clerk and ordered her routine bagel. While waiting for the bagel, she thinks of her morning objective at the office. "It's a challenging job staying on top of things especially since the economy is changing for the worse; tomorrow will be a better day once we find out if we won the latest contract" she admits to herself. "That would save so many jobs, especially mine. Heck, everyone is on the chopping block if business doesn't pick up. One day, you know it would be quite nice not to worry about jobs and just enjoy life. If only I had a partner who would support me while I venture into something I love to do. Right now it wouldn't be the right thing starting my own company. There are too many things I have to support first before stepping out on faith."

# Chapter 2

## *Understanding the Value*

"Aunt Marge, are you feeling better? Doctor Smith, will she be better or is it something more?" asked Sabrina.

"She is going to be fine," Dr. Smith reassures Sabrina. "One of her readings isn't quite exact, but it's in the normal range. I think we should keep her here for one more day so I can run one more test. You know its best to be safe than sorry."

Aunt Marge opens her eyes and sees Sabrina. "It's my favorite niece, how wonderful it is for you to visit. Is it the weekend baby, or is this a special visit?"

"Aunt Marge, it's a special visit. Do you realize where you are?" asked Sabrina.

"Sure I do baby, I am in my bed and that's why I am surprised to see you. Its early Tuesday morning and I have to get ready for my meeting at the church."

"No Aunt Marge, you aren't heading off to the church right now. You are in the hospital. Look around the room this isn't your home. It's East Medical Hospital. You forgot to take your medication and tried to go somewhere. If it weren't for the neighbors, you'd still be on the street. It's so nice of them to look out for others."

Confused Aunt Marge explains, "Dear, dear now. I know I took my meds before walking out of the house. I know for sure because I recall you reminding me to. Didn't you ask me before leaving for your home? I suspect I took them all and I do remember getting dressed. I even put my large coat on for the cold. I walked out of the door and started up the street. That's the last thing I remember before waking up here."

"There you go Aunt Marge; you have something troubling your health. I see why the doctor wants you to stay for another test."

A nurse enters and checks vital signs. "How are you Mrs. Blaine?" she asks.

"Oh I feel pretty good right now. I am ready to go home," replied Marge.

"The doctor will let you go home tomorrow. You are scheduled to give blood, and have a scan done. You will be discharged once you complete those two things. And the doctor will call you with a follow up appointment to discuss the results of those tests."

"Aunt Marge, I will be here for your discharge tomorrow morning. You don't have anything to worry about, I will take care of your things" said Sabrina. Sabrina walks out of the room while the nurse is still providing her routine care. She goes to the waiting lounge and using her cellular phone starts calling relatives. She informs them of Marge's condition and of tomorrow's tests. She suggests that they all get together and discuss options to help Aunt Marge.

Marge Blaine has no children, was married to Arthur Blaine who is the brother of Sabrina's father. Marge was an only child and gave lots of love to her nieces and nephews. Sabrina was her favorite but Marge treated all the kids with the greatest kindness. Each of the children would visit Marge at every trip to the city. They would make her place the first stop before heading to their parent's home. It's routine, that all of the family knows once the kids are in town, they always call from Marge's home to announce their arrival. Many of the grandchildren are following their parent's belief that Aunt Marge is an important person in the family. Every year Marge makes it a point to send everyone her famous cookies. She baked those cookies with such delight and made them her family trademark. Her recipe is secret to this day. In addition to her famous cookies, Marge attended and supported every child through college, military events, weddings and every coming of age accomplishment. All of the family wonders how she does it. How does Aunt Marge keep up with every member of the family? How does she seem to send things or just do the right thing when we least expect it? Always aware of the kids, Aunt Marge has a sixth sense of things. She could feel strife from others long before it became a reality. And with such knowledge, Marge prevented greater hardships by her actions. She just knew what to do, when to do it, and where to send it.

Many years passed since the family came together. Now, in light of the news of Marge's health, all the kids are pulling together and planning a large reunion for their favorite aunt. Its time for them to get the next generation involved with the angelic aunt. Sabrina started planning with her sister Simone. "You know Simone; we should have the family show love for Aunt Marge all week. It would be great to just give her something special for every day of a week. I know how she loves to hear us sing. Remember how we use to sing for her back when we were kids?" asked Sabrina.

"Sure, I remember, replied Simone. We use to start singing and all of the others would join in. We would make up tunes and she would laugh for hours. Especially Thomas, he was so silly with his lyrics. It's a wonder he didn't become a comedian."

"We should see if the little ones could do something like that for Aunt Marge."

"That is a good idea. The kids may not carry a tune, but Aunt Marge would love hearing them. She is so fond of kids trying anything together."

"What about having something at the civic center? Do you think we can afford it?"

"No, I don't think we need to get so far in debt. I am sure Aunt Marge will like whatever we do without being so elegant and expensive." .

"I know, but she has done so much for us. She deserves whatever we can do, sniffles Sabrina as tears begin to fill her eyes. Who knows how much longer she will be with us? Simone, if she died, what are we going to do?"

Hugging her sister close Simone reassures her." Sabrina, you know we've had the greatest time with Aunt Marge. We spend quality time with her at every chance. We support her without question because she's done so much for every one of us. We are here for her with our hearts and minds. I am sure we will miss her but be stronger from her love. And besides, the hard lady will not parish away from us. She is too much of an Angel and our love will heal her wound. So don't worry about losing her, she will be with us for many years to come."

Controlling her tears Sabrina tries to help Simon understand," Her dying isn't the only point, it's not quite that we lose her, it's the quality of life she has while aging. I know she wants a great life in her senior years and I worry for her. Every since she lost Uncle Arthur she's been alone."

"I guess that's why she is so active in church and community."

"It does take much of her time, but her health is what bothers me now."

"You shouldn't worry so much. It's going to be ok. Aunt Marge will pull through like a trooper." Simone says with hidden fear.

"That's easy for us to say. I plan on staying with her as much as possible. I hope you are willing to share some of the responsibility and actions with me. I don't know about the others helping out since they live so far away."

"You know my schedule is hectic, but I'm sure to give a portion of my time as much as possible. We have to stay in touch and create a schedule so one of us will be with her most of the evenings."

"Sis, you're ok with me no matter what others may say, just kidding. I am glad we had this chat. I hope our nieces and nephews look out for us when we're older."

"If we ever have any kids," says Simone but from the grimace on her face you can tell she is doubtful. "So what about the program? Do you think we can do it at her church?"

"You know she would love for us to include her church family. That's not a bad idea." Sabrina looks for a phone book. She leaves the hospital room and heads down the hall towards the nurse's station. She notices the back of a guy's physique wearing a white coat standing at the counter. She approaches with a sense of urgency. "Excuse me doctor, is there a phone book available that I may use?"

The young man turns around and sparkles with excitement replying, "I am not a doctor, well not yet, but thanks for the gesture." Taking a quick breath and thinking of a stronger comeback, he looks down at the counter for the phone book, grabs a medical reference book instead and gives it to Sabrina. Not realizing the book isn't the phone directory, he hands it to her. "This will cost you. Have dinner or coffee with me, tomorrow night."

"Oh, a phone directory is costly these days. Too bad it isn't a directory or I'd have to say yes to dinner or coffee."

"What? Oh my, it isn't the phone book. I am so sorry, wait." Reaching behind the counter once again, he grabs the correct book. "Here is the right one, sorry about that. So this means tomorrow night we're on, right?

"Yes, but we have to see how my Aunt is doing first. I'd love to chat with you before going. So why don't you give me a way to contact you."

"Sure will." Reaching into his pocket, he pulls out a business card, looks on the back of it to make sure he doesn't pass anything embarrassing, and gives the card to Sabrina. "You can contact me with either of these numbers. I am glad you accepted my invite." Smiling, he turns away, carrying a clipboard and heads down the hall.

Sabrina finds the phone number out of the phone book and records it on the back of the card. She walks back to Aunt Marge's room where there is laughter. "What are you two laughing about?"

"Child, your sister is just as silly as ever," replies Aunt Marge.

"I'm glad to see you in better spirits and feeling energetic Aunt Marge."

"Well, laughter is good for anyone, even when it hurts. It helps you keep the spirit positive and alive"

"Your spirit will be alive and well for years coming, I am sure of it."

Sabrina comments, "Yea, your spirit will be here long after our spirits leave us for that long journey down the Mississippi."

"Silly girl, she laughs, I'm still on the Chattanooga rolling with the current."

"Aunt Marge, you are so funny."


The apartment was warm and cozy when Rodney returned from his shortened run. He rushed to get dressed, as he is far behind schedule. While tying his tie, he thinks of Ms. Blaine lying on the block. "I sure hope she makes it. I'd hate to see a lovely elderly woman with no family fall by the way side. Isn't it hard for people to be left alone? I wonder if she has family close by and if there's more to this. If anything, I should check up on her health." Heading to the office he stops at the local coffee shop for his usual cup. "I know my coffee is going to make me late, but I have to get my first cup to handle the day. Nothing puts me in a better mood than my first cup of coffee."

After ordering his coffee, Rodney winks at the counter help. He and she are always flirtatious at every opportunity. Even though they haven't really exchanged names, they are warm and welcome enough to laugh together at their antics. Debbie loves to watch Rodney come into her coffee shop. She thinks of ways to catch him off guard to her flirtatious antics. She talks her way into his day starting with a quick come back to his good morning.

"Good morning Debbie" said Rodney.

"You gotcha some didn't you, Rodney?" she asks as she pours his coffee.

"Got What?"

"You know exactly what I'm talking about. Was it creamy and smooth too?" asked Debbie.

"Like when you dip your finger in my coffee," smiling.

"Like when you drop that load of cream to make things sweeter for the honeys."

"Oh, you mean the whipped stuff that you had before the bees came to attack you."

"Exactly, just before the bees walked in on your action attacking that butt while it moves up and down. Don't you remember?"

"Oh you wish I were there. Girl, I'd sweeten it for ya and keep the bees from stinging."

"Yea, you're all talk. You don't want any of this. You couldn't handle it because you'd end up fighting those bees to stop stinging your butt."

"Ha, ha, ha, you got something going on this morning, wait until the next round. I'll get you before the days out."

"Will that be all for you today," asked Debbie while passing his coffee.

"Just the usual and nothing more," replied Rodney.

Rodney drops a few dollars in Debbie's hand, smiles, and leaves the coffee shop heading for the office building. The building is relatively close; it's the first door on the right just after the subway entrance. The tall skyscraper with the dark mirror windows is full of different businesses and human traffic. For a city this size, it's the only building with so much traffic. There are people going in and out at all hours of the day, especially for his modeling agency on the 7$^{th}$ floor. They have a 24/7 studio in full operations with multiple photographers. The studio is rented to out to thrill seekers, novas photographers, and any photo related work.

Rodney is one of three senior marketing account executives that handle multiple major magazines and photographers. He doesn't mind the photo lab being rented for extra income; it helps when the business loses an account or drops a millionaire model. "Besides, I don't mind as long as I get a chance to see those expensive models? I know they would never talk to me; however one day, bam, I will get to smile with a jewel on my arm. Then there goes the agency and all those attractive models out of my life" he thinks to himself.

"The 9th floor is where the action is for tomorrow's executive. They seem to have a training program for all the guys there. It's a great network and full of surprises. Unfortunately I haven't been invited there but man it would be nice to one day have so much to live for. You hustle for the right manager, get selected for training, and with a wave of the wand, you're on the 9th floor. My floor is the 25th level with multiple cubes, a few window offices, and lots of every day people. My floor is where people interact without fear. Even though sometimes, I'd wish they had some fear before they opened their mouths. Even though things seem pretty good on the floor, and it's full of life, at least the focus is in the right place. Just consider yourself lucky being here and not on some floor where they receive damaging emails all the time. At least here, there's a positive environment. It's pretty late and I'd better hurry and login to my email account."

"Hi Rodney, What's the latest?" shouted Dan.

"Not much Dan. I suspect things are going as planned," replied Rodney as they walk to the elevators.

"Sure, things are as expected. The agency sent another model yesterday that has multiple looks for the McKenzie shoot. Man she's one knock out and with a wonderful personality!"

"It's nice hearing about sharp women in the business. It's always challenging working with egos. Unfortunate for me, it's the majority type of women I deal with. What's her name?"

"Sabrina Willingham."

"That's a new name I hadn't heard before. Is she new to the business?"

"No, she has a strong portfolio and worked with top name photographers. She started this shoot and was interrupted because of a family emergency. Because she has that certain look the magazine wanted, they changed schedules to accommodate her emergency. We tried to replace her to maintain the schedule, but McKenzie wouldn't allow anyone else to step in, which is an amazing twist from past shoots."

"She's got to know someone in right places; it's the only way a model doesn't lose a shoot opportunity to someone else."

Aunt Marge sits up bedside and places her feet on the floor. "Lord this floor is so cold; don't they ever consider having rugs or mats by each bed?" Sabrina looked at Aunt Marge, jumped from her seat and in haste grabbed Aunt Marge's arms to help her stand.

"Aunt Marge, where on earth are you trying to go?" asked Sabrina.

"I need to get out of this bed and try to make it to the bathroom."

"Why didn't you just call me, I could have gotten your bed pan."

"Why on earth would I want to do that when I am capable of going myself?"

"You aren't in the best condition right now Aunt Marge. You have to relax and get your strength back."

Aunt Marge takes slow and deliberate steps toward the bathroom. Sabrina walks with her adding a secure brace to withstand any unbalancing. Making it through the door, Aunt Marge grabs the sink, turns to Sabrina and says, "Child, I am not the little one as you were, I think I can do the rest from here. I'll call you if I need help."

Sabrina replies, "Yes mam, go right ahead and do your thing. I will be here if you need me. Please yell loud enough to wake up the next room."

"Sabrina, you're such a smart ass. That's one thing that will never change. Cute but smart mouthed as heck."

A nurse enters the room just as Sabrina returns to her seat. "Where is Ms. Blaine?" asked the nurse.

"Oh, she made it to the bathroom," replied Sabrina.

"That's a great sign of recovery. I think the doctor will release her in the morning after her test results come back. You should think of heading home. I know it's been a long day for you. I will be here all night and you can call me anytime you feel the need. She's in good hands."

"Is it OK for me to stay the night? I don't mind. But let's see what Aunt Marge would like first? I am sure either I or Simone will be here for the night. Simone will return in a few minutes."

Aunt Marge enters the room without assistance. She slowly walks to the bed, sees the nurse and says, "How are you sweetie?"

"I'm doing quite fine Ms. Blaine. I see you are doing pretty good too."

"I don't plan on being here very long. There are things I have to get back too."

"The way you're showing improvement in such a short time, I bet you will be out of here tomorrow. As a matter of fact, you'll be discharged tomorrow after the doctor briefs you with the tests results."

Simone enters the room just as the nurse tells Marge of the discharge plan.

"Aunt Marge, that's great news."

"Yes it is Simone. I am ready to go home and get into my own bed."

"You haven't been here for an entire day yet. How can it be that bad?"

"Hey Sabrina, is this what you wanted for dinner?"

Sabrina takes the bag, views its content, and says, "Yes it is sis, it's just the way I wanted it. You know sis, we have to decide who is going to stay for the night."

"No problem, I can stay for sure. My office doesn't expect me in tomorrow."

"Neither of you have to stay" said Marge.

"She's right," said the nurse. "We have it all under control and it's what we do best."

"Simone, it's a plan. You stay here tonight and I will stay with her at her house tomorrow evening. I will be there right after my shoot." said Sabrina. "Sorry nurse, it's for our sanity that we look out for our aunt."

For a short period, the three women watched television. The show is one of Aunt Marge's favorites. Comforting as it seemed, those hospital chairs were too uncomfortable to really relax. Sabrina started showing discomfort from being in the hospital all day. She started fidgeting and noticeably enough that Simone nudged her.

"Sabrina, do you have too?"

"No. Well yes I do. These chairs are so uncomfortable. Do you think you'll need anything from your apartment tonight?" asked Sabrina.

"No, I'll be fine."

The nurse walks in with an extra blanket for Simone. "Here you can use this and since the second bed is empty, you can sleep here tonight." Simone stood up, took the blanket, and replied, "Thank you very much. You are too kind."

# Chapter 3

## *Worth the Chase*

Sabrina steps into the hospital corridor with the intention of meeting that handsome guy from earlier today. Looking left down the hall, she hopes he'll enter the passage way so they can continue flirting. She thinks he is the most interesting doctor she had ever met. Not seeing or hearing anything reminding her of him, she steps lively towards the nurse's station; during her approach, she looks in each direction as if the doctor might appear. Still, no sign of him in any direction and multiple faint noises echo the halls, giving her a creepy feel. Even though it's past 10 pm, her hope of running into the doctor holds her close with anxiety. She dearly wanted the chance to talk to him again. Sabrina remembers the business card she'd gotten from him today. She pulls the card out of her purse, reads it again, and contemplates calling at this late night hour.

Doctor Lorenz Maynard grew up traveling with his family to every central city within the eastern region of the United States. The family comprised of his parents, three siblings, a cousin, and one dog that lived beyond years of expectation. Having lived in multiple cities as a child, he quickly learned how to communicate with every type of person, became well known to avoid childish conflict, and studied well to adapt in every school. His father was a federal government employee who traveled to rise through the ranks. His mother was an accountant who never settled for meritocracy in her profession or in the kids. His older brother Dan joined the Marines at 17, graduated college, and now owns a physical fitness business. His sister, the oldest of the three, attended college, married her college sweetheart, has two children, and works part-time at the child care center for her husband's corporation. Since Cousin Michael lives in another city, the three kids make certain there is a second effort to entertain their parents once a month. Monthly the family find themselves at a dinner or having a picnic event. Either it's at their parent's home, or someplace near so they don't have to travel far.

During Lorenz' childhood, many things happened that made him into the man he is today; from experiencing his father's repeated drunken stupors, to the drug addiction of his older and closest cousin, had an emotional impact one way or another. His family endured challenges of spousal abuse when dad went on a drunken binge, at first hand he disagreed with such behavior. After having multiple things stolen to support an expensive drug habit by his cousin, he read and communicated about every facet of drug abuse. After assisting his cousin to sobriety, Lorenz promised to help others as often as he could. From elementary school years, Lorenz would watch his mother's bad treatment and vow not to ever become physical with the opposite sex. Often, he would fear for his mom's life during the physical bashing and the verbal yelling. During those years, all the kids would gather in a bed room to avoid the horrible mishap of being slapped, or hit with such force that would break an arm or leg. One year that actually happened to his younger brother and they had to explain the broken arm to the doctors. Fortunate for them, those years didn't bring such penalty for abuse as they finally evolved to the 21 century.

Years would go between drunken splurges. By the time Lorenz and his little brother were teens, the drunken stupors became far between. One night, the father went into one of the most horrific drinking binges ever witnessed by the family. As things heated to a physical confrontation, Dan jumped to his mom's defense, and cracked his father's jaw responding to a wild swing targeted at his head. Blocking with the left, Dan punched his father with such force, that the three of kids felt the blow. Dad fell to the floor passing out from the alcohol and Dan's ferocious punch. Lorenz went to his father's side after he fell and tried to ensure he was still alive. From this, it was as if he found his destiny. He then vowed to always be able to apply special care to those in need, especially to the poor.

Years of education passed and Lorenz followed his calling. Class after class he achieved excellent grades, found the support of others, and climbed the ladder to High School leadership positions. He became class president just after leaving middle school. Every year, the class voted him in like clock work. During the year he decided not to run, the class penciled him in and he again won the popularity vote. His popularity goes back to those development years on the road. Each year he had to adapt to every type of person. Lorenz was a natural and could win the heart of the meanest pit bull dog if he got close enough. He had natural charm, communicated with anyone and everyone at a level of pure understanding, and made everyone amazingly comfortable. He showed a natural care to his fellow man. One year, Lorenz attended football practice when one of the new guys was trying out for the team. During a play, the new guy was clobbered and hit so hard that it practically knocked the kid out. After the other players picked themselves up off of the pack, the new kid laid there and didn't move. He didn't even nudge his head when the coach yelled for him to. Lorenz ran to the new kid, started looking for a pulse, breathing pattern, and any sign of life. Lorenz performed a mental checklist to find a problem or eliminate any dangers. Once Lorenz was sure of no physical injuries to the head or neck, he removed the helmet for a better feel of the kid's condition. Lorenz didn't get a heart beat from all the pressure points. He called the coach for an ambulance and started to perform mouth to mouth recessitation. The kid woke up with a few blows and heart pumps. Just in time, the ambulance arrived and took the kid to the hospital for further care. The EMT team applauded Lorenz for being so quick to save a life. Later in the week, coaches found out that the kid lied about his physical condition. He had a heart condition that didn't allow him to play contact football or be involved in any distant running type of physical sports.

Graduating nearly top in his class, Lorenz received numerous scholarships. He attended a local university for family reasons. He wanted to be close to his parents to encourage their retirement and set them on a path to finally build a smaller home. He wanted them to downsize because all of the kids were now out of the home and their living cost would be next to nothing. Graduating suma cum laude, Lorenz applied for numerous medical colleges and was accepted to one near a metropolis where multiple hospitals would embrace his internship. Being the intellect that he is, Lorenz started class with a strategy to succeed. His first year, he partnered with well established doctors who's practice involved them in both private and public organizations. Making the appropriate contacts, Lorenz contributed to multiple organizations by providing medical screening as a means of giving back to the public. Twice a week he would attend public assistance programs and provide medical services to the needy. During his third year of medical school, Lorenz found an internship in the hospital that admitted Ms. Blaine. He was hired in large part due to commitment to helping others during his weekly public service meetings. Word got around to the hospital executives that he does remarkable work and is extremely good with patients. This is what the hospital needed to change their image. Even though it's a public hospital, the traffic is overwhelming, and many of the interns and doctors have lost that one important perspective.

Lorenz arrived to his station and exited the train. He walked up the stairs to the street, turned left, and dodged people as his path led him to his apartment. In front of his apartment building were multiple kids playing on the sidewalk. Across the street, there is a play ground where younger kids can swing and ride the merry-go-round, climb on the jungle gym, and see-saw. On a spring day, there's always someone in the park with their kids. Summers are not quite as active in the middle of the day. On a hot and humid day, most people come out in early morning or early evening before dusk. Early summer mornings, Lorenz goes to the park to watch the sun rise or take in the new day. That is if he returned from his shift at a decent time of course. He normally takes time to meditate and focus on what he has to do to achieve his plan. Going to the park, he got to meet a lot of the neighbors, many of whom are mostly nice people. And as usual, once they found out about his plans and marital condition, they would always seem to set him up for a blind date with either a relative or friend. Fortunate for Lorenz, he's with little time to venture on a date and has too much on his plate from all the activities; he's way too busy to even notice women during public service programs or at the hospital. Today was very unusual for him because of empty time. He reminds himself of beautiful and impressive Sabrina.

Going inside the apartment building, he walks up to the second floor, turns right, and heads to the last apartment on the left. He unlocks the door, enters, and hears his answer machine beeping, indicating new messages. Thinking of Sabrina, he'd forgotten to stop at his mailbox before entering the apartment. Something outside his normal routine, the phone rings.

"Hello," answered Lorenz.

"Hi Lorenz, how are you," asked Sabrina. "Or should I say Doctor Lorenz?"

"Hi, is this Sabrina?" asked Lorenz. "I am very glad you called. You can call me anything comforting to you."

"Good, I'll call you Lorenz." She smiles and being silly chuckles over the line. 'Did I catch you at a bad time?"

"No, actually it's a great time. I just walked in the door and hoped to hear from you."

"I don't mean to be forward or seem aggressive, but I wanted to start our move to getting better acquainted."

"No problem. It's surprising to see a woman make such a bold and quick move."

"I am one of those type of women who makes a decision and don't wait for chance. Do you think it's a good way to be?"

"That depends on the outlook of who's answering that question. Are you asking for my opinion?"

"Sure, I need to know what you think of a woman who's kind of aggressive."

"First of all, you aren't aggressive, just focused. Secondly, I like the way a woman is direct and doesn't play around. And lastly, especially since you are greatly attractive, it's my dream come true for a woman to make the first move."

"So you don't mind me calling first?"

"No, I don't mind at all, especially since you didn't give me any contact information. And I like giving the lady the option to call or make a move. It helps me make sure of her interest, and most of all, it takes out the guess work."

"You mean the game playing?"

"Yes, playing the game is too time consuming and difficult to read. I like a woman who lets me know her interest without going through the typical checklist. Time is too short and precious and wasted if things don't move."

"I can respect that, and since you are ok with me being aggressive, let's make our first date. I want you to pick me up next Thursday night after your shift. What we do and where we go is up to you. I will tell you, I enjoy a man with creativity."

"Thursday 7:30 sounds like a charm. Will I meet you and do you like chivalry?"

"Chivalry of course, but if the activity you choose is convenient for us to meet, then I am open to either. Your call; let me know the logistics. Here's my cell number."

"OK, let me write it down to make sure I get it right. Lorenz records the number on a business card in his wallet. He highlights the number by writing Sabrina with a 1 centered in the circle. Repeating the number to Sabrina, he asks, "When is the best time to contact you?"

Sabrina answers, "Anytime is fine, I will get the message if I don't answer. Talk to you later, I have to go."

"Bye, and thanks for calling." He places to phone back on the stand, walks to the calendar and highlights Thursday by writing 7:30 date/Sabrina. Remembering he needs the mail, he walks out of the apartment heading to the mail boxes on the first floor. While opening the mail box, a neighbor walks in.

"Hi Lorenz, how's it going?" asked Robin.

"Hey, hey, Robin it's going pretty good today."

"Wow, that's the most you've spoken to me on any occasion. It must be a great day for you."

"Yes, it is. It was a great day," he replies with a dimple accented smile on his face.

"You know, it would be nice hearing what made you so happy. Care to visit for a while?"

"No, no thanks. I have studying to do. Talk to you later"

"OK, then maybe on another one of your good days."

Not answering, Lorenz heads back to his apartment, mail in hand, and thinking of what just happened. Without a second thought of Robin, he skips right to Sabrina and this coming Thursday. "What am I going to do for this date?" he asks himself. "I know she's probably spent a lot of time with better eye catching, classier, profound, and pretty financially stable men, but that doesn't matter. I know exactly what to do, so if my plan works, it will be one evening she'd always remember."

Robin Murray has an apartment on the second floor of the building. She always seems to notice Lorenz and his schedule of activities. From her point of view, he never has a visitor, he's always with books, and he seems to be quite busy with no time for friends. On multiple occasions, Robin would make a second effort to catch Lorenz when he's leaving or returning to the building. She attempts conversation at every opportunity, believing if they communicate, she has the ability to persuade Lorenz into an evening together. "How lovely it would be for us to just find our common interest," she thinks. "It would be hot to get him out of those scrubs and into my bath, candles, bubbles, wine, strawberries, and of course me. And explore our bodies to depths of hysteria." Breathing deeply, she finds herself envisioning the curves of his body. His muscular build, the smooth wet skin accented with flickering candlelight, the physique slim but defined, and of course his gift for women hanging with fullness like the finger in a hand of bananas, all run together in a single thought. Now in a pant, she finds herself trembling with desire, hot as a summer's day in July, leaning against her door frame for balance. She leans there at the door in her moment, feeling the goodness of desires, while throbbing nerve endings palpitate at her sensitive zones. She sighs in relief as her thoughts change to speed the decent to a normal state.

Walking into the apartment, she scans through her mail. She finds a card of some sort without a return address. Opening the card, she smells a wonderful fragrance. Not knowing who sent the card, she pulls it out with excitement and hopes for the best. The card cover is beautiful with a floral print and a heart in the center, floating over the ocean with glitter on the water representing natural light on the waves. A very romantic scene on the card's front cover, with inside words reading:

> If one night mist is not the time
> Then morning dew delight
> My wish or may to be with you
> Will come when time is right

Admiration near but far
From one with focused eye
Tempest of the heart's desire
Calmed by colored sky

You are the one I wish to see
Silence golden not true
When the chance presents itself
The one becomes the two

With no signature on the card, it's a total mystery to the sender. Can it be Lorenz who sent this to me? No, it can't be him. He barely talks to me when we meet. But it could be his way of breaking the ice and adding spice and excitement to our first private encounter. Oh, that will be a wonderful day to remember.

Lorenz finally opened his mail. Not noticing anything out of the ordinary, he places the mail on his desk. It's his normal routine with the mail. After his shower, he settles in studying before ensuring he pays his bills, and then falls into a deep sleep until the next morning. Thinking while in the shower; "Tomorrow is a different day to plan my date with Sabrina. I hope she is fond of children; at least she seems to be. I may have one kid at the center give me a hand for this date. They'd be obliged to see a top model and it could help her with having a public image. Giving back to the community while dating me could be a great thing for the both of us."

Sabrina hangs up the phone and wonders if she did the right thing. Whatever it is, she thought, I put my desires up front with him. Any man can handle being told what to do, or given the opportunity to think he knows what to do. I am proud that I picked up being straight forward in college. It paid off quite well, though it didn't help my image with the other girls on campus, it was great with the fellas. Deciding to finally listen to her phone messages, she taps the play button. Beep, message 1, called today at 11:00 am.

"Sabrina. Hi its Marie, I am calling to remind you of your shoot tomorrow afternoon. I scheduled the shoot for 1:30 so you can visit you aunt first thing in the morning. Call me if you need anything." End of message.

Beep...message 2 called today at 11:15 am.... "Sabrina, I heard about Aunt Marge. Call me when you get a chance and give me an update. My number is 898.324.0022 in case you didn't have it.   Love much and hang in there"....... End of message

You can count on Dale to find out things so quickly. I wonder if Simone called him.

Beep....message 3 called today at 12:00 pm..."Hi Sabrina, this is Dan from the studio for the McKenzie shoot. I hope things are going well. We are very sorry to hear of your family emergency. If there is anything we can do, please don't hesitate to call. We are here to help you get through your dilemma. Oh and please use us, but go through your agency first as a courtesy.  Hope all is well and we'll see you soon." ...End of message. There are no other messages... beep

Sabrina sat in her bedroom looking at the family pictures as tears rolled down her cheeks. The concern for Aunt Marge suddenly hit when the picture of Simone, Aunt Marge, and Sabrina glared back at her from the dresser. She couldn't hold those tears back any longer even though she tried to show strength in the hospital and with Simone. She bellowed with fear and pain, a true concern for her loving aunt who is supposed to be healthy. Even though the doctors for security sake advised Aunt Marge to have test done tomorrow morning, she wanted them over and a clean bill of health. Sabrina dropped to her knees on the side of the bed and began to pray in between tears.

"Lord, I know you are the almighty powerful one who bestows blessings upon all who seek your will. I ask that you look over one of your loving and faithful servants, my Aunt Marge. I ask that you watch over her and wash away her illness. Please give her the health to live a good life. She has been good to all and a true blessing to this earth. For all things and in your name I pray. Amen."

Wiping her tears, Sabrina rose and started her bed time routine. She took a shower, changed into her night wear, and crawled into bed. She started reading her fashion magazine for new options and ideas for her upcoming shoot. She reviewed some of her past working shots and thought of ways to present an ideal view for the next level in her profession. Turning the next page in the latest fashion magazine, she finally dozes off to sleep. The light's timer clicked and the room became dark, filled with silence, and solitude with all elements for a comforting slumber.

# Chapter 4

## *Health and Romance*

Early morning before Aunt Marge's tests, she wakes to Simone's light snore. "Poor child must have had a hard time sleeping in that bed. Reminds me of her younger years when her mother brought her to visit the first time. The child snored all night and had the nerve to yell in her sleep. She woke me up in a panic and I thought the world was coming to an end. She was so cute then. Because she did that as a youngster, it's my turn to shock her. It's time I wake her."

"Simone," yelled Aunt Marge. "Simone, wake up. Wake up you snoring hen. You're making all that noise so early in the morning."

Simone answers, "Huh? What time is it?"

"It's time you woke up and stopped making all that noise. You are in a hospital where most people need their rest. You're keeping people up all night. Listen…people are walking the hall trying to find where the loud noise is coming from."

"Aunt Marge, you can't be serious. I don't snore and you know it. Why are you bothering me and interrupting my sleep?"

"You are here for me right? And since I am up, you should be too."

"You haven't changed a bit. I know you are all right now, still crazy as ever. You never allowed us to sleep in when we visited as kids."

"You know it isn't good to sleep your life away. When the sun comes up, you should be too. Didn't I teach you anything at all when you were a child?"

"What time is it Aunt Marge?"

Marge turns the television on and searches for the information channel. "Its time you woke up and got ready for the day. I see the sun peeking behind the curtain, its up and so should you."

The nurse enters the door, softly speaking, "I thought I heard talking. Good morning Ms. Marge."

"Good morning," Marge replies.

"Good morning," Simone whispers. "What time is it?"

"It's nearly six thirty and you're up early," said the nurse.

"Six thirty in the morning? No way. I feel like I just fell asleep."

"Today is just starting and I am glad you are up. Ms. Marge you have the first test appointment. We start with you at 8:30 and all should be done by noon. I think you should try to have breakfast and be ready for the technician to take blood by 8:15. Is this ok?"

"Yes, its fine and I am ready to go home."

"Stop being cranky Aunt Marge. The nurse didn't ask for that comment."

"No problem. I get that all the time. People want to be in the comfort of home especially when they have to stay overnight."

"Well, at least the nurse understands the importance of comfort," replied Marge.

Marge moves her legs off the bed and prepares herself to stand. She is hesitant to stand because of her ill feeling that just came over her. She waits by the side of the bed with her feet on the floor. Her hesitation is noticed by Simone who stood up to come to her aid. Walking toward Aunt Marge, Simone asks, "Are you ok?"

"Child I am fine, you move slower when you realize you're older."

"Sure Aunt Marge, that's a good one to tell. Look we are here to ensure we know the condition of your health. If you don't tell us, we don't know the extent of your illness."

"Why do you think I am ill at all?"

"We are here aren't we? You were found in the street by some man jogging by your block. If it weren't for him; you'd probably still be there lying on the side walk. Let's get you to the bathroom."

While Marge is in the bathroom, Simone takes the liberty of ordering breakfast for her. Reading the menu card, she thinks, "She will have two eggs over easy sunny side down, cereal, juice, and hot tea. That sounds like a good breakfast for her. What will I have? I guess I can go down to the cafeteria and purchase a bran muffin and coffee. That will hold me over. I'll head down as soon as she gets out of the bathroom."

Its six thirty in the morning and Rodney is back at his exercise routine. He strides for the door to start his morning run. After the routine stretching, he takes off on his second route, six miles today he thinks. I feel good after a relaxing evening, a good night's sleep, and a great dinner last night. It's time for a good heart working, lose a few pounds run. I have the time this morning for the extended length. My first meeting isn't until 9:30. Turning the first corner, he passes on comers as they approach. Many people are up walking their dogs, sitting out on the stoop with coffee, or picking up the newspaper. He greets as many people as he can if his wind allows it. Huffing and puffing on his first quarter mile, Rodney has second thoughts to his six mile attempt. Pains are roaming through his legs, breathing is difficult, and his lower back is prickled with feeling from needle probes. "Gotta keep going," he thinks. Just as he gets to his first mile, a drastic pain falls upon his chest. Slamming into the ground he fell. As if one of the professional football team's defensive tackle suddenly closed the number four hole as he ran in that direction. He fell right on the grassy knoll next to the cement sidewalk. He rolled to his back and felt the pain grow in his chest. Breathing rather harsh, he almost hyperventilated as his heart raced. Lying there facing the morning sun, he grasped his chest from the pain and tried desperately to breath, He barely contained his breathing to stay conscious. The pain was crushing and his arm started to numb. "Oh my, I am too young for a heart attack." He rose to his feet and started walking back home. He moved cautiously not to make his heart beat rise and feared his lack of blood flow would reach his legs. He sat on a street bench for a minute or two before trying to make it back to his home. Slow moving, he made his way back to his apartment. Walking in, he immediately called his doctor's office for an emergency appointment.

"Hello, Doctor Tyler," he shouted with a painful panic.

"You have reached the office of Doctors Tyler and Willis. Our office hours are…"

Damn, the office is closed. It doesn't open for another hour or so. I better get there. Let me call Dan. Dialing with pain, Rodney fumbles with the phone while holding his chest. Increasing pain skipping through his chest cavity area, he slams his fist on the desk to catch his fall.

"Dan, hey I need you to take me to the hospital."

"What happened?" asked Rodney. Are you ok?"

"No, I have this excruciating pain in my chest and its not settling, it's worse than when it started. Hurry"!

"On my way! Keep the door opened."

Within minutes Dan arrives at the door. He enters and finds Rodney lying on the floor, still breathing, but faintly. Immediately he checks for a pulse and Rodney opens an eye.

"Dan, you made it. Help me up."

"Sure. Hang on man; we'll have you in the car in no time." After entering the car, they take off down the street. Racing to the emergency room, Dan breaks the speed limit and dodges traffic as best as possible. Not knowing for sure how dangerously ill Rodney is, his increase urgency helps him decide to drive faster with hopes of getting a police officer's attention. He speeds through the busy streets of the city screeching tires at every turn. In another block they're at the hospital. No police officers anywhere in sight. Arriving at the hospital, Dan jumps out of the car, grabs Rodney and places him over his shoulder. He runs into the emergency room and captures a nurse's attention. Rodney, slumped over Dan's shoulder, nearly passed out because his lungs are pressured in this position. He gasps for air and whispers..."put me down."

Dan does just that...hastily flops Rodney down in a wheel chair and rolls him into the nurse's legs. "Sorry about that, but my friend really needs attention. Can you help him?"

"Yes, said the nurse. What's the problem?"

"His chest, he is in dire pain, he can barely breathe, and he's nearly passed out."

"Is he allergic to anything that you know of?"

"I don't know, you'd have to ask him if you can."

"Who knows his medical history?"

"I guess his family will know, but unfortunately I don't have their number."

"What's your friend's name?"

"Rodney, Rodney Witherspoon."

"What, what?" answered Rodney in a squelched voice.

"Are you allergic to any type of drugs?" asked the nurse.

"No. Can you cure my pain?"

"I hope so, if you help me. Did you take anything within the last 24 hours?"

"No," Rodney answers while holding his chest.

"When did the pain start?"

"This morning during my six mile run. The pain stopped me dead in my tracks."

The nurse rolls Rodney into an emergency bed section for doctor's review. A young doctor enters the room and the nurse informs him of her pre-screening. Lorenz starts his review of Rodney and performs the routine checks. He asks Rodney, "What's your name sir?"

"Rodney Witherspoon," he replied.

"Does your family have a history of heart trouble?

"No," answering whispery

"Are you taking any medication at this time?"

"No."

Lorenz continues his check over Rodney and runs through the routine screening. He orders an EKG and fluids. He then tells the nurse to give Rodney a couple of Tylenol. "Give him a strong dose so the pain stops and decreases his chest swelling." Lorenz heads to another cube to view a patient who's screaming in pain. He tells the nurse to call him when the EKG results are back. "Mr. Witherspoon, we have to test your heart and see if you suffered a heart attack. It seems like you had an angina pectoris event. The right thing for us to do is run the EKG to evaluate my prognosis. After the EKG, I will give you some health instructions and everything should be fine."

Rodney replies, "Ok doc."


Walking down the hall from her aunt's room, Simone detours from the normal passage heading for the cafeteria. Earlier she woke with such a hunger and desire for coffee that she jumped out of bed, yawned, looked at Aunt Marge, and quickly headed for the door before a nurse could tell her good morning. Simone detoured because of a wet floor sign in the middle of the hallway. She decided not to head through the side where others were walking towards her, and it seemed as if the hallway had "patient traffic" for the morning appointments. She turned towards the emergency room hallway, which was a short cut to the cafeteria on the bottom floor. While walking down the hallway, out of the corner of her eye, she takes a snapshot of the excitement just as a nurse comes out to greet Dan with Rodney slumped over his shoulder. Without a second glimpse, she continues her journey to the cafeteria.

Arriving at the cafeteria, Simone makes her breakfast order. I'd like a ham and cheese omelet, lightly browned toast, and two slices of bacon." She pays the cashier and travel back to Aunt Marge's room. With the breakfast in hand, walking briskly so she can enjoy her feast sooner, she thinks of an earlier hospital scene when Rodney was slumped over his friend, heading for the ER. "That guy looked really familiar," she thinks. I wonder where or if I've seen him before.

Returning to the room, she encounters Rodney's friend just as she reaches the elevators. It seems that every time I recall meeting someone, I get a chance to ensure my thoughts are correct. Closer they walk to the elevator and with Simone's meal in hand, Dan says something different and blandish. "What's for breakfast to keep a fine honey like you looking so healthy?"

"Didn't I see you earlier with a guy on your shoulders?" asked Simone.

"Yes you did," replied Dan. "It's my friend Rodney who felt chest pains while running."

"Does this guy run a lot?"

"Yes, he runs nearly every morning. He's nuts but you have to admire his discipline even though it doesn't show. Not that he looks bad or anything; its just he doesn't workout the other muscle groups for balance. Why do you ask? Have you met him before?"

"I am not sure if I met him before. He looks familiar, so I wanted to see if my memory is right. Does he work downtown?"

"As a matter of fact he does. He works at the advertising agency near the center of town. And just looking at you, reminds me of one of our recent models. Are you related to a Sabrina Willingham," asked Dan.

"My sister," answered Simone.

"You two have a great resemblance. You wouldn't happen to be a model too would you?"

"Most people recognize me as her sister all the time. It happens when you have a popular sibling. No, not the life I'd like to have or profession I'd care to venture." So what about you, what is it that you do?"

"I am at the advertising agency as an account specialist. Hey I see Rodney's doctor and I should catch him before he gets down the hall." Dan walks down the hall and looks back and says, "It was nice talking with you and I hope your breakfast isn't too cold now."

"Nice chatting with you too." Breakfast, oh yea I'll have to zap it now. "At least I know I met Rodney for sure," she thinks while strolling back to Aunt Marge's room. Stepping off the elevator straight to Aunt Marge's room she walks with thoughts of Rodney and the conversation with Dan. "I hope Rodney gets better."

Sabrina wakes early in the morning for her routine palates class. She bounces out of bed, dresses in her workout clothes, and heads to the 5:30 session. The gym is relatively full with people doing multiple workout activities. Just in time for the class, she finds a spot on the floor, and waits for instructions from the instructor. After the workout, she runs back to the apartment, changes into a nice outfit, eats a quick breakfast, and heads for the train station to the hospital. Its 8:00 as the train stops at the hospital transfer point. She takes the bus to the hospital's front door. Entering the door, she heads for the elevators to get to Aunt Marge's room. Arriving through the corridor directly in front of the nurses' station she tells everyone, "Good morning ladies," before heading to Aunt Marge's room.

"Hello pretty lady," Sabrina directs her comments to Aunt Marge.

"Good morning to you little angel" replies Aunt Marge.

"Hey girl how was your night" asks Simone while still munching on breakfast.

"It was fine, and I slept very well. It's nothing like sleeping in your own bed. And speaking of such, when are you ready to get out of here Aunt Marge?"

"I have a few more tests this morning and I should be able to go home shortly after. I understand that the test results will be available to me by phone or a follow up appointment will take place. God knows I want to get in my own bed and at my home. It's nothing like being home."

The nurse enters the room, "Ms. Marge, are you ready for your first test?"

"Yes I am," replied Marge. She stands up from the bed and settles into the wheel chair.

"Aunt Marge would you like me to come along?" ask Simone.

"No, I think the nurse and I will be just fine. You get ready for me to leave by this afternoon or so. Simone, you should go get cleaned up and get some rest. Even though you slept here last night, I know you didn't sleep well. I will see you both or one or you back here this afternoon. Love you two very much," she shouts while being rolled out the door.

Simone stands and gathers her things before heading out. "Sabrina, are you heading to work now?" asked Simone.

"Yes, that's the plan" replied Sabrina.

"Are you working with a guy named Rodney?"

"Ah, I think so. Is he like an account manager or something for the Marketing Agency?"

"Yes, that's the guy. He is here in the hospital for chest pains. His friend Dan told me. I ran into him when I headed to the cafeteria this morning."

"Really, he is so young and in good shape too. It would be horrible to be in a condition so young. I should drop in on him and see how he's doing. Want to come?"

"Oh, I'd love too, but I look so bad now. You go ahead and I will call you later and see what we should do to pick up Aunt Marge and get her home."

"That's a great idea. Let's talk later and I will tell you how things went with Rodney."

"Why would you do that?"

"Let's face it, you only ask about those you're interested in. I don't think you've met the guy, sis."

"Ok, you know me so well. I met the guy in the parking lot nearly a week ago, got his card but never called. I'm waiting for him to call me."

"You are so old fashioned. How do you know he isn't waiting for you to call him?"

"I am sure; he is sitting by the phone every night just waiting to get my call. Yea, sure he's that lonely or inactive. Surely he must have things going on or he would have called me by now."

"You assume a lot of things don't you? He should be calling you right as he leaves the hospital. Just you wait and see. Remember the guy you were interested in back in high school? You waited for that phone call and it never came. Years later you ran into him and the first thing he told you was how much of a crush he had on you the entire senior year. But as usual, you never made a move to just see how someone may have interest in you. You're repeating that mistake again. I think you should just call him and see where the conversation leads. Better yet, why don't you go see how he's doing and get a feel if there's interest from him. You can do it on our way out."

"That sounds kind of forward and aggressive."

"No, that's just following or acting on your thoughts and interest. Go on sis, you can do this. If he isn't interested, at least you'd know and can move on to other opportunities."

"What other opportunities? We can talk about my love life another time. What are we going to do about the reunion?"

"Oh, that's next on my agenda of things to plan. I think we have to get a letter out to the family. I'll construct a sort of 'scare them to come but not in grief' letter, if you know what I mean. I don't think we can pull everyone here if we don't write a letter like that. You know, family normally comes only when there's a death or a wedding. I want them to come while Aunt Marge can enjoy seeing them without giving them the scare of her death."

"You know that's what their thoughts are going to be. If you send a 'scare them to come' letter, it's the only thing they'll think. And you know Aunt Marge will not go for sympathy. Let me think of a way to invite them and start the leg work on a letter and you start the activities for entertainment. These two things can make the reunion an event Aunt Marge will never forget."

"Yes, you can use those great communication skills to entice family cooperation. I will make some calls to the farthest distant cousins and see if we can pull a date off that saves them airfare."

"Sounds like a plan so far. I'll get up with you later tomorrow and see what progress we make. I have to head off for the office after going home to change. Are you ok here with Aunt Marge?"

"Sure, you go ahead, I have everything covered with Aunt Marge. I'll call you with an update if something comes up. Have a great one sis."

Simone heads out for home. She intentionally strolls past the emergency area hoping to see Rodney and his friend Dan. Arriving to the emergency area, she scans the room for those two; unfortunately she doesn't see either of them and walks out the nearest exit. "I wished at least one of them were around. I could have reminded Dan to tell Rodney to call me." Arriving to her car, she notices folded paper on the windshield. "No drawing so it's not an advertisement she thinks." Grasping the note and sitting in the car, she unfolds it began reading:

*Simone,*

*Thanks for asking about me. It's nice to know you remembered me from weeks ago. You too left an everlasting impression. I'd love to ask you out for milk (Doctors orders to cut down on the caffeine). Please call when you can.*

○ *Rodney*

▪ *P.S. If this isn't Simone's car, please accept my apologies.*

Smiling from the note, she starts the car, places her seatbelt in position, put the car in reverse, and prepares to back out of the parking space. Holding the brake, she turns around for a good look in the rear before pulling back. Just as the car begins to move, she thinks of where she put Rodney's card, turns forward, and reaches for her purse. Immediately she stops the car just before crashing into a person passing by. Reaching down into her purse, she rummages for any lose business card. Unfortunately not one is Rodney's. "Why didn't he write the number down? That would have been the right thing to do. I guess he isn't serious about calling. I don't recall throwing that card away. It must be at the office"

Rodney and Dan are driving back to Rodney's apartment. "Dan, do you think I did the right thing leaving Simone a note like that?"

"I can't explain that one for you man. I think you should have made it easier for her to call you. At least given her some clue to finding you if she didn't keep your business card."

"Yea, but that's the true test to her interest. I want to know for sure if there is real interest. It's easy for me to make it convenient for her to dial those numbers, but it's challenging for her to get in touch with me. When she does, it's an award for us both. I think she'd show true interest to going out with me the instant I ask her. Remember the note asked her for milk and I thought she'd get a chuckle out of that."

"But man that is a serious game you're playing or trick you seem to run on her. Do you really think it will work?"

"Believe me; a woman loves challenges especially for someone she's interested in. And I am sure if she doesn't like the challenge, then it's not worth the effort."

"OK, you may have lost a great woman there because of that note. What will you do if she doesn't call you within a week?"

"I may call her, if I find the right activity to invite her to. If not, then I'll invite her to a quick but short lunch."

Dan sighs, and makes a face of confusion as he listens to the latest groove on the radio. "Man, are you serious about this game? That's what you are playing with a woman you haven't met. I don't get it. I don't understand why you make it so challenging. Most women I know would toss the note without a second thought."

"You know, the types of women you date aren't really that interested in the challenge. Not to put your taste down, but they seem kind of short on intellect."

"Rodney, that's cold man, that's real cold."

"Just kidding Dan, it's a fact that you have wonderful taste. Look at your last girl, she was wonderful and funny. She held her own in conversation."

"That didn't last. She sort of fell off the fun wagon and was too much into non-active things. You know, the theater and museums were a little too much for me. And she asked too many 'What are you thinking questions?' even when I had no real thoughts. She would get furious about my nothing to share answers."

"I understand to some extent. So you keep the simple and interesting women close; easy to entertain, right?"

"I see them being much more fun and no pressures. I still think they are very bright women with other interest. I do have great taste and you have to admit that Rodney. Remember Crystal? She was fantastic, great cook, loved the outdoors, and was very active. I just couldn't take her to one office event. I don't thing she did well in those business crowds."

"She was a looker too."

"And that she is. A fine woman who hopefully isn't dating anyone and I shall call as soon as I get back to my apartment."

"You do that, but keep it simple, just joking."

Minutes later, Sabrina calls her agent for her shoot schedule. No answer. She leaves a message for a return call. Aunt Marge returns to the room for her discharge after all those tests. Waiting for the doctor's visit, Marge prepares herself for the trip home. Packing everything she can, she places all clothing items in a bag that Sabrina brought with her on the first visit.

"Sabrina, aren't you going to help me?"

"Sure Aunt Marge. What is it you'd like me to do?"

"Grab the flowers and all those cards for me sugar child."

"What are you going to do with those fading flowers?"

"Child, don't you know flowers can be dried for a very lovely decorating look. You'll see when we return to the house. Make sure you put them in the bag and don't damage them."

"Yes ma-am, I will take care of these flowers."

The phone rings. Sabrina answers "hello."

"Sabrina its Phil, how are you?"

"Fine Phil, it's about time you called?"

"I wanted to contact you this morning. I am glad you called. There is nothing strenuous or exciting happening today, but you have one shoot scheduled that's no real challenge. It's a basic studio shoot for a perfume account. I'm sure you'll look your best as you always do."

"Well, nice hearing it's something simple. You know me, nothing is ever as simple as you describe. What time and where is this shoot?"

"Its off Simmons and Yorkshire Streets, call Jamie at 843-949-1112. Make sure you call him early enough and confirm your time. I'd hate to pay a fine for bungling the shoot by not showing up. Don't be late, or it will cost us this time around. Last time I had to pay homage favors for a sick guy. It was gross as hell too."

"No doubt, a fine is the last thing I need these days. I'll call him as soon as we hang up."

"You do that and let me know if you need help. We have to do a bang up job on this simple shoot. It opens doors for so many other things and work for the future. Talk to you later, good luck."

Sabrina fumbles with her notes for Jamie's number. She looks at her writing and can't make the last number; 5 or 2 she asks? I wrote it down so fast I didn't write it clear enough. Five, its five, I'll try this number first.

Please coordinate the candles and control those youngsters so everything stays in place. Lorenz tried his best to communicate with the young group and the activities for them to distribute donated flowers to senior citizens. Every week or so, a local florist group donates flowers to the community health center. The youth group takes the flowers to multiple senior citizen homes throughout the community, sometimes there are extra flowers for other locations. Senior citizens love to see the kids and especially spend time with them. As each child shows up with flowers, the inhabitants have smiles and hugs to share. There is warmth for both the child and seniors. As a matter of fact, the children often spend time reading and playing games with those who seldom have visitors. It's a fantastic trade off as each person entertains the other and friendships are born. Such great friendships that people entertain each other in between the floral deliveries. Lorenz takes time out during his community services and in between studies to supervise multiple deliveries, communicate with kids on positive lessons of life, and encourage entertainment. During one visit, the kids started racing wheel chairs around the retirement homes. The funny thing was seniors were in the chairs enjoying the race. It was difficult to stop the action, but Lorenz felt responsible if something happened, so he stopped it after only a couple rounds. Just short of someone starting to complain about the races. "Doctor you should be ashamed of yourself, its dangerous for the kids to race around the building with the patients" said the on duty nurse, barely containing her smile at the rule breaking fun.

"I understand nurse; it's my mistake to let the kids have so much fun with the senior citizens. Thank you for correcting me and my short coming with the facility. I don't think the kids did any harm and of course, the patients loved it."

Lorenz walks to the administrative office to schedule future visits from the community center. Since the kids were having so much fun with the inhabitants, he thought it was fantastic for the home to adopt some of the kids for their patients. It can help most of the elderly with their health and emotional stability. Walking into the office, he hears a conversation between an administrator and a perspective inhabitant. That voice sounds really familiar he thinks. He walks closer to the receptionist desk to hear more of the conversation.

"I think it's an amazing place you have here. How do you select your patients or residents? What is it that you expect from them and is it only with the cost do you allow them to come here?" confusing asked Simone.

"It's a combination of many things besides money and character. It's a combination of residents interviewing new prospective people and having them select their neighbor. It's amazing how great life is when you choose your neighbor. And it's a happier environment for every individual" explains Ms. Whitmore.

"I see, it's a great way to have others come in and feel really accepted once they complete the interview process. I think Aunt Marge may be happy here if we present it well to her."

Immediately Lorenz recognizes the voice once she mentioned Aunt Marge. He recalls the fantastic patient who responded to his care so well. It's nice to remember patients that embrace you, but most of all, its great how the patient has a wonderful niece that is so attractive and lovely as ever. I need to make myself known to Simone before she leaves. "Hi Simone."

"Hi, do you I know you from somewhere?" answered Simone.

"Sure you do. I attended to your aunt during her stay at the hospital, and your sister and I are suppose to have a date really soon."

"Oh, I remember Lorenz. What are you doing here? Are you visiting patients?"

"No, I'm here trying to set up this home as one on the regular visit list with the community service I support."

" Oh, it's nice you do community service."

"Yes, it is. I love doing the service and finding great people whenever I can. What are you doing here, if you don't mind me asking?

"I am looking to see if it is appropriate for my sister and I to place Aunt Marge in this home. She's getting older and we can't help her living the way she did before the stroke. The info about the Aunt Marge having a stroke was never presented, and doesn't come out later either and we can't be afraid to live our lives without thinking of her welfare all the time. It just isn't possible for us to look after her as busy as we are."

"I understand, but how do you think she'll feel once you tell her of your idea? My impression is she wants to continue her life style and be the happy woman she is."

"Yes, Lorenz, it's going to be challenging for her to accept. It's something my sister and I need to discuss."

"Your sister, now that is a very energetic woman. When will you talk to her again?"

"Later today we are meeting for dinner. Right after she leaves Aunt Marge with the nurse we hired."

"She and I are going out soon. I am quite excited about it too. Its like a date that's needed, greatly needed."

"Yea, she told me about your date. I hope you two have fun. What are you planning?"

"I can't tell you that, but I will tell you its simple and nothing extravagant. Heck, I can't afford anything beyond simple. Just can't do it right now."

"She knows this, since being an intern brings limited funds. Don't worry, I am sure she'll like whatever you decide to do; no doubt."

"Well, I have to get back to the kids. Please tell your sister and Aunt hello for me. It was nice seeing you again."

"It was nice seeing you too Lorenz. Nice talking to you."

Lorenz walked towards the lounge room where large noises of laughter were. Walking into the room, he watched the wheel chair race, kids dressed like clowns in old clothing the citizens allowed them to use, a couple card games like black jack and poker, and a couple fellas dancing the swing with a couple of elderly women. Man theses kids sure know how to have a great time with senior citizens. "I hate to end all the fun, but its time for us to leave. We promised not to over do it this visit. Sorry folks, but the fun has to come to an end."

Immediately the kids knew what to do. Without any additional guidance, the kids and elderly began saying their goodbyes, cleaned up the mess, and started out to the center of the facility. The kids waved to the elderly as they walked towards the exits and told them how much fun they were today. The elderly says in unison "We can't wait until the next visit."

"See you next time" the kids reply.

"Yes, we'll see you again soon," says Lorenz. "Let's get in the van kids and head back to the community center. We haven't much time to get there."

Everyone climbs into the van and finds their seat. Lorenz takes the helm and starts down the road

"Hey Lorenz," Rick calls.

"Yes Rick"

"I hear you have a date. You know it's the first time we've ever heard of you going out with anyone. This has to be a special person for you to find time. I want to know is she really pretty?"

"No, Fred jumps in; she's just a girl that he likes. Looks have nothing to do with it right Lorenz?"

"She's awesome looking, smart, and I think sassy. She's the kind of girl you definitely take home to your aunt before she visits your mother."

"What type of girl is that suppose to be?" asked Elaine.

"Um, you know, the kind of girl you want everyone to like and have your aunt present her thoughts first. You'll understand as you get older and start dating Elaine."

Almost in unison, Fred, Rick, and Elaine asks, "What's the plan for your first date?"

"You know gang, I really haven't thought about it just yet. It can't be something fancy just yet. I am not at the point where I can afford the great fun things yet. I guess it's got to be something simple, a little romantic, and of course cheap." They start laughing and snickering about being cheap for a first impressionable date. Elaine whispers to Rick, "You know we can help him out. I have an idea, are you game?"

Rick answers in a low tone, "sure if it won't cost us too much. Fred, are you in?"

"In what?" Fred replies.

"Not so loud, silly. Are you helping Lorenz on his date/"

"Are you crazy, I don't have the money to help him? He's going to be the doctor and all. He can handle his first date impressing the lady."

"You know interns don't make much until they become doctors. Didn't you know? So, are you in or not? We want to do something nice for him."

"I'm in. So what do you two have in mind?"

"We can talk about it after we get to the community center."

Lorenz stops the van in front of the center and tells everyone to get out here so I can park the van in the drive. The kids jump out and head into the center just as they normally do. There is nothing exciting at all when they head to the meeting room except the receptionist holding a note for Lorenz.

"Didn't Lorenz drive you guys today?" asked Jalissa.

"Yes" replied Fred, "he's parking the van and will be right in."

Lorenz enters the center and immediately is handed a note from Jalissa. "You had a visitor today and she left this note. She was very nice and really interested in you; and she asked a lot of questions too. I didn't think she'd ever leave."

# Chapter 5

## *Bringing Things Together*

"You know Sabrina, the family will not like Aunt Marge in a home. They will be outraged if we place her there," said Simone.

"I know, but its best. Who is going to be with her now that she isn't in the best of conditions? Are you going to schedule your work and life around her? I can't do it. I don't see any of our relatives jumping to her aid. And why should it be us who steps up and take the lead on these things anyway?"

"Did you call anybody about the reunion? I didn't get a call, email, or letter from anyone."

"You know I called and wrote everyone on our original list. I guess its time to make phone calls. Oh, one of our cousins called and offered to help."

"Let me guess who, the crazy one."

"Yep, that's the one. You know he may be crazy, but he's always willing to help at a moments notice. And we need his help now."

"So, did you return his call?"

"No, not yet, I wanted all the information for the retirement home first."

"We've got to bring the rest of the family in on this one. And as I always say, the sooner the better."

Rodney stands in the doorway of his apartment waiting for his friend. He looks over to the next apartment and observes the next door neighbor fumbling with her keys. She seemed so distraught that she drops the keys with no other items in her hand. "Hey, Diane what's wrong? I haven't seen you this nervous about anything before. Can I help you with anything?"

"Nothing is wrong Rodney; she tells him between sobs and sniffles, nothing is wrong. It's been a bad day and I am ready for a serious wind down: A glass of wine is calling my name."

"Can I assist you with the door? It doesn't seem to be cooperating with you right now." And in a swift move, Rodney picks keys from the floor, points at the one he'd hope the right one and with a nod from Diane, he inserts the key into the lock. The door opens and he grabs Diane's hand to enter the apartment. "Please have a seat, I can pour you a glass of wine and you can start telling me about your day."

"Thanks, but I don't feel like talking about it. I appreciate your help but I need some alone and wind down time for a few. Can you do me one favor though? Can you just sit here and have a wine of glass with me?"

"Sure, I don't mind. Whatever it takes to get you back on track; what are neighbors for?"

Rodney finishes pouring two glasses of wine and sits squarely in the recliner next to the couch. Diane sets on the couch with her head in her hands, reflecting a despair of drama and confusion. "Rodney, I appreciate you sitting there and opening the door for me. I had a hard time at the office, received a call from my displaced boyfriend, and my cousin called about our favorite aunt being in the hospital. All I need now is for my best friend to call and tell me something bad. You know, a person can only handle so much in one day."

"You know, sometimes its just bad timing for all things to happen at once. It doesn't mean it's the end of the world. We just have to find a way to cope with the rough time." Moving over to the couch, Rodney places his right arm around and pulls her close to him. In a swift move and in sync with the rhythm of the soft music he turned on when he entered the apartment, he pulls Diane closer to him and offers to hold her for a few minutes. Diane accepts the gesture and moves closer as her thoughts are "this is just what I need for the moment." They sat there, said nothing, and in a very flaccid move, reach for the wine, place it up to their mouths and sip a swallow or two. In no time the wine glasses are empty, the moment seems much better in Diane's eyes as she turns to Rodney and says, "Thank you for being here for me. I appreciate it so much. I guess I may get a chance to return the favor in the future."

"You are welcome. What are neighbors for? We get a chance to do something for each other all the time." In a swift motion, Rodney rises from the couch, reaches for Diane's forehead and place one gentle kiss upon her. As Rodney stands tall, Diane gives him the look of contentment for the moment. "Thanks Rodney, I really needed this. You have no idea what it means. I know the woman who gets close to you will have a wonderful man in her life."

"You are special and never forget it. Things will look up tomorrow and as a matter of fact, if you want, we can make it get better now if you let me fix dinner for you."

"Oh, that's nice but I have to take a rain check. I have too much to do this evening and besides, I still don't think I will be great company."

"It's only eating. Tell you what, you can come and get a plate if you change your mind. I'll make sure one is set aside for you. Just give me a ring if you like or whenever you like."

"Thanks again Rodney, you are too sweet."

Rodney leaves the apartment and heads for his place next door. He heads for the kitchen and starts dinner. Having a second taste for wine, he pours himself a glass of Chardonnay and starts his creation. Having told Diane he'd cook, he motivates himself to create a dish to remember just in case she decides to pick up a plate. The master at work in the kitchen or better yet, the wizard of creation; I think chicken and rice, strawberry and nut salad, and a green veggie will do. Dessert will be a cup of chocolate pudding with whipped cream. That's a good meal for an evening of hard work and misery. I'll flavor the chicken and rice with my secret spices and flavor the veggies the way my mother use to. I am sure she'd like the meal. You know, I kind of like this cooking gig for a woman. It's motivating and I can probably get use to this. Simone will have to call me really soon, but not too soon because I'd like to try a few dishes on Diane. I am sure she wouldn't mind being my guinea pig, he thought. In a little effort and 20 minutes later the dinner is complete and smells wonderful. Rodney hears a knock on his apartment door; he's thinking as he laughs out loud "She changed her mind after smelling my cooking."

"Just a minute, be right there," shouts Rodney.

"OK," answers Simone. Being surprised by a man's voice from Diane's apartment, she waits for the door to open.

"Who is it? Is it you Diane?"

"No. Is she home?

Opening the door, he answers the woman, "I guess so, but she isn't here," in mid sentence he gasps and recognizes Simone as the woman at the door. "Well, I'll be a lucky son of a gun, as a smile cracks his face ear to ear I must have wished you up to reality, I was just thinking about you," said Rodney.

"Oh, my goodness, you mean you live in my cousin's apartment."

"Diane is your cousin?

"Yes, has been all of her life."

"Oh my goodness you are cousin Simone right? What a coincidence! No, this isn't her apartment it's the one next door."

"I didn't mean to disturb you, but I should check up on her. She didn't take the news of our aunt too well today."

"Yea, she told me about her bad day."

"When you get a chance, maybe you can get her to have dinner over here. I offered to cook and please include you as my guest as well. I'd love to have you here for a taste of my cooking."

"You cook? Are you a good cook?"

"No doubt, one of the best if I have to say so."

"OK, I'll try to get her over, but if all else fails, I'll return and take you up on dinner. I wanted us to talk anyway."

"Sounds like a plan to me. I look forward to seeing you really soon."

Simone leaves for the next apartment and Rodney returns to the kitchen after closing the door. Rodney goes into the closet and pulls out an ice bucket, takes a bottle of zinfandel and places the wine on ice. He takes three wine glasses and places them in the freezer. He then checks the meal and makes his final touch for flavor and quality. In no time he sets up for three in the dining area of his apartment. Not to seem a little too feminine, he sets up the table with simple tools of the trade. At least they are all matching and presentable. From napkins to dish selection, he coordinated his apartment content to be with quality and flare. Having good taste as a man is a best kept secret amongst his male friends. Besides, they all think everything in the apartment was selected by a former girl friend or his mother who visited nearly twice a month. His apartment was a smooth bachelor pad. Yes, smooth as his color coordination must have been the result of a contract with the popular designer. His furniture selection is a class of modernistic simplicity, the quality in décor is just like his flare of dress. Presentable and fashionable, many would emulate if they could. No, he isn't not the fashion trend setter, just plain good looking in clothes, as his selection tipped the scale to exquisite. Rodney looks great in any type of clothing, his mother and sisters would always say.

The chicken and rice dish has an awesome aroma which fills the apartment complex. People are always commenting on Rodney's cooking. Once he was the host of the apartment mixer and every dish was emptied within minutes of its start.

All were items were from Rodney's cooking, and with such a talent in his possession he is always asked if he'd open a restaurant. Back in the kitchen, Rodney takes a sneak peak at the veggie dish. He adds a little flavoring and turns the fire down a little. "Its just about ready and I do hope Simone and Diane comes over soon." The phone rings, "hello" he answers.

"Hey Rodney, we smell dinner and its lovely. Diane and I will be over in a few minutes if that's ok."

"Are we on some kind of mental connection? That was my thought just before you called. Dinner is ready and waiting, so come quickly before it over cooks."

"We'll be right there. Bye"

Simone replaces the phone receiver and starts gathering her things to head next door. Diane is standing up from the couch and places the last glass of wine down on the coffee table. She slightly stumbles as she heads to the bathroom to freshen up.

"Diane, you know, Aunt Marge will be fine but we have to think of a way to take care of her. You surely aren't available to come in every day. Sabrina and I think we, all of the kids, should place her in a senior citizen home," said Simone.

"No way, it just isn't like her to want something like this," replied Diane.

"Well, it's not what she wants, but its something we have to do since we all have our own lives."

"I can understand, but maybe we can share the responsibility or work some sort of schedule to maintain her home and support her."

"That is a good thought, but our dependability isn't the greatest. And the object is to share our time and not take one over the other doing our own thing. Which of us is willing to start sacrificing our careers?"

"I see your point. But she is so sweet and loving. You know she is awesome and we love her to death."

"Are you ready for dinner? Rodney has everything ready and we need to head over right now."

"Yes, I'm coming right behind you. I need to lock the door right behind us."

"Ok, we are there. I hope the dinner taste as good as it smells."

"Oh, girl, Rodney can seriously cook. You won't be disappointed."

The girls head for the apartment door. Simone makes it to the hallway and turns toward Diane just as the phone rings. Diane turns around and heads for her house phone. "Hello" she pauses, "This is she; No I will not accept the charges." She shakes her head from left to right while her eyes are connected to Simone. She hangs up, and returns on the journey to the door. "Some people never give up."

"Oh, was it someone you're trying to get rid of?"

"Yes, it is just that. A dead beat who I should have never got involved with. We can talk about it later. But right now, let's get that dinner going. I'm famished."

"Ok, let's knock on the door and hope for the best."

Simone knocks on Rodney's door. Rodney yells, "Just a minute," and does the finishing touches to the dinner table. Ok, all set for three. I hope they are ready and just in time too. Rodney briskly walks to the door and turns toward his counter and grabs two lilies from the flower arrangement. He opens the door and says "welcome ladies to my humble abode, presenting them with the lilies."

"Thank you for inviting us to dinner. We really appreciate it and the timing couldn't be better."

"Anytime, what are neighbors for?" smiling Rodney.

"Its nice having great neighbors that looks out for one another. You are so sweet. Where should I sit?"

"Simone, you sit here," Rodney pulls out the chair and places her at the east side of the table. "Diane, you are here" as he repeats the courtesy and places Diane at the opposite end of his position at the table. "I have wine prepared for you. If you don't mind, I'd like to serve the wine first and you two can sip on it while I prepare the plates."

"Sounds good to me" said Diane.

"Yes, its darling for me too," answered Simone.

Rodney gets the chilled wine glasses from the freezer. He places the glass in front of each person and then opens the wine for consumption. He pops the cork and pours each glass to the near rim. He places the wine in a chilled bucket for later. He then runs over to the entertainment center and starts his music. All CDs were planned to provide a not too funky crowd or atmosphere, but one of true relaxation and enjoyment. Numerous love ballads start playing over the air as each song has a hint of island flair.

"Rodney, this is a nice CD. Did you compile it yourself or is it something you picked up?" asked Diane.

Still in the kitchen preparing plates, Rodney answers, "Something I picked up from a friend. He dabbles in mood settings and such."

"Oh, this is supposed to set our mood to eat? I don't need to be in a mood to eat, just be hungry enough and you don't care about the music," said Simone.

All three chuckled at Simone's comment. Rodney moves back to the kitchen and retrieves the plates. He places a dish in front of each of the girls and returns to the kitchen to get his. Returning to the dining area he takes his position at one side of the table. Sitting at the table, he asked, "Is there something you'd like to help you both enjoy your dinner."

"No," they answered in unison.

Settling in, he raised his hands asking the two to join him in dinner grace and with one motions, he grabbed their hands and said, "Father, bless this meal as it provides the goodness of the earth, the multitude of strength through the fuel for energy, and one connection of three spirits as we enjoy the savory taste of your creation. Thank you for my guests and their hunger, and may work in the kitchen please the hunger pain of the day. With all things of your grace and goodness, we pray. Amen."

"Amen" they said.

Together they picked up their forks, filled them with food, and with a swoosh gave a taste.

"Umm, if it were any better, we'd have to hire you for life," said Simone.

Smiling, "I told you he could cook," said Diane.

"Thank you ladies for the compliment, but you haven't gotten to the good part yet, wait until you taste the main course."

"Is that something you made especially for us?" asked Simone favoring him with a smile.

Taken back by her quick comment, he plunders for a conscious and decent remark without seeming overly confident. "Ah, that's a for sure thing. I want you to open your arms for every time I prepare a meal. I need you to want more at the drop of a hat and the mention of my name. You need to just get hungry and allow your mouth to water at the thought of me cooking."

"As if I don't every time I smell you cooking in the evenings," said Diane.

"You mean he cooks all the time?"

"I try to cook as much as often, but my schedule only allows certain nights. I try to be creative as I consider my next move in the office. You know what I mean, don't you ladies?"

While eating the meal, drinking wine, and enjoying the moment, Diane and Simone nearly finished while Rodney talked about his cooking. Rodney noticed how they both were such quick eaters and commented, "No one has ever eaten my dinner so quickly. Did you taste it all?"

"Of course, we tasted it," they said in unison.

Laughing, Rodney finished his last bit of his chicken. He started on the veggie mix and just before placing the next fork full in his mouth, he looked over towards the kitchen to see if his soufflé was still warming on the stove. Simone saw his look and immediately moved closer to his hand and sensually placed his food in her mouth. "Mmmm, that's great for a second taste of those great veggies."

Looking surprised and stunned, "You know, you took the best portion of the veggies and especially flavored from my fork," he said with a smirk.

Diane looked stunned and extremely surprised. "Simone, uh, we need to talk" she whispered.

"No, not now, later," she whispered back.

"Simone, you know we should talk, now!"

"OK, ok, let's go into the hall."

They both stood up and walked across the apartment into the hall. Rodney stood up looking puzzled by the ladies heading toward the apartment's front door. "Hey is there something going on?"

"No, just a moment," they both said in unison.

"Oh, ok, it's good, I guess."

The made it into the hall way and immediately Diane touched Simone's shoulder, looked into her eyes and said, "What are you doing?"

"What? I see someone very interesting and I'd like to snatch him up. Smiling, "isn't he fine? And the man can cook, keeps a clean apartment, and has a great taste."

"He is a great catch. But should you throw yourself on him? You just met the guy."

"Oh, no, I met the guy a few weeks ago. He walked in the art gallery and we hit it off. I don't know if he remembers but I'm going to remind him of our encounter."

"Then you do what you must. He is a great guy and let me warn you, he's amazingly attractive. There are women dropping by here all the time."

"Shouldn't we talk about this later?"

"Yea, we should get back. Just remember to take it easy and not be too aggressive. He can be a player, so watch your step."

"You sound as if there's history between the two of you."

"No, no history, just observation."

"Sure. Thanks for the info. Let me work my magic. By the time I get my grips on him, he'll not need another woman in his life."

Returning to the apartment they find, Rodney just finished washing the plates and started cleaning the kitchen. "I didn't know you two were returning."

"Oh, come on, we were just out in the hall way. We weren't out there but so long. Besides your cooking is fantastic and I wanted to finish the rest of the food. Not to make a pig out of myself, it's just a compliment to your cooking." said Simone.

"Thanks, I appreciate the compliment. And since I didn't put everything away, I can make you a plate to take home."

"Thanks. What about that dessert?"

"It's coming right out."

"Great. Is there more wine?"

Rodney moves about in the kitchen and quickly brings out three bowls of his special chocolate pudding, with a touch of chocolate sprinkles and places them on the table. He returned to the kitchen for the new bottle of wine. The girls glance at the dessert and like young teens in unison say, "uuummm, this looks delicious."

"I thought you'd like it. It's a creation I'd like to leave to my off spring. Just haven't found the right partner to make that commitment yet."

In one spoon swoop, the two ladies took the first taste of the soufflé and their eyes expanded to the size of quarters. "Wow, this is really good. I mean really good," said Simone.

"And I agree," said Diane. "You can market this. This is really good, really, really good, and I'd be the first to buy the recipe if you publish it."

"Thank you ladies, I am honored you like my cooking."

Returning from the kitchen, Rodney pours more wine in the ladies glasses. Looking directly in Simone's eyes, Rodney says, "I hope you ladies enjoyed the meal, the music, and the wine. Is there something else I can do for you to make your evening better?"

"Yes you can," said Simone.

"No, you can't, everything is fine, actually it was excellent," said Diane.

Immediately Simone gave that look to Diane signaling for her to head back to her apartment. Diane looked back and winked, shaking her head from side to side indicating 'bad move'. In a heated whisper, Simone said, "are you sure there's no history between you two?"

"No" she whispered back.

"Rodney, everything was great. I think your meal hit the spot. It was wonderful, really wonderful. When can we do it again?" asked Simone.

"For you, it's just a phone call. As a matter of fact, I have an opening for this weekend. What's on your schedule?"

"Let's say my schedule matches your weekend events."

"Ok, we're on. Let's make it Saturday night."

"Saturday night it is."

Diane takes the last bit of her wine, stands and walks towards the door. Moving with a frustrated face, she whispers to herself, "it never fails, nothing changes with Simone. Every guy has to be someone she dives for. It didn't matter if I had my eyes on Rodney. She always moves on a notion and throws her claws at him. It could be a hundred guys in a room and she always go for the one I like best. Never fails." In her regular voice, "Good bye, Rodney."

"Good night neighbor" replied Rodney.

"Simone, are you coming?"

"No, I want to talk to Rodney for a moment or two."

"Ok, great. The door will be open. Just walk in."

"Thanks Diane, will be right there."

Simone picks up the bowls and silverware off the table. She collected the wine glasses and walks toward the kitchen. Rodney meets her at the kitchen entrance and grabs the wine glasses from her hand. In one smooth motion, he positions himself for a quick brisk kiss on her cheek. "Thank you for the glasses."

"Moving, just moving, you are so moving and with nice moves. You are something aren't you?"

"Something?"

"Yes, something quite different from other men, I sense there is much more to you than you reveal."

"There is always something special to every person. And showing all your cards at one time leads a boring life."

"A boring life, you mean showing all leave little to the intrigue of finding a life long partner? You know how challenging that is in today's society"

"Intrigue, you mean finding someone that tickles your fancy from the mental capacity instead to the usual physical one?"

"Yes, finding that one. You have an idea of what we have to go through. Aren't you tired of searching?"

"Searching is half of the fun. The problem is the players expecting too much too soon."

"You mean the commitment question before you know the person?"

"Yes, you do look for that commitment and partnership in every person you date don't you?"

Moving to the sink, Rodney runs hot water for washing the glasses. Not saying much he makes faces to her last question as contemplating his answers. Simone sees his facial reflection in the window. "Don't think too hard on that last question. You know all of us seek one special person to spend the rest of their lives with," said Simone.

"No, it's not what you think. It's different for me. Or should I say for guys in general. I don't see every woman as a potential life long partner. It's just not my way and I do believe most guys don't see it that way either. I mean, when you find the right one, you immediately know."

"That leaves room for a question or two. It also leaves room for assumptions. You have an idea of what type of girl is your dream woman, right?"

"Yes, I have an idea, but nothing I'd like to share with you tonight. I like to take time and find out more about you and our start is Saturday night. That way we can ease our way into something if we are compatible."

"Oh, I get it. Keep it as interesting as ever and the more you keep in the dark, the better it is at finding out. Isn't that a game people play?"

"No, no game. You don't lay all your cards on the table unless there is something specific about the guy you like right?"

"Ah, right. You are right. Let's keep this conversation open for the weekend."

"Exactly, let's keep this open and our eyes keen on each other."

"One day at a time and build on this night."

Moving closer to each other, Rodney embraces Simone, gives her a tender kiss on her cheek and says, "Here is the beginning of tomorrow and a step on a journey to the rainbow."

Returning the kiss Simone says, "As long as we walk hand in hand, explore with an open mind, we'll laugh and play along the way, and fly the big blue sky."

"Fly the big blue sky?"

"Giggling, I couldn't come up with anything else that quickly, but it works for the moment."

"Great" with a laugh he agrees

Simone breaks away and walks towards the door. She looks back and smiles, "Good night and I look forward to Saturday night."

"I can't wait myself" as he walks to the door. Right after Simone walks out, he quickly closes the door, turns around and thinks, "What did I just start?"

Sabrina dials the number 843-949-1112 and waits for the ring. "Hello," answers Jamie.

"Jamie, is it you? Thank goodness. I thought I miss placed your number," said Sabrina.

"Sabrina, it's about time you called me. I've waited for sometime now and you are pushing it so close to your next shoot. You need to be at Market Square, 9:30 in the morning, and meet the photographer today, 7 o'clock at the bottom park by the lake. He's doing a shoot there and wanted to meet you and review the shoot strategy."

"Why tonight?"

"I don't know. I'm just the messenger. You need help getting there?"

"No. I can make it. Just don't understand those strategy meetings."

"You know, it's a part of the deal and profession."

"No it isn't. Every time I see a photographer in the evening, it turns out to be some kind of sexual advancement. I am so tired of this. I can't wait until I find the one guy who respects me for my mind and spirit."

"Don't worry about this Sabrina. It's going to be different. Trust me on it."

"You say this every time Jamie. You say this every time. Don't worry I'll be there."

Ending the call, Sabrina turns to her calendar for notes to her shoot. It's a shoot for a charity organization. I see, so why should we have a strategy meeting for a charity shoot? It can't be something out of the usual charity organizations. I hope it isn't for hunger as I am sure to eat at the restaurant. She turns to her wardrobe and selects her outfit for the evening meeting. Nothing seductive, nothing too plain, but something enticing and comfortable will do the trick. Let's see, the pants suit will do.

Lorenz arrives at Market Square around 6:30 pm, walks in the door and scans the room for a table. He finds an empty table, moves towards it and dodges other people moving towards the door. "Excuse me" he says as he bumps one gentleman. The gentleman nods and says, "I'm sorry, excuse me." This is a courteous place Lorenz thinks. Doesn't seem quite that fancy but simply nice. Lorenz pulls out the chair at the table and one beautiful woman walks past with a camera around her neck. Looking at the woman, Lorenz compares her beauty to those of models; her face is very unique and slim in its shape, luscious lips, eyes of gold, and a proportionate build most women would envy. Her skin is olive, and seems quite smooth. Her hair is dark, brunette like. Needless to say, guys gawk in awe in her presence, and looking around the restaurant, that's exactly what men are doing. A waiter comes to Lorenz' table and proceeds to inquire to his drink preference;

"Welcome to Market Square" as he hands Lorenz a menu. "May I start you with a drink while you look over our menu?" asked the waiter.

"Water is fine. I'm looking for a photographer named Mikel, do you know of him?"

"Yes, and it's a woman not a man. She is right over there," the waiter points at the lovely woman.

"No way," said Lorenz.

"Yes way. Is there a problem with a woman being a photographer?"

"No, no problem. I just didn't expect Mikel to be a woman."

"Most people don't. Should I bring your water to her table?"

"Yes, that will be the right thing to do. Thank you."

Mikel makes her way through the restaurant, waving at multiple people. Without a doubt she's a regular patron. Multiple people smile and wave to her as she moves about the place speaking to a select few. Some are younger than she, some are extremely older, but they all seemed to know her well. Mikel stopped at a specific table, large enough for 6 people. As she takes a seat, two other guys walked up to the table and immediately take a seat after their artsy air kiss near each cheek greeting. Lorenz thinks, "I sure hope she doesn't expect me to do the same as those two. It might be fashionable, but it's not quite in my circle of things just yet." Mikel places her camera on the table and immediately start reviewing the menu. "I guess I'll have the usual" she told the other two. Her usual is a Calamari appetizer, Blackened Salmon steak, steamed vegetables, and coffee as her dessert. The guys nodded and turned to a waiter who is standing by. Given their order the waiter walked away. Lorenz stood up and started walking toward Mikel and her friend's table. Just before arriving there, the waiter who took Lorenz's drink order dashed to the table and places the glass of water on it in front of an empty place. "Who is the drink for?" asked Mikel.

"It's for him, the guy walking to the table" answered the waiter. "He said he has a meeting with you."

"Thanks Tom."

"You're welcome Mikel" answered Tom.

Lorenz arrives at the table. "Hi folks," he says. Extending his hand he speaks "Mikel, I'm Lorenz and I represent the community center. I am suppose to be a part of the advertisement you are shooting. The director asked me to meet you here."

Mikel takes his hand, looks him over quickly, and says, "They made a good choice. As soon as the other model arrives, we can get started. Please take a seat and give Tom your order."

Lorenz ordered a salad and asked that it comes out with the main meal.

Sabrina walks in the door of the restaurant in a great silky pants suit. Nicely fitting, and showing her features but conservative in revealing her skin. She stops a waiter and asks for Mikel. The waiter directs her to the table in the rear of the room. She sees one woman with the three men and immediately thinks "it's already different than the other meetings. What a relief, at least there is another woman at the table. I wonder which man is Mikel." Arriving at the table Sabrina asks, "Which one of you is Mikel?"

"I am," Mikel replies.

Shocked and surprised she starts to giggle, you're a woman. Lorenz sees Sabrina smiles and immediately stands.

"Yes I am. Most people find it shocking" answered Mikel.

"Sabrina," Lorenz says with a smile.

"Lorenz?" she replies.

"You two know each other?" Mikel asks.

"More of an acquaintance," Sabrina answers.

"Not for long I hope," comments Lorenz.

"Please have a seat. I can get a waiter for you so you can order." Waving her hand and signaling for a waiter. "One is on the way; shall we get started with the meeting?"

"Sure." They agreed in unison.

"This shoot is for the community center. I hear they are doing a great job but they need our help in raising funds. It's that time of year when we have to give back to the community and I have support from your organizations to do this shoot. My objective is to make it simple, clean, and interesting. So I've asked you here to discuss how we may present the community center. First, let me introduce everyone. Sabrina is our model from the agency, Lorenz is a representative from the center, Ted is a publishing writer for a magazine, and Paul is a marketing director for one of the agencies. We are all here to pull this off with minimal funding.

"They didn't tell me I am doing this as a contribution," said Sabrina.

"I don't think you are here as a contribution. Your agency will make the contribution" answered Mikel. "We can start with Lorenz telling us about the community center."

"First let me tell you my activities at the center. I contribute time and medical skills to the center. Therefore, my exposure to the entire program is limited. So I can only tell you about the things I see. Twice weekly I hold a health clinic, once a week I drive the teenagers around to senior citizen homes, and that's the extent of my exposure. All other things you'd have to get back to the director."

"You give three afternoons to the clinic?" asked Sabrina.

"Yes, I do and it's worth every minute."

"We can get enough ideas from you for the shoot. Just your activities will be a start," said Mikel.

Tom the waiter shows up to the table and takes Sabrina's order. She orders Calamari, salmon steak, and a dish of steamed veggies. Mikel looks at her and winks "Good choice."

Ted asks, "Lorenz, do you mind if I follow you around on your days at the center?"

"Sure, I don't see why not."

"Good, this will give us an idea to what the public will embrace as a campaign. It will also give Mikel an eye to some great snapshots of common people and where to throw in Sabrina."

"Paul, are you open one night this week to meet at the center?"

"Sure Ted, just give me a call when you're ready. I only need a tour of the facilities and one day of observation to create a marketing scheme."

"Then we are looking at next week as our time of discovery and the following week to have a complete package. You guys are wonderful. Let's agree that all questions should come to me as the coordinator. I want to make sure we stay on the same page for this fund raising commercial shoot." said Mikel.

One after the other, they all agreed to Mikel being the coordinator. After the agreement all meals arrived to the table. "Dinner is served," smiles Tom.

"Sabrina, its surprising to see you?" said Lorenz.

"Same here and I look forward to seeing what the center is all about."

"You're going to love being with the kids there. Once you get with them, your world changes."

"What about the others there? Isn't there some training classes for a change in professions?"

"I am not sure about that, because I focus on two areas, the kids and the health clinic."

"So what do you do for a living when you aren't at the community center?" asked Mikel.

"I'm a medical intern at the hospital near the clinic."

"Yes, that's where we met. My aunt took ill and he gave me a phone book." Sabrina giggles.

"A phone book?" Ted laughs.

"It was to dial a doctor right," laughs Paul.

"No, no, Sabrina wanted the phone book for another reason."

"Don't get angry Lorenz, we are only kidding" said Mikel.

"I know, I know Lorenz mumbles as he shakes his head from side to side."

"He's a good intern there. My aunt liked him and so did my sister."

"Oh really, and what about Sabrina, does she like him too?" asked Mikel.

"Let's just say opportunity is knocking."

"Opportunity knocks loud but will the door open?" asked Lorenz.

"Sure, it's opening for dessert right now" exclaimed Ted.

The dessert cart came around the table. Ted chose a pudding dish, Paul a cake, Lorenz asked for coffee, and Sabrina rejected it all. "Mikel are you ready for your coffee?" asked Tom.

"Yes, would you please bring me a cup? Sabrina, are you sure you don't want anything else?" asked Mikel.

"No, I'm fine."

Small talk between the men occurs while Mikel and Sabrina have a woman to woman conversation. "You know Lorenz is drop dead gorgeous. You better get on him."

"Yes I know. I am on it believe me. We are supposed to go out this Friday night."

"You mean the date is set up and you two didn't know you'd be working on the same project?"

"No, I didn't know it was shooting for the community center. I just know it's a shoot coming and we needed to meet tonight."

"You know what this means don't you?"

"I think I do, but tell me your thoughts."

They look at each other and immediately lip the word "fate." Smile at each other and then glance at Lorenz.

"He's too good looking to be alone. Is he alone?"

"Yes, he doesn't have time to do much of anything. I wonder how he gives three evenings to the community center."

"You do what you can to get him off the take. I have an idea to help you if you need it."

"I need all the help I can get."

Ted, Paul, and Lorenz called the waiter over the table. Mikel says, "I have these guys."

"Thanks Mikel" they said in unison. Ted and Paul stands and motion for the door. Mikel stands repeat the cheek to cheek greeting as they say good bye to each other. Lorenz looks over to Sabrina and ask, "Do you have a ride home or can we share a cab?"

"I have my car. Do you need a ride somewhere?"

"As a matter of fact, I do."

"Are you ready now or do you have a few minutes?"

"I have a few minutes. Only a few minutes because I have to be at the hospital, with a glance at his watch he adds in six hours. I need to get some sleep before the shift."

"If that's the case, we should leave now. Mikel, do you mind us leaving?"

"No, go right ahead. I will be fine." answered Mikel

Lorenz and Sabrina both rise from the table and head for the door. Sabrina leads the way out and Lorenz follows gazing at how luscious her body is. "Stop looking at my ass Lorenz" Sabrina giggles.

"But a nice ass it is for sure. Lovely specimen if I have to say so."

Exiting the restaurant, they head to the parking lot for Sabrina's car. Sabrina stops and turns towards Lorenz. "Are you sure you want us to go out this Friday? Or was that a conversation piece?"

"Sabrina, I seriously want to take you out this Friday. I've thought this over a number of times. I see us having a wonderful time together."

"Then why haven't you confirmed a time and place for us?"

"You know, I am very limited until I complete my internship. I am trying to find a place suitable that I can afford for such a lovely woman."

"You shouldn't worry about impressing me, I'm very simple. I'd like to get to know you, soon to be doctor."

"OK, we are definitely on for Friday. Can we get to your car now?"

"Oh, I'm sorry. Yes we can."

They enter Sabrina's car and she starts the engine. As she backs up, she asks 'Where do you live?"

"You know where the community center is?"

"Yes"

"I'm two blocks from there. I can show you once we get near the center."

"OK" she answers. Sabrina push radio buttons to find a soothing channel. She finds a channel and looks over to ask if he likes the music. In minutes, Lorenz is asleep. A few miles later, Sabrina arrives at the community center and wakes Lorenz. Lorenz immediately directs her to the next block and asks her to stop the car there. He exits the vehicle tells her good night and he'll be in touch. Before Sabrina can pull away, Lorenz disappears into the darkness of an alley. "He has to get some rest. How does he keep going with little sleep?"

Simone returns to Diane's apartment, knocks on the door and waits. Diane opens the door, waves her in, steps aside and says, "Are you that desperate?"

Simone enters saying, "Desperate? I don't think so. You know, Rodney is a great guy and when you have an attraction that's all there, then why play around. You have to go for it. Obviously he has the same idea as we have a date this Saturday night."

Both girls sitting on the couch, Simone stretches for a magazine form the coffee table.

"Look Simone, Rodney is a great guy, very good as a matter of fact. He is worth taking care of. He is considerate, helpful, focused, and on top of all, attractive. He is all of that and I know how you like to go after the opposite type of guy. He isn't your norm so please try to control your emotions."

"Like you control yours?"

"What do you mean? Of course I control my emotions and I always find the right one."

"Like the one who called before we left for Rodney's apartment."

"Simone, he is not the one. You know, you think you have one and they either hide something from you, pretend to be someone they aren't, or just plain play on your emotions."

"Then your choice of men happens to be someone like Rodney. Why didn't you try to date Rodney?"

75

"I thought about it, but it was too close for comfort. And besides, he is too good of a guy in my eyes."

"Then what's this conversation about. I thought you had something for him and wanted me to back off."

"No, I'm just doing the family thing, We have to look out for each other even if we aren't sure what they are about to get into."

"Then tell me everything you know about Rodney. Start from the first time you met him."

"I told you earlier. He is all and everything I'd want in a man. No, I haven't seen many women come by. He had a girl friend, but something happened and we never talked about it. Or, let's just say he didn't spill the beans when I tried to get it out of him," Diane said with a mischievous grin.

"You sly woman; it's amazing how investigative you can be at times. Is that the good ole college training? Or is it just being interested enough as a good neighbor?"

"Just interested as a good neighbor, and could have been more she adds with a wink at Simone.

"So there is interest. I thought you just said there weren't any physical or mental attraction."

"No, I didn't say it wasn't. I said he wasn't quite the type of guy I normally date. But I almost got him to tell me about his past." A quick way to cover up my comment without revealing my actual thought; whew that was close, Diane thought.

"So you wanted to but didn't have the opportunity. Are you sure we aren't trampling on each other's ego or turf?"

"No Simone, we aren't traveling down the same path. You go have fun on this date. But, don't expect me to be a spy for you since he's my neighbor."

"Don't worry, I'll only ask sensible questions and you will tell me" said Simone with a wink. I better get back to my place. We can talk about Aunt Marge later in the week. I'll call you. Thanks for everything tonight. Thanks especially for letting me hang with you at Rodney's apartment. I'll let you know about the date." Simone stands and tracks to the door for a quick exit. Diane moves right behind her to lock all the locks on the door once she exits. "Good night cousin."

"Good night, talk to you soon."

Rodney calls to make reservations at Restaurant De Marco for Saturday night dinner. The restaurant has an Italian cuisine, is fairly romantic with its booths, tables, and has a relaxing atmosphere. Not too ritzy, but right on for conversing and setting the right impression. "Hello" Rodney said.

"Hello, thank you for calling De Marco's. May I help you?" asked the receptionist.

"Yes, I'd like to make reservations."

"Sure, reservations. Please hold while I transfer your call to reservations."

"Reservations, may I help you?" asked the clerk.

"Yes, I'd like to make reservations for two on Saturday night around 6:45pm. Is there a table available?" asked Rodney.

"Yes there is. I have a booth or table. Which do you prefer?"

"I prefer the table near the east window overlooking the city lights."

"Sir, 6:45pm will barely be dusk. Would you prefer another table since the view will not be as expected?"

"No, that's the table I want and with reason. Tell me, is Tyrone working now?"

"The table is yours. Can I have your name and phone number to hold the reservation?"

"Sure, Rodney Witherspoon; 500-234-3456"

'Thank you Mr. Witherspoon. Yes Tyrone is here. Would you like to speak to him?"

"Yes please thank you." Waiting for Tyrone, Rodney thinks of a way to really impress Simone. Let me see, I can order one dozen roses and have Tyrone place half of them as the table decoration. The second half I'll tip him to have one of his waiters bring and present them to Simone. I hope he allows me to bring over the dessert and keep it especially for us. What else will impress Simone? Let me think.

"Hello, this is Tyrone.'

"Hello my friend."

"Rodney. What a surprise? We haven't seen you around the restaurant lately. How are things?" asked Tyrone.

"I have been quite busy, had a health scare, and lost with intrigue. Can you help me out with a date this Saturday night?"

"Sure no problem, but remember you'll have to make some advancement in our marketing scheme this summer. If you give us your all with the advertisements, I will help you with your date. Is that a deal?"

"No problem. You guys are the greatest to work with and your meals stand alone and needs no marketing. Working for you is a no brainier. Just display one of your common dishes and everyone will drive thousands of miles to eat there."

"You're still funny Rodney. What do you need for your date?"

"First, what do you think of this. A dozen roses, six for the table arrangement and the other six you have delivered to the table once we settle in. Second, allow me to store her dessert in your fridge. And third, isn't there a violinist available for hire? Do you know him very well? If so, can you coordinate the violinist for me for two songs once the dinner comes to the table? Is this too much?"

"She must be a special woman for you to go out of your way. Are you popping the question?"

"She's special all right and I am not asking her anything. Well not asking her about anything long lasting. I might ask her for a little physical attention later. You know what I mean."

"Rodney, it's me Tyrone. I know what you mean and I am surprised you haven't asked her for that already. You always get that sexual attention first before you bring her to this place. When you finally bring her around here, she's considered your girl. What's so different this time?"

"Gut feelings Tyrone. This woman has something more and it's just a gut feeling I have about her. Do I need to send you an email or are you ok with my request?"

"I've got the request down. When are you bringing the roses and dessert?"

"I will have them there around 2:00 on Saturday. Will you be there or will you leave a note with the receptionist?"

"Don't worry about anything. Everyone will be instructed to look out for you and we'll take it from there." said Tyrone.

"Great. I will see you at 2:00 Saturday. Thanks you guys are the greatest."

"You're welcome, and remember our deal; less charges for our advertisement on the next shoot."

"Not a problem Tyrone. I have it under control. Talk to you later."

"Have a great one Rodney."

"You too Tyrone, see you Saturday. Bye" said Rodney.

Rodney is happy with his planning for Saturday night's dinner arrangement. "Now, what else can we do after dinner?" he thinks. Let me see what's happening that night. Concert, Theater, Park, River Cruise Jazz, Cloak Room Club for old school dancing, or a night under the stars at the club play house. I am not so sure what she'd like, but I'm thinking a combination of things after that dinner. Have to keep it simple so we can explore in conversation, be comfortable with our dress, and continue my romantic notions. What to wear? The clothes will answer the question to activity. Jeans are out. Suit, over dressy. Sports coat, ok.

Black slacks, black shirt, blue sports coat. River Cruise Jazz seems to fit in my mind. No, maybe not have to check show times. I'd hate to purchase tickets and miss the boat because we started talking deep into the evening. How about the concert? What time will we finish dinner? Maybe the best thing to do is head to the Cloak Room with a drive through the park by horse and buggy. That may be a little too much. The Cloak Room for sure.

# Chapter 6

## *"It's Preparation"*

Sabrina makes it home, walks in the door, turns the foyer light on, and looks to find Lorenz' phone number to confirm Friday's date. She finds the number on a folded piece of paper torn from the local telephone book in her navy blue jacket. She thinks to herself, "it's late, and it wouldn't be a good time to call. I know he's out asleep for the night for sure. He was so cute sleeping in the car. I know he has much to do in the morning. What a coincidence being on a shoot together? Is this fate or what?"

Smiling, Sabrina prepares herself for bed, still thinking of Lorenz and their opportunity. Washing her face, brushing her teeth, and changing into her night clothes, she completes her routine for the next day. "God, please allow Aunt Marge to get better. And please get Lorenz and me together. Amen." It's her silent prayer before hitting the bed. She sets the alarm, cuddled under the covers, and found her perfect position. Trying to fall asleep, she continually runs over the dinner conversation and the upcoming event with Lorenz. Pictures start to snap in her mind of Lorenz and her at the community center presenting the great work that goes on there. Lorenz is wearing nice slacks, no shirt, and a white lab coat unbuttoned to show off his chest. Sabrina is wearing a tight white blouse with the bottom tied at her waist, pushing her breast up to fully expose her assets to Lorenz, a nice dark colored short skirt exposing her legs, and the make up of angels to really indulge his attention. She falls deeper into a trance and off to sleep.

Lorenz wakes to his alarm fully clothed from last night's dinner. He reaches over to the alarm, pushed the off button, places his feet on the floor and sits up. Leaning forward he places his head in his hands and thinks, "What am I suppose to do today?" He stands and prepares himself for his daily routine before heading to the hospital. Running in his mind is last night's dinner and something else but he can not remember. "Oh my, what was it? What else? I know there is something else." Moving about the apartment he finds all he needs for his day. After a quick breakfast bar from the kitchen, he grabs his pack and heads for the door. Looking back, as he opens the apartment door to exit, his thought returns to something he's forgetting but can not place what it is. Nothing comes to mind so he closes the door and exits. He then ensures the bolts are locked.

"Good morning Lorenz." said Robin, smiling as if her sun just rose at the sight of Lorenz.

"Hey, Robin, how are you?"

"Good. Are you going to the train station?"

"On my way there now, do you want to walk together?"

Smiling, she answers, "I thought you'd never ask."

The two leave the apartment building heading North on the main road. The train station is four to five blocks. Every morning, the same people are out and about. The traffic is picking up as life comes to this part of the city. "Robin" called Lorenz as they continually walk to the train station.

"Yes, Lorenz"

"Have you ever thought of something you are suppose to do and just can not for the life of you remember what it is?"

"I've done that a few times."

"What did you do to get your mind to remember?"

"You go through a checklist of events that either you talked to someone about, or you wrote somewhere as a reminder."

"A checklist; let's see. Appointments, Community Service Center, Spokes Person, Emergency Room. So far nothing comes to mind."

"Don't worry it will come."

"Yea, let's hope so. I don't like dropping the ball on anything."

"Remember, you normally don't. Don't worry about it, it will come."

"I have too as it could be very important."

Silently walking next to each other they observe more life. Step by step they pace towards the train station. She thinks of the opportunity as it presents itself. We shouldn't be so quiet while walking to the station. Now is my opportunity to get his attention. "Lorenz," called Robin. "What does it take to create interest from a man?"

"What?" answered Lorenz. His mind wonders about her question as if it were a slap to the cheek. Is she actually thinking about someone I know?

"You know. What does it take to get interest from a man?"

"I guess its dependent upon a number of things. First it is the man and the opportunity." Why on earth would I answer her like that?

"That doesn't tell me anything. What do you think will get attention from a man? And be honest."

"Attention from a man. Let's see. There are things you can do with appearance. Does he see you often?"

"Often enough, but I know he doesn't recognize me."

"Well, some men like the way a woman dresses. Some men like the way she smells from her perfumes. Some guys don't mind being the recipient of gifts and messages. Some men like to be plain told about a woman's interest."

"So you are saying it could be a number of things to get a specific guy's attention."

"Yes, you can say that. Watch your step."

"Thanks"

"It's too vague to get a guy's attention when you don't know the individual and what he likes. What do you think would get his attention?"

"Well I can use the seat to write a note when we get on the train."

"OK, a note is a good place to start."

"Sounds like you have a plan or two. Does he have any idea to your interest?"

"No, I don't think so. He is kind, very nice, has a great physique, and is very smart."

"Seems like a nice guy so far. What does he do for a living?"

"He's in school and plans to graduate with a purpose."

"Oh really, he's in school. Aren't you in the last year of your undergrad?"

"Yes, my last year. But my guy is in graduate school."

"Oh, really. What does he study?"

"Yes. Really, as a matter of fact, he is in graduate school for a specific profession."

"What profession?"

"Something in the medical arena, like a doctor or surgeon specialist."


Both reach the steps to the train station. They walk through the gates and submit their electronic pass for entry. Each one walks in sequence to the exact bench location perfect for waiting on the next train. Lorenz sits on the left side opening a book to review a chapter before hitting the hospital. Robin sits on the right and glances at Lorenz as if they were the only two at the station. She glances at him from head to toe, from toe to head, sighs and stares exactly at his features. She sighs louder and clears her throat to get his attention. "Uh hum," coughs Robin.

"Bless you," Lorenz exclaims.

"What are you reading?"

"My study guide to emergency room operations."

"Is it a hard subject?"

"It's challenging. But not too difficult since I'm applying everything right now."

"Do you perform any operations yet?"

"No, not yet. I am generally helping patients with all sorts of emergencies, from applying band aids to saving lives without intense surgery."

"Oh, that sounds exciting."

"It can be at times. But I know my work helps a lot of people. And it's rewarding, tiring but rewarding."

"Can you tell me something else?"

"Depends on what it is."

"When do you have free time? You never seem to be home, not that I am watching, and I never see you with friends or girls. Do you go out or have a social life?"

"I get around and free time is limiting. As a matter of fact, I have a date coming soon. I don't know what I'm going to do just yet, but there is a girl who's interested."

"Do I know her?"

"Oh, you might."

"Does she know about the date?"

"What kind of question is that? Do you think I'm imagining a date to appease your conversation?"

"Oh no! Don't get angry. I just never saw you with anyone. Where did you meet her?"

"I think at the hospital."

Specific tunnel lights are flashing announcing the train's arrival. The lights align the tunnel at the corner of the round curve just before the tunnel's top center. They flash every time the train arrives; flashing very bright, quickly and in cadence. The lights stop when the train passes them. The train arrives right on time. Lorenz and Robin gather their things and quickly step onto the train in one of the cabs. The cab is lined with multiple seats, facing both directions and with lots of bars for those standing to hold on for safety reasons. Lorenz stands while Robin finds a seat. She tries hard to get close to Lorenz but decides to back off since their last conversation exchange didn't go so well. Lorenz stands holding the top rod that's attached to the cab's roof. He looks around the cab at the various faces as they ride the train to their destination. Riding from station to station, the driver announces every stop just before arriving. People constantly moving on and off at each location. The train moves quickly and pauses just enough for people to exit and enter. Bells rings as an alert for the train's take off. The train driver announces the next stop, "Medical Center is the next stop. Please exit on the left side of the train."

Lorenz prepares himself for a quick exit. He looks for Robin in a seat near the cab's rear. He finds her, nods his head upwardly indicating a farewell. She waves back just as Lorenz moves towards the exit. He steps quickly onto the deck just as the cab doors close. Stepping lively, Lorenz moves immediately towards the stairs leading to the street. He maneuvers around others moving slower and each step brings him closer to the open exit and to the hustle and bustle of the street. He moves into the flow towards the general hospital area. Routinely there are multiple people who seem to arrive on his schedule. He waves his hand greeting each one of them, and without a sound, they return the wave as if there is a common language for them. Each step closer to Lorenz' destination, he starts thinking of his date with Sabrina. He recalls his ungentlemanly like exit from Sabrina's car. Over and over again, he questions his intentions with her as if he is the one in pursuit. Not like anything else in his past, he contemplates how to process the actions of last night so he will know what to say to her once he calls and makes sure they are still on for the coming date.

Arriving at the locker room, Lorenz opens his locker, places the bag on the bench and reaches for the white coat. He places the bag in the locker, secures the lock, and heads out to the nurses' station for instructions. Without hesitation he stops at the station, picks up the phone and calls the community center to check his schedule. "Hello. Is Mr. Hicks there?"

"Hello, yes he is. May I ask who's calling?" answered the receptionist.

"Yes, this is Dr Lorenz Maynard. May I speak to him please?"

"Please hold." The receptionist places Lorenz on hold and announces the phone call to Mr. Hicks. "Mr. Hicks there is a Dr. Maynard on line two."

"Thank you, answered Mr. Hicks" Picking up the phone, Mr. Hicks answers, "hello."

"Mr. Hicks, this is Lorenz Maynard."

"Hey Lorenz. I've heard great things from the kids and other people here at the center. Are you coming by today?"

"That's why I'm calling. Can I change my schedule?"

"Is there something wrong? I know the kids will miss you if you don't come today."

"No, it's not today, its Friday. I have something I need to do that evening."

"Oh, you mean your date. Oh sure you can switch days on your schedule. No problem."

"How did you know about the date?"

"When has a kid ever kept a secret? Did you tell them to keep the date under wraps?"

"The kids. I guess you're right about the kids. They are fun and quite helpful. I didn't expect them to mention the date. Anyway, thanks for understanding."

"I am glad to see you do something more with your social life. You spend so much time here; I can't imagine you'd have a social life. How did you meet the young lady?"

"I met her here at the hospital."

"Coincidence. Right?"

Smiling, Lorenz answers, "Yes, as a matter of fact, a nice coincidence. Thanks for understanding and I will make it up to you."

"No problem. You don't owe anything; you've done more than enough. Just enjoy yourself. Let me know how it goes."

"Thanks again. Take care Mr. Hicks." Lorenz disconnects the phone call. He returns the phone back to the nurses' station and immediately grabs charts for his round.

Robin walks from the train station directly into her office building. She sees a co-worker arriving at the front doors. "Hey Missy, how are you?"

"Hey Robin, I'm fine and you"

"Great. I had an awesome ride into work today. I got a chance to spend some quality time with my dream guy."

"Wow that can always make a girl's day."

Blushing, Robin replies, "Yea, it made mine for sure. Now if the rest of the day goes as nice it will be a good day."

"You're smiling and it must be love. Does he make you like this every day?"

"Yes, every time I lay my eyes on him my day gets better. Every time I hear his voice, my day is brighter. Every time I smell him, my day becomes awesome."

"You've got it pretty bad. I'm quite happy for you. When will I get to meet him?"

"One day Missy. One day."

They both arrive at their cubicles and perform the daily routine to start the day. In no time, the office becomes hustle and bustle. Periodically, Robin finds herself in a daze thinking about Lorenz.

Sabrina wakes in one of the greatest moods. She recalls a part of her dream with Lorenz as the main character.

He stares deeply in my eyes, as if a message from his heart alludes to his secret desires. His arms are strong, shapely as a Greek God. His chest is muscular in definition. His abdominals are cut like a middle weight boxer. His legs are shaped like a 100 meter track runner. His voice sounds like the melodic whisper of a deep voice radio announcer playing love ballads in the late evening. His touch, gentle, smooth, and effective, coupled with his focus has a tremendous effect on the spots that counted the most. His thrust was consistently smooth as the push rod of a locomotive. His eyes were deeply entranced into mine as he passed multiple messages from his heart. His embrace, strong and firm, holding me in one spot where moving is difficult, like cornering me into a position of pleasure. His move, his touch, his strength, my breathing changes, a moan comes to my throat, and the combination brings me to.......WAKE UP.

No wonder I'm in such a great mood. If that only happened in real life? What a dream, girl what a dream. I haven't had one with such intensity in such a long time. If this isn't excitement before a date, I don't know what is.

Preparing for her day, Sabrina showers, brushes her teeth, put on her make-up, and styles her hair just enough to leave it for the artist at the studio. She walks to the closet and selects a cozy dress that's easy to slip on and off for quick disrobing. She looks at the clock in the bed room and estimates her minutes to her departure time. Fifteen minutes before its time to leave. I have just enough time for a quick breakfast. Moving to the kitchen, she grabs the box of cereal, a bowl, milk from the fridge, and a spoon from the drawer. She pours milk and cereal into the bowl and takes one quick bite. She returns the cereal to the pantry, milk to the fridge, and immediately returned to her breakfast. The phone rings. "Hello" she answered.

     "Good morning sis," said Simone.

     "Hey, you sound really energetic."

"Yea, I had an interesting last night. I ended up with a date for tomorrow night."

"You too! What a coincidence. I have a date tonight too."

In unison they ask, "Who's the guy?" Giggling, they immediately reverted back to their teenage days. Challenging who goes first.

"Sabrina, you go first. Who is he?"

"Remember the intern at the hospital when Aunt Marge was there?"

"Yes, is that him?""

"He's the one. What about you?"

"It's Diane's neighbor. We had dinner there last night. Girl the man can cook, and cook great. I mean great."

"That's nice. I have to get out of here and head to the studio. Can we finish sharing this later? I want to know all and everything. As a matter of fact, let's just compare dates Sunday."

"That sounds good. I will talk to you then. If you don't hear from me earlier today, you will tomorrow. Ciao"

"Ciao"


Sabrina finishes her quick breakfast, washes the bowl and spoon, place them in the strainer and heads for the table by the front door of the apartment. There she picks up her purse, jacket, and keys. She heads out of the door and locks it before leaving. She then walks to the parking lot to her car, enters it, starts the engine and heads off to the studio.

Simone places the phone back on the receiver. She immediately moves towards the bathroom. Her typical habits start from toilet to shower. Right after the shower she prepares her color coordinated clothes in line with her meetings for the day. What impression she needs to make with whatever client enters the office suite. She recalls one marketing executive requiring the firm's services as the schedule for the day. It's the meeting of the day for the right clothes. Ideally, she made the appropriate power arrangement with her clothing selection. Dressing, she remembers her conversation with Sabrina. One great smile appears reflecting anxiety to tonight's date with Rodney. Brushing her hair right before pinning it up, she walks to the compact disc player, presses play and her favorite singer blows the melodic tune. Finishing her dressing routine, she sways to the music and sing verse to verse of three songs on the CD. One more look over before walking out the door, she turns around in the mirror, walks to the CD player, turns the player off and strides to the foyer. She picks up her keys, picks up her purse, and exits the home. She immediately secures the door by locking multiple locks. She walks to the drive way and gets into her car. Ensuring everything is done; she thinks of her morning actions before leaving and finds herself happily singing one of the tunes on the CD and realizes all is ok. She starts the car, places it in reverse, looks around and proceeds to her journey to the office.

Down the street after one intersection there is a coffee shop. Simone normally stops there to purchase a cup of coffee to drink during the drive to work. Her drive takes nearly 45 minutes to complete. The traffic is often demanding of her attention and sometimes very hectic, specifically if she doesn't leave at her opportune time. This morning there is a difference. She is extremely ahead of schedule, has ample time to stop for coffee, and this time she walks into the coffee shop instead of using the drive thru window. Parking her car, Simone walks into the shop, looks at the menu board and makes her selection. She orders a mocha vanilla swirl coffee specialty coffee instead of black with room for cream. Waiting for her coffee, she stands near the window and watch cars and people pass by. Immediately she recognizes a neighbor out on his morning run. She waves at him and turns back to the call of her name from the coffee shop attendant. Simone grabs her coffee, picks up a napkin and heads out of the shop for her car. Once entering the car, she places the coffee in a cup holder, and proceeds to drive on the journey to work. Stopping at the exit of the parking lot, she looks both directions and proceeds into the roadway without incident. "This is amazingly easy during this time of morning" she thinks. "Normally it's a challenge to ease back into traffic. I've been here in the past for nearly 15 minutes just trying to get into traffic." Easing down the roadway she sips her coffee, listens to the radio for the morning news, and observes her drive. Nothing out of the ordinary for an early drive, she thinks of her planned date and what she should wear. "I have three dresses that will do the trick. You can never go wrong with the little black dress, but that might be too simple. The red dress with bare shoulders is a knock out, but that might be a little too formal for a first date. The blue dress with a floral arrangement might be the one. Yes, the blue wins. I am sure he'd like that one, it fits well and shows a little of my figure, lets say a little more of my figure and I want him to notice all of me tomorrow night."

Simone is closer to her office as traffic seems to finally pick up to normal levels. Just as she turns in, she notices an office worker whom she isn't quite familiar with. She waves at the person and surprisingly the person waves back. Driving toward her parking spot, Simone finishes her coffee. In one last gulp, she finds herself at her reserved parking space and sizes her parking to ensure she has equal space between the white lines. She's happy with her parking and changes the gear to park, turns the car off, and exits. She locks the door and turns towards the open lot to travel into the office building. She turns left and as she steps a car screams by locking its breaks. She looks at the driver, smiles, waves, and crosses as if nothing happened.

Arriving to her office, Simone has a message light flashing on her phone. She immediately dials in the code to listen to her messages. She presses the numbers and then depresses play.

Rodney's voice sounds out on the answering machine, "Good morning Simone, I am excited about seeing you tomorrow night. I hope you're just as excited. I think we're going to have a great time. Please don't be mad at Diane for giving me your work number. I made a deal that she couldn't refuse. Also, I'll pick you up 7:00 at your place so if you don't mind, please call and give me your address. Its something we left out in our conversation last evening. I think it would be nice and courteous if you'd give it to me. I hope to hear from you soon. Bye for now"

Immediately Simone scrambles into her purse for Rodney's numbers. She looks frantically for the card. She dumps the purse contents onto her desk in search of the card. Still, no card found. She thinks of what she did with it or when was the last time she'd seen the card. She recalls having it before and never used it. She remembers pulling it out when she read his note left on the car windshield from sometime ago. It seems that she didn't return it back to her purse. Simone figures to have left the card either in her car or her house. Right now, no card and she would like to return Rodney's call. "No problem, I have time," she thinks. "I have to get into business and start my day; I will figure out how to contact Rodney later." And immediately with one thought, the professional Simone returns to her work routine.

Rodney starts his day with the usual run. Early morning habit followed with the calisthenics and weight lifting. During his run, he contemplates his date for tomorrow night. "I should wear a royal blue blazer, black shirt, black slacks, black shoes, black belt. That is a lot of black, but the shirt will hit it off well. I think it's a pleasant outfit for the occasion. And the cologne, 'what if she doesn't like it?' Maybe I should call Diane and ask her about her taste. No, that's going a little over board with it. I am sure she'd like the cologne I use. I haven't heard anything bad about it yet and don't think it's a factor, unless she's allergic. I don't think she's allergic. I know every woman likes a nice smelling guy. Nice smelling, oh, that could be defined differently with every woman. Heck, it's a chance I have to take and sweating over the cologne is not that important. Let's see, the meal is coordinated, the pick-up time and location. Location, she has to call me for the location. I haven't any idea where to pick her up and I don't want her to drive. "That wouldn't be much of a date now would it? Of course not, you're too classy to have her meet me" he speaks to himself. .

Another quarter mile passes in no time. Rodney continues his checklist for his and Simone's first date. "Let's see, what activities will we do after dinner? I think we can listen to jazz in the park after the horse and buggy ride. That's it. We can always go dancing later. This gives me time to explore her mind and not fight to hear every word. Man this woman is awesome, and quite impressive. She seems to have the right chemistry for me. Only time will tell. It all starts tomorrow night with a little quality exchange of thoughts." Turning the last corner of his run, he picks up the pace for a strong finish. Rodney immediately lays in the area in front of his apartment, starts his cool down exercises, leg lifts and sit-ups. After finishing, he jumps to his feet and heads inside for a shower, get dressed, and heads to the office for another exciting day. His energy level and attitude is awesomely high. Without a doubt he's going to have a wonderful day and in no time he is back to the routine office journey.

# Chapter 7

## *The Dating Game*

Early Saturday morning, the city is alive after Friday evening's events. City sponsored jazz concerts flare at most public parks. Clubs with Latin dancing, R&B jingles, Rock – n-Roll, in the entertainment district were live and active for most of the night and until early morning. Traffic with families and friends are heading out for multiple activities, social club events, city sponsored races, and of course park games. Sporting games where kids ranging from 5 to 18 years of age in organized team sports bombarded multiple parks and fields, going for hours with parents in observation.

At the community center, the kids from Lorenz' group met to plan his date with Sabrina. The kids jumped at the opportunity to put Lorenz in good standing with his first date. Knowing that Lorenz is not a man of great resources, Fred, Rick, and Elaine comes up with a quick plan instead of their routine sporting event. "Let's see," said Fred. "Let's meet at Lorenz' apartment building. I know his neighbor Robin who'd let us use her apartment to set things up. We should meet there around three."

"Three sounds good to me" answered Rick. "What about you Elaine? Are you in?"

"I wouldn't miss it for the world. Besides, you two think you can set up something romantic?"

"Oh heck yes," answered Fred and Rick in unison.

"Oh heck no, and you two shouldn't think you have romance in your heads. Thank goodness I'm here or this date could be devastating. You need a woman's touch"

"You girls think the same thing all the time. We guys just don't know anything about romance. It isn't like you know much more than us."

"I know much more than the both of you in my pinky finger. Not including the simple things like setting a table."

"Well, you may have a point, but we know lots of stuff. We have girl friends too. Right Fred?"

"Sure, right Rick. We have girl friends. I remember taking my girl to a burger place for a bite. She was really mad. Does that seem like romance? I thought it did," said Fred.

"Yes, really romantic. That could have been nice if she wasn't led to believe the date would be something more. Didn't you tell me you wanted her to dress nice?"

"Sure did. She looked good too, really good. Nice dress and shoes, I thought she looked very nice indeed. Even had her mother drop us off when I went to her house to pick her up. It was nice of her mom to drive us to the burger joint. She looked funny at me when I told her the restaurant. And as a matter of fact, so did my date."

"Explains it all Fred, you have no idea to romance."

"Yea, Fred, you have no idea."

"Rick, as if you had a better date. You haven't had a date since…you've never had a date."

"Yes I have."

"No you haven't"

"Yes I have and you know it."

"No you haven't and I'd know if you had one."

"Stop before you two get carried away" piped Elaine. "Let's get this rolling. Are you going to get the rest of the crew involved?"

"That's the plan. We can get at least five for the chorus and two to help cook" said Rick.

"You leave the cooking to me; it needs a woman's touch."

"Do we have a woman in the group? Do you see one Rick" said Fred.

"Will you cut it out? We don't have time to play around. Let's get serious. The date will be here in no time."

"I'll get the three singers and rehearse one song. I think we can pull that off. You two figure out how to get the meal set up. Fred, you contact Robin and get the key to the roof while you Elaine go to grocery store for the meal. Here is the money we collected from the rest of the community center."

"OK, we're gone with the winds making this happen," shouted Elaine and Fred.

Rick called Lorenz to find out what time his date is suppose to start, and where were they suppose to meet. "Lorenz, hey it's Rick."

"Hey Rick. What's happening today?"

"Not much. Just thinking of your date tonight; what is your plan?"

"What? I have a date, not you."

"Look Lorenz, you know as well as I that you don't have much money. You borrow from us all the time."

"Don't say that, I never borrow money from you. I make a few dollars here and there."

"You're right. You never borrow money. But I know you are limited as being an intern doesn't pay very much. I noticed you cutting corners all the time."

"OK, you are right about the funds. But, you still shouldn't try to get involved with my date."

"Look, you do lots for us at the center. Just let us show you how much we appreciate your time and efforts. We promise not to do anything too expensive or extravagant."

"Well, ok, you go ahead with your plan. I will not be home until 6:15 or so. My date is suppose to be 7:30. What do you have in mind?"

"Just something un-costly for you, I am sure she'd like it too. It should be great, don't worry."

"Now I'm worried because you told me not to worry. The last time you told me not to worry, I got my butt chewed out from the center's director. Will it cost me again?"

"No, totally different. Things are all together different this time."

"Sure, they are. You should be glad I trust you. What do you need from me?"

"I need you to promise to bring Sabrina to your apartment for the date."

"What? Are you serious? Don't you know Sabrina will think of me trying to make moves on her instead of going out to a public place?"

"I don't know about that. I'm only a kid remember. Just get her to the apartment and don't have dinner until after you bring her by."

"OK, I can pull this off. DO NOT do anything crazy. Remember, I trust you and I know the rest of the gang's involved. So please tell them to take it easy on her. She is important to me."

"Sure, sure, the gang knows to take it easy.'

"No really, I am not kidding, I trust you and this may be the one."

"I got it. Don't do anything crazy. What do you consider crazy?"

"Don't play with me. You know what I mean."

"Just kidding, I know what you mean. Just remember to have her there at 7:30."

"OK, 7:30. I'll see you then. Bye Rick"

"Bye Lorenz."

Rick walks to the center's game room where the rest of the gang is waiting. "Hey, it's on. Lorenz will bring his date by at 7:30 tonight. We have to get thing on track."

"We have a song picked out and practically rehearsed while you talked to Lorenz," said Fred.

"I have the dish planned and collected a few dollars for the meal. Do you want to contribute?" asked Elaine.

"Yea, here is a couple dollars. Man that kills my allowance," replied Rick.

"Don't worry, we are all broke now. But at least Lorenz will have a great first date with this lady. Did you call his neighbor Robin?"

"No, not yet, it's my next thing to do. What time are we meeting?

"Let's meet at Robin's apartment at 5:30 to get things together. As soon as I get her on board with this call we should get out of here."

"Sounds like a plan."

"Yup, sounds like a good plan to me."

"OK, I need to make the call. See you guys at 5:30." Rick walks to the office again to use the telephone. He reaches into his pocket for the number. Dialing, he turns to see Elaine talking to the community center's director. Curious, he waves at Elaine with a high signal not to let him in on the plan. Elaine winks back. The phone rings, once, twice, and Robin answers on the third ring. "Hello" answered Robin.

"Hi Robin, its Rick. Rick Hillman. How are you?"

"You mean little Rick from Worcester Street?"

"Yes, it's me."

"How are you? How's your mom and sister?"

"They're fine, doing great. Sis moved in with her friend a few months ago. She seems happy now. Mom is hanging in there; even though she sometimes gets on my nerves. But I seem to stay out of trouble with her."

"That's nice to hear. What can I do for you? I know you want something because you always did when I lived near you."

"Oh, there is something but not elaborate. I just need a favor."

"Nothing elaborate? Money involved?"

"No money involved unless you'd like to contribute. But that's not what I want. I want to use your apartment to

99

prepare a meal and give us access to the building's roof. Can you do it? We are counting on you."

"Give you and your friends access to the roof. What the heck for?"

"You know Lorenz right? Well he has a date tonight with a girl he met. Since he's always doing for us at the community center, we thought it would be nice to do something for him. So we decided to cook, serenade, and create a nice atmosphere for his date. Can you help us?"

"For Lorenz and with another girl, how could you ask me to do this?"

"Is something going on Robin? Did he do something to you? If he did, I know he didn't mean it."

"No, he did nothing to me. I'm sorry for yelling. He doesn't know, I mean he hasn't done anything to hurt me or offend me. He is a nice guy and a good neighbor. I guess you can use the apartment and I will give you access to the roof."

"Great. We, my friends and I, will be there at 5:30 today. Is that alright?"

"Yes, come on down. I'll be glad to see you and say hello to your mom for me."

"Thanks Robin. You're the greatest." Rick ends the conversation and places the phone receiver back on the home base. There is a touch on his shoulder just as he turns to exit. It's Elaine. "How did it go?"

"We are in there. It's set as planned. Did you tell anyone about our plan here at the center?"

"What do you think, I'm stupid? NO!"

"Good. You know it's against policy for us to have activities outside of the center when it comes to a counselor or volunteer. They don't like the possibility of something going wrong."

"Glad to know that. It's a good thing because fortunate for me the conversation was on a ping pong tournament."

"Let's go buy the groceries."

"Let's go." The two walked out of the community center heading for the nearest market. Along the way, they discuss the menu. "Elaine, I thought you had this all together?" asked Rick.

"I have it together. Let's just say I know how to make a quick meal. Nothing fancy of course. But it's going to be interesting."

"Interesting? That's a scary thing to say."

"Are you going to cook?"

"No, that's your area. We decided that you'd handle the food."

"Then I'm handling it."

"What can you cook?"

"Lots of things; the simpler the meal, the better it is of course. So let's see my best dish for the occasion. I can make Mac & Cheese, Green Beans, and Fish Sticks. How's that for a meal?"

"Sounds great to me. I like them all but fish sticks?"

"Yea, they are easy to make. Put them in the oven and minutes later they are done."

"I guess you're making the macaroni & cheese from scratch, right?"

"Yes, scratch right from the box. How much money do you think we collected?"

"I see your point. Simple and inexpensive."

"Now your eyes are opening."


Lorenz calls Sabrina to coordinate the date. "Hey Sabrina, how are you?"

"Hey, I'm doing pretty good. How are you?'

"Excited. I'm really excited to seeing you again. Especially tonight."

"Me too, I was thinking of you earlier."

"Since you know I don't have transportation, do you mind driving tonight?"

"No, of course not silly. I don't mind at all."

"Good, then can you come over around 7:30. The kids at the community center have something up their sleeves. I promised you'd come over at 7:30. They are nice kids and I spend my off time with them mostly. I guess they are trying to impress you for me. Will this bother you?

"They sound very nice. I will be there 7:30 on the dot. You can't disappoint those kids. Or you'd never hear the end of it."

"Right you are. Thank you for understanding. Talk to you later, I have to get to my rounds."

"Bye Lorenz."

"Later, beautiful woman."

Rodney calls the restaurant to make sure everything is in place. It's nearly 6:00 pm; he selects his clothes, presses them, and jumps in the shower. He pulls out his best cologne, the one that he gets the most compliments when he wears it, splashes it on, and starts dressing in his underwear. He checks the shoes for shine and a great appearance, and cleans them just before putting on his socks. He inspects the shirt and pants for additional wrinkles, and then steams his blue sports jacket. He looks himself over once more before getting completely dressed. His pants are perfectly creased, the shirt is tucked neatly, and his belt is just tight enough. "Immaculate and clean," he thinks, "I look great and I hope she sees the same." It's amazing what a man does for a date.

Simone arrives to her home from the cleaners. She picked up the dress for tonight, heads into the showers, hangs the dress near the bathroom door, and immediately strips for a quick shower. Singing in delight, Simone blares her tune as if singing for a church choir. She is excited about tonight but doesn't want to display the overly excited girl characteristics; that is being too anxious. "Why am I so excited about tonight?" she wonders, "What makes Rodney so right for me?" she asks herself. As she finishes showering and towels off, she finds herself in deep thought as she moves around the bathroom in preparation. "Is it his charm, or is it my need that's driving me for this? Is it because we've bumped into each other over these past weeks, or is it the intrigue of him being such a handsome gentleman and I just need attention from a man?" she ponders. "Just go and enjoy even though you practically threw yourself at him at his place." She continues dressing, putting on her make-up one stroke at a time not to make a mistake. "No doubt, it's the thing to do. Don't read into anything more, just go and enjoy the date. I don't foresee anything happening between us. Heck yea, he's a nice man and I want things to happen. Who am I fooling," she argues with herself.

Completely dressed Simone takes another look for perfection. Her dress is immaculate, off the shoulders, tightly showing her figure, and a smashing blue. The dress color accents her skin tone and hair. Her shoes are nicely attractive as open toes sandals. She makes a 360 degree spin in front of the mirror to get the last look over and prepares for Rodney to arrive. Simone walks to the kitchen, grabs a wine glass, pours a glass of wine and turns on nice melodic music to set the tone for the date. At least in her mind the tone is set as being smooth and comforting so her excitement decreases to controllable levels. Even though Simone is enthused to go on this date, she doesn't want to seem over anxious when Rodney arrives. Simone takes a sip of wine, walks over to the door, and peep out for Rodney's arrival. "Not yet, no car in the drive way," she thinks. She looks at the clock in the kitchen and realizes Rodney isn't supposed to arrive for another 20 minutes. She returns to sitting in the kitchen and drinks her wine as she waits for Rodney. "No one is here yet, is it me or is the time creeping along. I shouldn't be so anxious but he is a fine man with nice attributes. You know, the body, the mind, and the spirit. The man can cook too, has lots of style and I've waited for him to come in my life for a long time now. Let's hope he continues to show me his true colors. If he maintains what he's showing, life can be really good." The phone rings. "Hello" answers Simone.

"Hey Girl, Is he there yet," asked Sabrina.

"Hey. No he isn't," answered Simone.

"I have to go to Lorenz' place in a few minutes myself. I hope you have a wonderful time and let's get together after our dates."

"Do you think we are going to be in early or something?"

"Well, let's call each other in an hour and a half to check on each other. If things are going bad, maybe we can use the call as an escape."

"Do you always have to have an escape plan in case of a bad date?"

"You haven't gone out with the guys I have in the past."

"That bad?"

"That bad and you only know the surface. We'll have to laugh at it when we get a chance."

"I don't think we will have to call or at least I don't think I will. But I will call you anyway, just in case."

"You call, I like Lorenz, but just in case you never know when you go out with a poor man."

"I'll call. At least I hope to hear you're having a good time. If nothing else it will be an experience. Look forward to it and enjoy."

"I'm heading out of the door now. Don't forget to call."

"I will. Bye."

"Bye."

The sound of a car enters her drive way and immediately she finishes the glass of wine and places the glass in the sink. She peeps out of the window to see if it's Rodney. She immediately runs to the bathroom for a once over and to brush her teeth from the wine. Rodney rings the door bell with a fist full of flowers and wearing his blue blazer, he stands close to the door for Simone to answer. Waiting, he smells his breath and gives himself a once over as best he could without a reflection. A minute goes by and there is no answer. He rings the door bell once again and waits. He looks at his watch, straightens his jacket once again and waits for Simone to answer the door. Another minute goes, now its three minutes at the front door. He reaches for his cell phone and just as he starts dialing, Simone opens the door. "Hi Simone," he says, "These are for you."

"Sorry I didn't come right away; it took too long to come to the door. You look great, very nice Rodney"

"It's ok, you look ravishing yourself. How did you manage to wear blue?"

"Oh, I see we have a serious vibe going here. Blue happens to be one of my favorite colors. I always like the way I look in blue. It's a nice color on me. And I see it's the same for you. How nice, another thing in common."

"Well, it seems like we have lots of things going on here. Are you ready to leave for dinner?"

"Yes, I'm ready. Let me get my sweater." Simone opens the closet door and reaches for her powder blue sweater. She starts to place the sweater around her shoulders and immediately Rodney reaches to assist. Simone then turns and remembers the flowers. "Let me put these flowers in a vase and then we can leave."

"Sure thing, it's a good idea for you to do."

Simone moves hastily into the kitchen with the flowers in hand, takes a quick sniff and grabs a vase from the cabinet. "These are so nice and how thoughtful" she exclaims to Rodney.

"Glad you like them. I wasn't sure if roses would do, especially on a first date. They send a strong message."

"And what kind of message is that?"

"You know, roses claims love and affection. Not quite the impression I'd like to make too soon."

"You think I'm in love with you because of roses?"

"No, just the message of love I'm sending by the roses. I mean to impress not direct emotions. Let me stop before I put my foot deeper in my mouth.'

"You should. Just know I love the roses, not you. Not that falling in love may not happen, but it's the flowers and they do impress me. Shows you are a man of style and class. Thank you again."

Rodney turns for the front door. Simone follows behind. Rodney stops, opens the door and waits for Simone to exit first. Simone pulls her key out to secure the lock. Rodney reaches out for the keys. Simone steps back and ask, "What are you doing?"

"I'm reaching for the keys so I can lock the door. I will return the keys as soon as the door is secure. Please allow me to lock your door."

"This is a first. I've never had a man ask for my keys on a first date. That is different" says Simone and gives Rodney the keys. Rodney takes the keys, locks the door and turns for the drive way. He passes the keys back to Simone. He steps in front of her and walks to the passenger side of the car, opens the door, and waits for Simone to enter. After she enters, he closes the door. Simone thinks "he's laying it on tonight. It's rather nice he is such a gentleman." Rodney enters the driver's side of the auto and places his seat belt in position. He looks at Simone and asks, "Please put your seat belt on."

"You drive that bad?"

"No, it's just a safety habit" he answers while starting the car. The roar of the engine and the cool breeze from the air condition port blows right at Simone. "Ooh that is cold" she says, "Can you turn the air off? Please."

"Oh I'm sorry. Not a problem" he answers, then turns to look in the rear to back the car into the street. Once the car goes into the street, he changes gears and starts the car forward. Music from the compact disc player starts. It's a love ballad sung by Luther. "Is this music ok for you?" he asks.

"It's nice. I like Luther. I like all of his music. They really hit the spot for all moments in life. Don't you agree?"

"Yes I do. As a matter of fact, I have all of his albums. Luther and I go back for years."

"Who else is a favorite singer of yours?"

"Will Downing. A smooth melodic singer with a deep voice and it places many in similar moods like Luther. Except Will's albums are not as consistent as Luther's. I think his last album was for true Will lovers."

"I like his music too. But I don't follow him as close as I do Luther."

"What did you do today?"

"My usual weekend routine"

"Yea, the routine, we all have them. I did the same as usual for a weekend until now. You've made a variation in my routine."

"Yes, you and I both actually since you put it that way."

"Are you famished?"

"No. Just hungry" she answered. They both laughed at her comment.


Rodney drove in silence thinking he shouldn't talk too much too soon as they will not have much of a conversation over dinner. "What are you're thoughts on the current economy situation? Do you think its going to change?"

"Funny you mention this. It's been a subject I've wanted to discuss over some time now. I think we are definitely heading for a recession. I don't know how much of the GNP will impact our current market analysis; however I do think the local economy will bounce back after the recent spiral and with local investments the city will grow. I heard the city made some deals with a few fortune 500 companies to build offices and assembly plants here. If my information is right, it would be interesting to find a few properties and hold on to them until the change. Now is the time to do it."

"You know, that is a great idea. With information like that, it would be wasted if someone like us doesn't take advantage."

"You have to have money to do so. Do you have any money to invest?"

"Now you're asking me about money? I don't have money exactly for a home purchase, but I do have a few dollars stashed for a rainy day."

"Well, its raining" she laughs.

"Oh, you've got jokes. Yea, it's raining and I can respect a woman with a business sense. I see if there is a way for people to build a partnership, we could make a large investment and reap greater profits."

"That's the idea."

Rodney pulls into the restaurant's parking lot. He quickly finds a parking space, parks the car, and immediately steps around to open Simone's car door. She reaches out her hand and he grabs it to assist her to exit. "I can get used to this" she thinks. Rodney holds his arm out for Simone to grab and they walk in stride towards the restaurant's entrance. Just as they reach the entrance, again Rodney shows his consistent charm and gentleman like actions by again opening the door for Simone. "Good evening, can I help you?" asked the Mait-re-de.

"Good evening, yes you can assist us. We have reservations. Witherspoon."

"Yes, Mr. Witherspoon, your table is ready. Please follow me."

Rodney waves his hand for Simone to follow the Mait-re-de first. He follows right behind and walks close enough to have everyone recognize they are together. Reaching the table, the Mait-re-de pulls out the chair for Simone to take a seat. Then he places the napkin on her lap. He then walks to Rodney and places a napkin on his lap while he announces the specials for the day. Immediately after the Mait-re-de leaves, the waiter appears. "Hi Mr.

Witherspoon, could I interest you in a cocktail from the bar or start you out with drinks?"

"Simone, do you have something in mind as a pre-dinner drink?"

"Sure, an apple martini will do for me."

"One apple martini for the lady and a black Russian for me please?"

"Thank you, I'll be right back with your drink orders." The waiter leaves for the bar area, orders the drink and heads back to the table with two bottles of wine that Rodney previously coordinated. "Sir, I think these are our best suggestions for the dinner you're having."

"Simone, do you mind doing the taste test and making the selection?"

"How did he know what we're having for dinner? I haven't opened the menu."

"I took the liberty to order for you earlier today. I think you'll like this dish as well as dessert. Trust me a little please"

"OK, then I'll be glad to select the wine."

"Please do."

Simone has the waiter pour a little of the first wine in a glass. She takes it, swirls, takes in the aroma, and sips a little. "Ooh, I like this one. But before I say ok, I'll have to taste the other." Immediately the waiter pours a taste of the second bottle of wine. Simone does the same as before. "Ooh, this one is nice but the other is better."

"Then, we'll take the first bottle. Thank you" Rodney tells the waiter.

"Sure Sir" the waiter answered, prepared the bottle and took the other away.

Another waiter returns with their drinks from the bar. "Apple Martini for the lady and a Black Russian for the gentleman."

"Thank you," they both exclaim.

"Rodney, this is really a nice place. I'd heard about it but never got to try it out. Is it true about the food? I hear it's a great place to dine, and the ambiance is rather nice. Are you planning to ask my hand in marriage?"

"Let's not get silly so quickly. Let me answer your first question about the meals. Girl you are in for a treat. How's that for an answer" he said smiling. "Second, I chose this place because of its ambiance and charm, as well as the service. I come here with family and friends on special occasions. And finally getting out with you is a very special occasion."

"Oh really," she smiles "A date is that special to you?"

"It's a first date that's special. You see, every one in the dating scene has a first date. It's a beginning and we wish to remember our beginning even though we have no idea to what the future holds of this beginning. Yet, we remember important things and I want the first date to be important and have a memory of a lifetime."

"I see your point. So I am to remember this event for a lifetime. You, so far, you've been pretty good at impressing my memory. I think I can remember this so far. But my saying so does include the event that something bad may happen tonight. If the date changes to something bad, then I will definitely remember it as well. It will be the date to remember!"

"Now don't get negative on me," sipping his drink, "you shouldn't have negative thoughts because it causes bad things to happen, you know, subconsciously."

"Don't worry Rodney, nothing bad will happen; at least from my part." Simone's cell phone rings. She reaches in her purse, pulls out the phone and looks at the face of it. "I'm sorry Rodney, I need to take this."

"Please go right ahead."

Simone leaves the table and immediately answers, "Hello."

"Hey sis, it's me. How's it going?"

"Girl I can't talk. It's going really good so far. As a matter of fact, it's going so well that I forgot to call you."

"No problem, I haven't gotten upstairs yet. Lorenz is waiting for me now. I wanted to call you because I am behind time. Listen, you should call me in an hour or so to check on me OK?"

"I'll try, but if I don't that tells you things are going really well and I'll have to tell you about it tomorrow."

"Girl, you better call. You know our pact. Don't let me down."

"I'll call. Bye little sister."

"Bye."

The dinner is served as Simone returns. "Oh my, this looks wonderful."

"I'd hope you liked it. I was sure of it after you had dinner at my place with Diane."

"Yes, you cooked a wonderful meal. How did you know I like sea food?"

"I paid attention to your conversation and to your comments about the dinner. You put two together and it made it easy to order for you. Besides, this way our meals are much faster than the normal wait."

"I see. Are you trying to get me going here for something else? Or are you just doing the things for quality time?"

"Its quality my dear lady, quality."

"Well, its working for sure."

"Allow me to say grace before the meal" said Rodney. "Father, bless this meal we are receiving as nourishment for the body, mind, and spirit. Allow this fellowship to lead to greater events for two of your children. May our union become the beginning of a wonderful friendship and the building of a great partnership for future endeavors. In your name we pray, Amen."

"Amen" said Simone.

In a stroke of the fork, Simone takes her first taste of the meal. Rodney observes waiting for a response. He then pours a half glass of wine for Simone. "Well, what do you think?"

"It is awesome Rodney. It's awesome."

"Good. Please enjoy. I wanted you to know, since the first time I ran into you, I've wanted this moment."

"You mean me stuffing my face?"

"Yes, exactly, you being in a vulnerable moment where I can take advantage of your heart if I wanted too. I think you have what it takes for us to be wonderful, so I'm breaking away from my old dating habit."

"What do you mean dating habit?"

"I mean, with you I'm going out on a limb without really getting to know you. It's a gut feeling I have about you that drives me to you and makes me want a path to us."

"Isn't this a little fast? Don't you want to know more of me before you get ideas?"

"Like I said earlier, I know you in my heart as if you were there for many years. I can not put my finger on why, but it's a gut feeling that I've never experienced."

"Ok, I see. I've never had anyone come to me so strong. Or have I ever had someone go to the extremes for a first date. Even though we are acquaintances, it is still a first time we gave time to each other independent of others being involved."

"Well, how do you see things now? Is this too much or is it enjoyable?"

"It makes a woman wonder if this is a show and you're hiding something, or is it schmoozing for an ulterior motive?"

"No, it isn't a motive for anything more than what you see and I am not hiding anything other than fighting the old cliché of "love at first sight."

"Oh, Rodney, you are kidding right. Love at first sight. And you let me throw myself at you during dinner at your place. Why would you do so?"

Rodney takes a bite of dinner and a sip of wine while he listens to Simone's answer. "You think about that one. Throw yourself at a man who is already crazy about you. Why would he complain or stop you? That would be crazy for him to do. He'd love it as you see fit to throw yourself. And why did you throw yourself at me?"

Simone continues eating, all of a sudden; she places the fork down, wipes her mouth with her napkin and looks directly into Rodney's eyes. "It isn't love at first sight, but its interest beyond the norm. Let's say there is a fantasy world that we often embrace and I'd like to see it come to life."

"Fantasy world? You mean there is a fantasy about me going on in your mind? How could you go there without knowing me? That was a dumb question; fantasy is nothing close to reality, duh."

"Don't be hard on yourself, I met you before, and I was impressed from earlier moments. You've been on my mind ever since. Just so happens I've allowed you to enter into my deep thoughts and subconsciously I think of things we can do together. You know a man can run on that statement as if being a dream comes true" he smiles.

"Do you ever understand why women don't share their sacred thoughts with guys? That's exactly why. You run as being a gift to women, and this isn't the case."

Dinner is nearly over and they both have completed the major portions of their meals. The waiter appears and asks, "Are you done sir or m'am?"

"Simone, are you pretty finished?" asked Rodney.'

"Yes, I am pretty much" and reaches for her wine glass to take a quick drink. Immediately Rodney picks up the wine bottle and pours the contents into Simone's glass as soon as she places it back on the table. He then turns to the waiter and says, "We are both done. Can you please bring out the dessert?"

The waiter immediately grabs both plates and turns to retrieve the desserts. "I'll be a moment with the desserts," he replies.

"Did you like the meal, Simone?"

"Sure, it was fantastic. I know dessert is going to be exactly that, wonderful."

"I know you're going to like it. But meanwhile since we're waiting for the dessert, let's finish our conversation. Not to harp on anything, but I'm not the general guy who capitalizes on the dreams of women. Well, let me tell you, not this time. I've been known to jump on opportunities to find short term warmth and affection, if you know what I mean. But this moment means the world to me. And you are much more, much more than a whim of affection, more than a moment of warmth, and more than a fantasy to please. You are," Simone looks at her watch and immediately interrupts Rodney. "Hold on a minute. Keep that thought I have to go to the ladies room." In an instance she rises from the table, picks up her purse and leaves for the ladies room. Rodney is caught off guard, rises at the table when she stands, and immediately sits down thinking, "Did I say something to offend her? I hope not."

Simone enters the ladies room and immediately dials Sabrina on her cell phone. Waiting for the ring, she looks into the mirror and checks herself over. Ring one, two, three, four, and the fifth ring Sabrina answers. "It's about time you called. I thought you forgot."

"I told you I would but if things were going well, you may not have gotten it. It's a good thing I remembered. I walked away from an interesting conversation too. I want to get back so tell me how's your date going?"

"It's really nice and different. I have lots to share and I too want to hurry back. Thanks for calling; I know I can always count on you. Later." Sabrina disconnects without giving Simone a chance to reply. Simone's thinking, "She must be having a good time and next time I'll not stop in the middle of someone to call her again, she'll have to learn how to escape on her own."

Sabrina returns to her date on the other side of the roof. It is a lovely evening, the stars are out and the intensity for her and Lorenz is in thick abundance. Oh, in great quantities as she has never had anyone so intently focused on her beyond the physical as she finds Lorenz to be. She has never had anyone do something so simple for a date, and have so many invested to its success. "Amazing, just amazing and quite appropriate for a first date," she thinks on her walk back to Lorenz.

The date started when Sabrina arrived at Lorenz' apartment. When she walked to the stairs a young lady greeted her at the door and escorted her to the elevator. "Are you Sabrina?" she asks.

"Yes, I am. I am here to see," Sabrina replied, but is interrupted.

"Lorenz, right."

"Yes, Lorenz is he in?"

"Please follow me." The young lady leads Sabrina to the elevator presses the up button and turned and said, "He's expecting you and I want you to have a wonderful time. Lorenz is very special and we wanted to help him with your date, so we'd appreciate it if you'd go along with us. Please go along with it OK."

"OK, since you put it like that. I think Lorenz is nice too. That's why I'm here."

"Good," she answers. The elevator doors open and she walks in first, and Sabrina immediately follows. She presses the 12$^{th}$ floor button which provides roof access. "You're going to have a lovely time. I just know for sure. We are really excited to get things going."

"What things going exactly?"

"You'll see. Please remember your promise to enjoy it no matter what."

"No matter what, I guess I can do that, or give it my best shot."

"Please give it your best shot. I am counting on it and from woman to woman, Lorenz is a great catch."

"OK young lady, woman to woman, Lorenz is a fantastic catch and I'll take your word on it" and she winks her eye towards the young lady.

The elevator arrives at the 12th floor and when the door opens, a young gentleman smiles and says "Please follow me," then turns away from the elevator and heads to the stair way for the roof. He opens the door and waves his hand towards the entrance. Sabrina enters the stairwell for one flight and immediately hears music as she rises closer to the exit. "Oh my, this is really something" she thinks, "He said to be open and there were kids involved." She opens the door and immediately sees a really different set up. There is a table for two, white table cloth, folding chairs, candles in jam jars, a mixture of flowers, sparkling grape juice in a carafe on ice, and of course the view of the city with the moon rising and the sun setting. "How lovely" and impressive she thinks. The music is playing melodic tunes that are quite soothing and Lorenz is immaculate in his attire. Oh, nothing really fancy, but jeans, shirt and blazer makes him look so different from his white work coat. He is a handsome man, I mean really handsome, darn near breath taking gorgeous. His height is just right and his build is slim and muscular, which allows him to dress well. And he has the most charming smile which he shows while standing and waiting for me to come to the table. "Hi, this is lovely," said Sabrina.

"Hi lovely woman, yes it is. The kids did it; I give all credit to them. And for our surprise, there is more."

"More? You mean they did this and you had nothing to do with it."

"As I said earlier, you have to go along with it and just enjoy what we can." Lorenz leans closer over the table after he pushes Sabrina seat into position for her comfort. "And I have no idea what's for dinner." he whispered.

"We'll have to take it one step at a time. So how was your day?"

"It was full of anxiety to this point. I want this to go well and have fun all at the same time. Do you love the view?"

"Oh my heaven's yes. The view is lovely and I admire what the kid's have done with the table setting. They did a lovely job."

"Yes they did." Just as Lorenz replied, the kids filed into a group formation. Three in the front and four behind, one stood in the very front as a maestro and coordinated the group. The maestro raised his hands in the air and upon dropping them the group started singing. Harmonizing tunes, the song echoed on the roof top and windows opened to hear the melody. People looked from the street towards the building top to figure where the sound is coming from. Other building dwellers jumped at the opportunity to see where the choir sung from as their angelic voices heralded the air. Many people in buildings across from Lorenz's gathered at their windows and eyed the romantic escapade the children put together. Sabrina looked in awe at the children, smiled in wondrous agreement and glanced as Lorenz's face as he too embraced the kid's voices. "Wow," he whispered as he looked at Sabrina. "I had no idea they'd sound so lovely. Or is it because of you being here with me?" he asks.

In a whispering tone she answered "It's because they are just good."

"Aren't they amazing?" asked Lorenz.

"Yes, and for them to do this for us, means you must really mean something to them."

"They are my crew. I spend a lot of time with them during my community service. You have to give back to the community and these kids are the greatest. No trouble from them at all. I love being with them. They remind me of my youth from time to time."

"It isn't like you're far from being like them now. The only difference is that you're an educated kid with a wonderful heart."

"You think I have a wonderful heart?"

"Sure you do. And I'm not the only one who thinks so. Look at what the kids have done for us. If they didn't think you were special, then why would they go to this extreme just to make our date successful?"

"I see your point. I love them too."

At the end of the first song, all people started clapping as if they were in a concert. Lorenz and Sabrina clapped and smiled at them. Just as Sabrina started to stand and head to hug them all, two kids approached the table with their dinners.

"Please be seated so we can serve the dinner to you" said Elaine.

"OK" replied Sabrina, and returned to her seat.

Elaine placed the plate of food in front of Sabrina, and Fred placed Lorenz' meal in front of him. They both looked at what is being served. Elaine then spoke as if she was the head waiter, "You have the house specialty macaroni and cheese, fresh fish sticks, and tossed salad with Italian dressing. Please enjoy." Just as she turned to walk away, she turned back and said "What do you expect from 13 year olds?" as she shrugged her shoulders.

"Looks fine to me," Lorenz said.

"Really nice to me too" Sabrina smiled.

In an instance they both started enjoying the meal. Still, the choir started another song and this time the crowd started coming up on Lorenz' building to hear them sing. In a few minutes there were nearly twenty people on the roof top listening to the kids' angelic voices. Lorenz and Sabrina continued to consume the meal and never noticed the crowd as they looked at each other and held a silent conversation. Neither one said a word to each other but held continued focus on each other. Just as Elaine returned, they both looked at her as she returned to the table and poured more sparkling grape juice in their cups. "They practiced for a couple days for you two. I knew they sounded good, but I never expected them to get so many interested in their singing."

"I never knew they could sing like this. Who helped them put this together?"

"No one helped; it just happened to work out this way. Don't they sound great?"

"They sound wonderful, really wonderful" Sabrina and Lorenz said in unison.

Elaine walked back to the other side of the roof top to stand in the crowd. The kids are singing the last song and really poured their hearts out with it. The last chorus the kids moved towards the table and formed a semi circle around Sabrina and Lorenz. The song was so moving that many of the crowd nearly had tears. And on the last note, a thundering applaud burst into the air as if a storm appeared out of no where. Clapping the crowd asked for an encore. The kids turned away from the table and walked towards the stair well. "That's it for tonight folks, no more songs. We'll announce our concert in a few days. Thank you for your support." All the kids bowed and waved as each filed down the stairs and the crowd still clapped.

Fred went over to the table and said, "When you're finished, please let Elaine know and she'll bring out dessert. Take your time we don't have to be in until 9:00 tonight." Immediately he waved at Elaine and turned on his way out. Downstairs the singers grouped together and reflected on their performance. Then they disbanded going their separate ways. The crowd disappeared off the roof tops and in moments Lorenz and Sabrina were alone with one young lady waiting to bring dessert out. Lorenz waved his had towards Elaine and said, "You don't have to wait on us; we have it from here ok."

"OK, but I want to bring out your dessert anyway. I'll go get it and be right back."

"Sabrina, what do you think?"

"I have never had anything so lovely in my life as this date."

"Me either. I never thought the kids would do such a thing for us."

"And they did wonderful. I'll have to tell them thank you one by one."

"We can do it together. I'm sure they would love to see us do it as a couple, don't you?"

"After what they put together for us, I'd have to say yes they would."

"Then let's not disappoint them. We can tell them at the next community center meeting next Tuesday."

"Maybe we should do something special for them as they did for us."

"That's a nice idea. We can do something special but right now let's focus on us. If we don't it's a possibility there isn't going to be a we."

Elaine returns with the dessert. Two chocolate covered Twinkies. "Dessert is served," she says to both Sabrina and Lorenz.

"Thank you Elaine" Lorenz said as he looks at Sabrina.

"Thank you Elaine" said Sabrina.

They both looked at the Twinkies and started laughing. "What do you expect from pre and early teenagers?" asked Lorenz.

"I think it's great" said Sabrina, and in a wave of the hand she takes one Twinkie and bites it. "Oh, just as I remembered when I was a kid. It's still great."

"Yes they are. But I thought the dessert would be something more the way they kept forcing the serving."

"Oh, they just wanted to complete the meal, you know kids. They have to do it all and it's not a bad thing."

"Sabrina, it seems you know something about kids. That is a wonderful thing. Are you planning to have a family one day?"

"Well, it has been on my mind but not in the near future. I have to find the right partner first. I mean, the right partner not a sperm donor."

"Oh, I hear that all the time; sperm donors that is. I understand what you mean by partner. It is very important for two people to see life as partners and not just mates. Not that I don't like mating or dating for that matter. But partners, is having someone at a different emotional level."

"I agree. It is having someone at a different level that can work things through and keep the family vision."

"Vision?"

"Yes, vision on what makes the family a family; a vision on what is love and how to maintain it. You know the importance of roles and the responsibilities of each role; the importance of nurturing and developing children, the relationship, and partnership to reach greater levels."

"You mean really be in tune and maintain the general focus on each other and the family. Maintaining the unit as the gift from God."

"Exactly, family is a gift and I want my man to be that partner in life."

"I see, you have a great philosophy on family. I like it."

Music from the radio plays as they continue to talk about anything and everything from child bearing to modeling. In no time the darkness overwhelms the candles. Lorenz looks at Sabrina and says, "Would you like to continue our conversation at my place?"

"Sure, I thought you'd never ask."

They both rise and make head way to the door. Lorenz first grabs the paper plates, the bottle, and leaves the table with the blown out candles and thinks of a return in the morning to finish cleaning up the mess. Sabrina looks at the city once again and gives a once around to the lovely view and remembers how the evening started. "You couldn't ask for a better first date" she thinks before stepping into the stairwell. Lorenz follows with the exact thought and in silence steps lightly behind Sabrina.

Rodney stands as Simone returns to the table. "Is everything ok?" he asks with a hint of concern in his voice.

"Sure it is. Why would you think anything is wrong?"

"You took off so abruptly. I thought I said something heart breaking."

"No way. Everything you've done and said so far has been exactly great. You are very good and the best gentleman."

"Sounds like an exit statement."

"Don't be silly, I'm going nowhere."

"Well, then, where did I leave off?"

"Let's just say love at first sight."

"You were listening."

"Of course I was listening. Are you going to finish or move into a different direction?"

"I'm finishing, really finishing. Dessert looks great doesn't it?"

"Yes it does. Looks kind of familiar, what is it?"

"You don't recognize it?"

"No, not at all."

"Taste it and I'm sure you'll remember.."

"OK" and with a stroke of the fork, she tastes a little, smiles and looks at Rodney with a smile. "You made this the night I ate at your house. How did you get it here?"

"I come here so often that the owners and I are quite friendly with each other. Once I told them about you, they allowed me to bring in dessert and keep it here for us."

"You went to that extreme to impress me?"

"Of course, remember the love at first sight comment earlier? Well, you impressed me so much that I wanted tonight to be perfect and impressive for you. And I wish that my actions are received as being genuine."

"Oh, they are genuine alright. I don't think anyone would do so much for a first date as you've done. The only thing you haven't done is feed me as a child."

"It isn't that I hadn't thought about it, I have to have something to look forward to."

"Oh you thought about feeding me. I'm glad you didn't; at least there is something I get to look to do some other time. How nice?"

"Simone tonight is just the beginning of us, it is the spark to our everlasting flame of affection, and each interaction from now on is our fuel to burn stronger with desire. Every time the fire grows, so will our love get stronger, our minds meet as one, and our will to move closer to a union becomes our focal point. I am sure you know what I mean because you have the desire to be with me as I for you. I would like this first step to be something everlasting."

Simone is taken back to how serious Rodney's emotions are towards her. Immediately she thinks of this outpouring is more of an out cry for sex and isn't genuine enough for a woman to believe. "If he thinks I'll fall for this, he has another think coming. What a line of crap he's telling me," she thinks before responding. "Rodney, I don't quite know how to respond. I mean it's nice for someone to feel the way you do. I am enchanted but not quite to the extent as you. Intrigued with thought of tomorrow having a love and commitment; what woman doesn't have that thought. But for now it's just a thought. Don't get me wrong, I like you and want to find out more, but build a life together from one date, fall in love from interest, it isn't me. So I don't want to lead you down a path I'm not willing to travel."

"I said earlier, I didn't expect you to be here with me. It would be nice if you were, and that would make my effort of showing you my emotions easier, but I wanted you to know my feelings. As uncommon as they are, I wanted to make an early stand and profess my feelings. I know it scares you, and it scares the heck out of me. This is a first on my part, especially since I've dated quite a bit. So bear with me please and let's just enjoy the rest of tonight. I vow not to bring it up anymore."

"I'll bear with you for a while. It isn't that I don't enjoy the attention or the company. I do like you Rodney that's why I'm here."

Tom sends the waiter with six roses to Rodney's table and presents them to Simone. Just as he bows a violinist appears and plays a love ballad Rodney then reaches for Simone's hand and winks at her with a glisten in his eye.

"Rodney, you're going way out for this first date"

"As I said earlier, it's not just a first date, it's an investment of what's to come. Well, not in those exact words, but you get the jest."

"Yes, but, again, it's a little much for me" Simone replies and pulls her hand back to her side of the table. "I'll think about it, really give it some thought."

Pouring the last of the wine, Rodney raises his glass towards Simone. "Here's to you having an open mind and heart." Simone reluctantly raises her glass and taps Rodney's before taking a drink. They drink the last of the wine in their glasses and the waiter appears. "Did you enjoy the dessert?" he asked.

"Yes I did, what about you Simone?" replied Rodney.

"Oh, yes the dessert was fantastic. Thanks for asking."

The waiter took all the plates and silverware from the table. Rodney waived for the check and sat in silence for a moment. "Should I ask her where she'd like to go or did I blow the evening professing my emotions so early?" he contemplates. "The park should be fine and whatever happens, I'll bounce back with the next date." he decides. Looking directly at Simone he starts to speak as she says, "What's next? I'm anxious to see what you have planned?"

"Oh, I was just going to tell you. I think a carriage is waiting for us that will take us to a nice jazz spot."

"Really, you're kidding right."

"No, I'm not kidding. Remember I wanted it to be right for the first date. Besides, it is a perfect night for a ride. Are you ready?" Just as he asked, the waiter returned with the check and Rodney signed the receipt. He stands and moves over to Simone to pull her chair out as she stands. "Please" he says, as he leads the way with his arm extended towards the front exit. He grabs the coats from the coat rack and places her sweater around her shoulders just as they exit the door. In front was a horse drawn carriage. The horses were dark and tall, the driver waved at Rodney. Rodney returned the wave and took Simone's hand as a gesture to come along. He then approached the carriage and pulled down steps so she can safely step into the carriage. He assisted her and she found a comforting spot near the middle of the seat. Rodney walked to the other side and entered. "Hi John, thanks for waiting."

"No problem. Still heading for the same place?" he asks.

"Yes, the same place and take your time; I'm sure the lady wishes to see it all."

"You've got it." he replies and in one snap of the leather reins, the horses start moving.

The night sky is clear with stars scattered about, the air was cool but not so cold to cause bundling for warmth. The air was fresh and the park street was filled with on lookers as they passed each block. The old town buildings displayed candles in the windows as if there is a holiday to celebrate. "This is lovely Rodney. I've never done this before." said Simone.

"It is lovely and very nice," he takes her hand and holds it affectionately. "Yes, wait until you see my favorite spot in the city."

"Your favorite spot?"

"Yes, my favorite. It's a building with this fantastic tower, bells, and the architecture is geometric from the

Renaissance era. It is sort of Gothic but cathedral. It has its charm and every time I see its beauty, I feel the architect had ideas way before its time. The building isn't quite like the ones today, the workmanship is awesome."

"It sounds lovely, are we near it yet?"

"Not quite, but there are other things I'd like to show you."

The horse drawn buggy continues the journey through the town, traveling the winding road around the old town's center. A park in the old town has a band gazebo and tonight there's a concert and dancing. The closer they arrive to the location, the louder the music. They arrive just as the band in the gazebo stops for a break. "Whoa Missy, Mick, whoa" the driver yells to the horses as he pulls the reins towards him. The horses stop and the buggy become stable. Rodney jumps out, goes around the carriage, and takes out the stairs. Then he assist Simone's exit off the buggy. "We'll stay here for a short time then finish our buggy tour."

"Oh, how nice, a concert at the park."

"Yes, it just so happened to coordinate well with my plans for tonight. I hope you like live music and cozy dancing."

"Of course I like it. I love to dance, not that I am the greatest, but dancing is quite fun."

"Then let's find a seat before the band returns."

They walk along the path to the table area and find two available seats. "Are you interested in a drink?"

"No not now thank you, maybe later." Sabrina replies.

Sitting close to each other, Rodney places his arm around Simone as they observe others in the music area. People of all ages are walking, talking, and sitting in the area seemingly enjoying themselves at the event.

"Nice evening to be out at a park concert. It is something I've never attended even though I've heard about it for years," Simone said.

"Oh, it's been quite active in concerts every year and the groups coming are more popular. I mean the mainstream jazz groups show up for either free or a fraction of their usual cost. You can't beat the entertainment the city provides."

"It is quite nice. Do you know who's playing tonight?"

"Sure, it's a band from Philadelphia called" in unison they say "Pieces of a Dream."

"How awesome! This is free for the general public. Are you kidding? You mean a mainstream group like Pieces of a Dream is here and the park isn't over populated?"

"That's just it. The park isn't overly populated because the marketing for the music isn't a city focal point. No funds for marketing which I guess they use the money to pay the bands instead."

"Oh my, and I am like the average city dweller and not know anything like it. My Aunt Marge use to invite me out here all the time. I never attended, not even once did I entertain the thought."

"I'm sure your Aunt caught a number of great acts. One year there were Santana, Bobby Womack, Isley Brothers, Bob Dillan, and others at that level. And the kicker was they were all free. The city picked up the cost."

"No way, those are nice groups. As a matter of fact I paid $85 for my ticket to see the Isley Brothers back in the day."

"Free."

"Free and sponsored by the city."

"Yes, sponsored by the city and it's every summer."

"We need to get the word out."

"No, let's keep it quaint. The city will increase its marketing or publicity project soon. So let's keep this one to our immediate friends before they start charging."

"I see your point."

The band returns from their short break. The music starts and Simone really seems to enjoy the show. Song after song and without skipping a beat, Simone taps her foot, applauds at every change, and stands for the soloist to clap in appreciation. She glanced at Rodney from time to time and smiled at each glance. Rodney returned the smile and observed the beauty he admired in Simone. "She has a mind, a great figure, and a wonderful personality. No wonder I'm crazy about her," he thinks.

The concert in the park is nearly over; the band is playing its last song for the night. Simone looks at Rodney and says, "What's next. I'm enjoying everything tonight. I can't believe you showing me so much for one evening."

"We have to complete the carriage ride." Reaching out his hand as an invitation to take hers, he stands and upon her placing her hand in his, he leads her back to the carriage, but walking by her side. "The carriage is right over there and the last part of the ride is only 15 minutes. There is one more thing I'd like to share with you. It's my favorite building in the city."

"I'm learning more about you Rodney, so lead the way. I bet it's wonderful."

Rodney assist Sabrina into the carriage and this time sits really close to her. He places his arm around her and pulls her close to him. The night air is cool yet the sky is still filled with sparkling stars, like glitter on a child's face. The ride is slowly moving along the way as the horses pace themselves traveling block to block.

"Tell me about this building you want me to see Rodney," said Simone.

"The building was designed in the late 1800s. The architect was not very popular as his work was a fluke that's never been repeated. This is the only building of its kind even though it's Gothic in style. But the architect made this work for him and the owner. A family lived there for years, generation to generation. And as they sold pieces of their estate, the property became enclosed with neighbor after neighbor. Now the house is on the national historical list.

The family donated the house to the city which uses it to house special offices. This way the house is public property and can never be destroyed.

You should see the interior. The stairs are hardwood, with hand carved rails. The chandelier is crystal, authentically designed and one of a kind. The walls are made of solid oak, and the door trim is carved with symbols of wealth which is quite decorative in nature. Over the years, the owners added something important that represented their generation. Each oldest child of the first born on their 18th birthday had to design something that they felt represented the family and his generation. Throughout out the house, you'll see multiple pictures, hand carved sculptures, family symbols, jewelry with wood carvings, and the likes that multiple kids left for the house. Don't think the house is cluttered, because it isn't. Some of these items are small, and some really stand out. However, that was a genuine tradition.

"What happened to the original owners? Why did they give it to the city?"

"Well, the family out grew themselves. They became modern and moved away from the city. It's kind of like they became suburban Americans. Except for one member of the family, he maintained the tradition of staying in the house and continuing the family's tradition. When he passed, the family decided to create an endowment for future generations and expand the house's beauty for the general public. The family now lives across the world and annually returns for their reunion. To this day, each extension of the family will bring one artistic item to add the décor. They bring art and sculptures from new and old eras to decorate each room giving it a dynamic theme."

"It is really different from what I see. It seems more like a place from Europe than from this country. What you've described, sounds quite lovely."

"I wish it was open tonight so I can give you a tour."

"We can do it the next time."

"I'm already excited about it. It sounds so well put together from the way you describe it. Now that I know its history, it seems like a different place."

The carriage strolled closer to the house with each hoof beat sound as the horses stepped on the pavement. Each building in the neighborhood depicted a different era and architectural style. There were Georgian style houses most of the East side of the street, Victorian style houses were next, some accented with French windows and doors. As the carriage approached the next corner there was this overshadowing house, bricked home, gothic in style and Rodney's eyes sparkled and his enthusiasm showed. The house was exactly as he described earlier in the evening. Pulling Simone closer, Rodney whispered, "Can you feel the strength of the house the closer you get to it?"

"I guess so. I feel something over shadowing."

"Yes, it's over shadowing, because it's the strength of the house and the neighborhood."

"It is over powering and seems almost as it should be in a scary movie."

"Scary movie, you really think so?"

"Yes. It's kind of eerie, but somewhat intriguing."

The full view of the house appears. The moon light strikes the house with its glowing rays and shadows of the gargoyles standing firm against the building's steeples. The shadow of gargoyles made it seem as if someone was standing on the roof. The rose colored glass at the top of the foyer reflected moonlight and gave a spectacular show to any on looker. And from a distance the glittering light gave harmonic dances like a child's kaleidoscope reflecting the sunlight. The front door is those of a castle, thick and large, handles of iron rings, and doubled to swing outward. The porch is tiered concrete, with pillars rising to the second floor meeting the roof's overhang. The round pillar design is like Roman architecture at the forum and solid rock. The porch rose from the ground, with six stairs, as if it were leading to the entrance of a great monument.

"I wonder what gave the builders an idea to build such a different place?" asked Simone.

"It was the love for something different and a reminder of home," answered Rodney, with a smirk on his face.

"It seems like you know so much about it. And it is different especially for this part of the country. I never knew the building was here."

"It's my favorite. One day when it's open we'll have to take a tour of the inside. Then you'll see why I love it so much."

"That might be a day in the near future."

"Yes, in the near future." Rodney says with a smile.

The carriage ride rounds the lake, with its glittery glow from the wading water, as if it were a path leading to the opposite shore. "Beautiful ride and the night are so lovely. I like our first date" said Simone.

"You made it great, no whimsical mysterious side of you came out and I too enjoyed our time together."

"These were unusual events for a first date, the most different ever. And you are such the gentleman. What a breath of fresh air you are to me."

"And you are the breath I await to take whenever I'm in your presence."

"There is nothing more than having time with a wonderful man. It's early to be so impressed. But I am definitely impressed for sure."

The carriage stops at the restaurant; the valet opens the door and reaches out for Simone's hand. Rodney quickly steps around to Simone from the opposite side of the carriage and arriving to her side, he reaches for her hand to walk to the car. He smiles as his eyes gaze upon her to observe her stride like an angel. She seems to have a glow of contentment accompanying her in the night; a look of total pleasure and happiness from a wonderful event taking her mind into the future of "us" and a will to open the door. "What should I do next?" he ponders.

Simone surely loved the evening, including the activities leading to the ride back to her place. He was silent and played a touch of jazz on the radio as he drove the car to her home. "It was awesome not to be asked a million and one questions about our date. How was I feeling, or am I feeling great as a temperature check for his success? He did the impressive to allow me to soak in the moment and enjoy the silent conversation." Thinking about it, "he is very impressive and such a lovely man. He knows exactly what I want and seems to provide it without effort. Or at least it seems."

Nearing her place Rodney breaks silence and asks, "Will you allow me to call you tomorrow or do you prefer giving time for us to let things settle in?"

"Oh it would be nice hearing from you tomorrow. I don't mind being shown a little interest," as she smiles with her answer.

"Great, I will call you and probably make an afternoon of it."

"I'd wait to see what my schedule is like before making plans. I normally do many things on the weekend."

"Well, at least I'll get to hear your voice if nothing else. But keep your door open with a little time for me. I'd love seeing you again."

Rodney stops the car and immediately exits, steps around the car and opens her door. He extends his hand to provide assistance to Simone. She in turn takes his hand, exits the car and rise into his arms for a quick embrace. Her move of course. Surprised, Rodney immediately responds and capitalizes on the hug he's receiving.

"Thank you for a lovely evening Rodney," says Simone.

"Oh my, you are more than welcome. It was my pleasure to spend quality time with you on our first date."

Looking into her eyes, he tilts his head for a cheek kiss, and waits for a response. She immediately faces the other direction so it is not a kiss on the lips. Not yet in her mind. She then steps back, grabs his hand and leads him to her front door. And the entire way she smiled with joy and heartfelt emotions to open a greater door to Rodney. But, second thoughts prevailed to being too soon for a second base maneuver. A kiss good night will have to do.

Rodney follows Simone to her front door and along the way observes the sensual beauty she posses. It's a night of passion in the making, but rushing could be a mistake so I'll have to push back for a different night if she makes a move. How should I do this? It's a better position to talk your way out of it but being smooth about it.

They reach the front porch and the light from the motion sensors took away the still of darkness. Bright on the porch, they both sway in a different tone since the night is interrupted by the porch light. Another hug and a quick peck on the lips ended the evening. No words spoken until the key enters the door and Rodney quickly says, "You are a wonderful woman and I can't wait until the next time I see you. Good night and I will definitely call you tomorrow."

"Good night Rodney, I can't wait."

Sabrina moves closer to Lorenz for a quick embrace. Lorenz lifts one arm over Sabrina's head to grasp her shoulders to show the strength of his hug. A quick peck on the lips, a sigh of passion and an in depth kiss follows. No words spoken. Just the physical nature after an enjoyable conversation of mind blowing connections takes both to a step closer of joining pleasure in the making. No sooner than the deep kiss ends, they both start stripping their clothes to bare minimums. A quick kiss on the cheek, a nibble at her breast, and tender kisses down her neck, Lorenz follows a sensual ritual. Sabrina replies with a bunch of sighs and stronger grasps for him to be closer and do more. More she wants and Lorenz oblige. Sitting on the couch, she pulls him closer to certain body spots with the strongest nerve sensations. Shudders flow through her body as Lorenz kisses the spot ever so gently. Without pause, Lorenz moves closer and closer to her lips for continued seductive kisses. He follows the line of mid drift as following a yellow line of a road. From her stomach navel to her lips, he stops every few inches after placing her on the couch. She lies on her back and embraces Lorenz at every opportunity, with a sigh and ah. Such responses he thinks and how a desire for more.

Lorenz stands and pulls her up from the couch heading for the bed. Sabrina immediate follows, hesitates a moment, and without reluctance gives him a push towards the bed. He steps clumsily and falls face first on the bed. She burst into laughter and jumps right on his back as if she's riding a pony for the first time. Quickly he maneuvers under her ending face to face with her still on top. Hugging her with a great move, kissing her lips with conviction and desire pouring from his entire body, he entices her to respond as if every muscle in her body relaxes to his every wish. He strokes her hair, gently touching her face, and with the other hand keeps the pressure of body closeness.

With excitement and passion combining for a great union, the two stop for a moment to finish stripping their clothes. In a moment they both pause and view each other's body. "What a fine man," Sabrina thinks. "Lorenz, you are so beautiful."

"And you are a queen of any man's dream Sabrina."

Both move around on the bed and without hesitation involve themselves in a body embrace. Intertwined, caressing, kissing, and heated. Lorenz starts exploring her body with his empowering limb, and just before further exploration, he stops and reaches for the protection of life. He downs the cover in seconds and without hesitation he rolls on top of Sabrina, to fully indulge himself to their first union. Slowly he penetrates the cavity and in no hurry he concentrates on one spot, kissing her, she responds in sighs and small moans and circular hip motions, spreading her legs for more entry. He continues to penetrate for a spot of passion and finds a spot on her neck that sends chills down her body. Feeling the results of her body, he makes one thrust to full engulfment of affection. A screech of passion comes from Sabrina and she grabs Lorenz with her legs and arms, still shaking from her chills and this time increased body response with goose bumps all over her body, holding him tight as if she doesn't want him to move. He continually moves his body in rhythm and in a moment stands on his feet holding her up with out disconnecting. With his strength, he moves her body up and down upon his masculine prowess. Moments later, their bodies start to shake from pleasure and in a controlled movement; they both fall onto the bed while still deeply embraced.

No words are spoken between the two for moments later. No release of passion as they continue to hold each other close, as if a comfort zone both overwhelms with relaxation as if this were a routine moment after years of involvement. Hours pass with them holding each other, Lorenz moves to take a full view of the beautiful woman lying in his arms. He stares as she continues to relax with her eyes closed. She is so lovely, a beautiful spirit, and seductive to the eye as well as the mind. I haven't seen a woman of this caliber since my first year in college. And not knowing the quality of women then as I know now, I'm sure of my past exposure to the total woman. Making love to her is a gift, the icing on the cake, the strawberry dipped in chocolate, and the greater fuel to my desire for more. I need more of her to satisfy my need for love and affection. She is the one, I know it, and tonight confirmed it for sure.

Sabrina wakes with Lorenz staring at her. She automatically thinks something is wrong with her look. "What's wrong?" she asks.

"Nothing is wrong. I'm admiring your beauty, your mind, and the ways you make me feel," responds Lorenz.

"Oh really? You have so much going on yourself and after tonight, I am so sure you're the one I've never met before. I never thought anyone could be so passionate the first time sharing their bodies sexually. It is such a wonderful experience. This may sound silly but are you like this with everyone you have sex with?"

"I can't say I have. I know there is something more with you that I've never experienced. However you know the first thought is always an honest response and without a doubt, you are special."

"Special?"

"Really special and I don't want to sound childish, but you're one of a kind. I'm sure to many others it's the same with them. No woman has ever made me drive to explore such great pleasures, especially from the first encounter. Special, yes, you are extremely special and an angel to my spirit."

Smiling and blushing, "you're such a lovely man."

"I'm glad you think so. And you haven't seen the best of me yet. Would you like anything for breakfast?"

"Just a glass of juice would be nice. I have to get going pretty soon. I hate to love and run, but its business and nothing against you." Sabrina moves to gather her clothing and directs her walk to the bathroom. There she looks in the mirror and starts dressing. She pulls her bra around, snaps it and twist the bra to position. She then slides her panties on before running water in the sink. She splashes water over her face, grabs a towel and dries off. Then she places one arm into her blouse and repeats for the other side. As she stands in the mirror, she notices how blushed she seems to look. In no time, she creates a finished polished look with no tools but her hand and water. She wets her hair just enough to manage a very attractive image. She then pulls her pants up and just as she closes the waist, Lorenz appears.

"My God, you're a fine piece of work. I'm sure you hear this all the time."

"Believe it or not, in my profession, you hear just the opposite. You get more professional rejections than you do work; especially when you're a struggling model."

"You're struggling?"

"Yes, no doubt I'm struggling."

"Oh, then what on earth can we offer each other?"

"That's something we need to discuss when there's time. Right now I have to head out to a shoot." Taking the orange juice Lorenz offered, she takes a couple of sips and passes the glass back. "Thanks. Can I call you later?"

"Well, I hope you do. If not, I'll call you."

# Chapter 8

## *Marge's Relapse*

"Aunt Marge, are you feeling better today?" asked Simone. It's early morning and Simone drops in for a quick check on her favorite aunt. "Is there anything you need from the store? Is there anything you'd like to have?"

"I'm doing fine child. I can't think of anything at this moment. I haven't had a feeling or desire for anything special lately. I don't seem to be the same as before."

"Don't worry; you're fine according to the doctors."

"Well, let me tell you the same as I told them. I don't have the greatest feeling about myself lately, but my soup isn't cooked yet.

"We'd hate you leaving us before your time. Please pay attention to the doctors Aunt Marge."

"I take all the drugs like a good patient. But nothing seems to get me feeling as before. It's like there's this decrease in energy. I suppose those vitamins the doctor prescribed should help me there."

"And what about the other prescriptions?"

"Oh, I follow the directions. I just want more soup these days."

"Huh?" Simone asked, while thinking that's a strange statement. Going into the kitchen, Simone notices the stove fire hadn't been on for sometime, and the soup is in the pot. "No wonder you don't have soup yet, the fire isn't on. How long have you been waiting for your soup?"

"Not long before you came in. I started it nearly thirty minutes ago. I went to check on it and the pot seemed slow at getting warm. So I let the burner warm up slowly."

Surprised at her answer, Simone says "Real slow for sure," she then turned the burner up high for a quick response. "Aunt Marge, you need to pay attention to your cooking. You didn't turn the burner on. That's why it's taking so long to warm up. You should have it in a few minutes. Is there anything else you'd like besides soup?"

"Soups all for now baby."

Simone leaves the kitchen and wanders to other rooms of the house. She walks into the bathroom and takes a look around. She finds nothing out of the ordinary and continues her walk through. Each room she's trying to find something out of the norm or any indicator of Aunt Marge being different. So far each room there's nothing to be alarmed about. There are a few things out of place on the hutch, which is normal for a lived in look and nothing to take great interest. Returning to the kitchen, she finds the soup boiling and immediately reduces the heat. "Aunt Marge, soups done. Do you want it in the kitchen or the dining room?"

"Dining room and I'll be right there," replied Marge. Marge slowly moves from the den to the dining room, stops for a moment to catch her breath, and stands next to a chair as if the back is supporting her. She moves to the seat on the east side of the table. The east chair faces the window to the street and provides a fantastic view of street activities. It's similar to sitting on the porch in the summer or spring. And it gives Aunt Marge a sense of company when no one's around.

"Here you go Aunt Marge. I hope its cool enough for you to enjoy right away. Since you've waited so long for the soup, there's no doubt you're hungry. Is there anything else you'd like with the soup?"

"No dear, the soup should be just enough. Thank you." Aunt Marge takes her first sip after cooling the soup with a blow from her mouth. She repeats for a third taste and Simone is being really observant and attentive. "What did you do last evening Simone?" asked Aunt Marge.

"I had a date Aunt Marge. It was lovely. This was the first date with a guy who has a lot of class. I bet you'd like him."

"Oh, you think I'd like him. Is he anything like the one I was supposed to like before who had lots of class?" she giggles while asking.

"No, nothing like that guy at all. He was a jerk and I didn't realize it. This one seems quite different. He has true style, is a gentleman, and seems to be really patient. He knows lots of people, comes from a great family, and smart. I mean, he's special and I know this from our first date."

"He sounds lovely. But you haven't said one thing. Is he handsome?"

"Aunt Marge, no doubt. He is one handsome guy. He has a build that's awesome. You know, like the model guys, nice complexion, good muscle tone, and has a smile that will light up Texas."

Aunt Marge takes another sip of her soup while she listens, and realizes Simone hadn't spoken of a guy with such enthusiasm for nearly two years. The last guy turned out to be a real jerk. Very selfish and centered on everything around himself; even as they tried to have a relationship. That girl cried many a nights for this guy to change and just open up. It's nice she's giving dating another chance. "Are you making him out to be something great so you can bounce back from the last guy?"

"No way, he's really a great guy. And as a matter of fact we did something you would have loved. It was just like the dates you use to tell me about with Uncle Arthur. He took me to a concert in the park. It was under the stars, in the moonlight, and there were other couples from giggly teens to sixty something." Simone ballerina around the floor in the dining room while she explains; "He is something for sure. Yes you're going to like him."

"All of this from one date. He really impressed you and I'm so happy to see you in great spirits. It's a good change."

"Oh, yes it is. I know it's been one date, but this one has promise."

The door bell rings, twice as if there is someone in a panic to enter. Ding dong, again it sounds louder than the first two rings. "I'll get it Aunt Marge," said Simone. Simone walks to the door, peeps out the peep hole, pulls the door open and says, "Why are you ringing the door like that, Sabrina?"

"Oh you're here. I thought Aunt Marge was alone. I didn't know you were here."

"You always ring the door bell like that?"

"No, of course not, but this time of day Aunt Marge is normally asleep. How long have you been here?"

"Just long enough to feed Aunt Marge and check the house over. Things seem normal," she exclaims as they walk into the dining room.

"Well, that's nice to hear. Everything normal." said Sabrina. "Except one thing."

"What's that," answered Simone

"The date last evening was awesome. And I'd have to admit this one is a keeper for sure. He's so humble and giving; handsome, witty, has great work ethics, and quite spiritual."

"Yours turned out great too. I kind of knew it would when you forgot to call me. I didn't think it would be the best ever though, what did you do?"

"Nothing much except have dinner on the roof top of his apartment building. And get this, he had his youth choir serenade us and serve us. I mean it was a different dinner, you know, kids made it, it was good. But the events were awesome. The kids sang so well that crowds of people around the building applaud after each of their songs. Amazing date. Hi Aunt Marge."

Simone and Sabrina walks into the dining room, take seats at the North and South sides of the table, then watch Aunt Marge continue to eat her soup. "Hi child" said Aunt Marge.

"Are you doing ok Aunt Marge?" Sabrina asks.

"Just fine! I think being home helps with my recovery."

"Recovery?"

"Yes, recovery from those symptoms the doctors identified as the cause of my illness."

"You aren't ill; you're as healthy as an ox."

"No I don't think so. I know something's wrong but I can't place a finger on it." Said Aunt Marge.

"If you don't have indicators to something then we can't make assumptions."

"No, there isn't anything that would cause you to think there is a problem. Is there?" replied Simone.

"Nothing other than a gut feeling, and sometimes those feelings are right on point. I can't seem to put my finger on it. Since I left the hospital, I've been feeling really weird and not myself. I'm sure it's nothing to alarm you over. I'll be fine and of course with more rest and good diet, things will get better."

"Ok," Simone and Sabrina replied in harmony.

"Finished the soup?" asked Simone.

"Yes, I have. But I'm enjoying hearing about your dates. Let's hear more. Tell me everything, and leave nothing out, even the nasty parts."

"Aunt Marge" they both giggled in reply.

Doctor Fitzmerrik calls for a quick session with a couple of specialist. One is a neurologist and the other a cardiologist. They gather in an office just large enough for three people, a desk and three chairs. On the wall is an X-ray reader, displaying Marge's x-rays and in the hand of the cardiologist is the test results from her test the other day. In the other doctor's hand is a test result from neurology. Each doctor sits for a moment and reviews the tests. In their analysis, there is nothing different for a woman of Marge's age. As a matter of fact, she seems to be in great health, and that's why Doctor Fitzmerrik called for special opinions. Each doctor reviewed in depth and openly discusses what the evidence is showing. They bring up scenarios and historical events making them wonder the cause of Marge's fainting the morning she was found. Why didn't she get to another level of sickness, show why or something that would highlight a prognosis while being in the hospital. Her normality is quite interesting or refreshing for a woman of her age. But there has to be something causing her faint spells.

No doctor can find a definite cause for her condition. Her charts were indicating common everyday symptoms to the cold or early signs of a foreign virus her body feverishly fights. But nothing in her symptoms leads to anything outside of the simple cold. Baffled to the extent of all doctors and specialist conversing intermittently between them, nothing seems to jump out at either one as a cause of her fainting and high fever. Doctor Lorenz Maynard was called into one of the conversations on Marge. Not knowing the name of the patient, he adamantly listens to the multiple case discussions. Taking notes, he graphically identifies each area of medicine in reference, and later heads to an office and pulls multiple reference books off different shelves. He searches for like symptoms within the group of notes he recorded. Nothing seems to match for a definite cause of Aunt Marge's faint spells. He then circles a trend of events those specialists identified. Nothing jumps out as a definite probability. Last, he contemplates contacting the patient for a follow-up visit. Before getting up from the desk, the makes notes for future questions to ask the patient. Within no time, he's got a list of items that would give him clarity.

Contacting the main doctor on the floor, Lorenz inquires to meeting or visiting the patient. He inquires to her location so he could make his call. The leading doctor directed him to patient services to locate her and provided Lorenz with his permission to find out as much information as necessary. Before heading out to patient affairs, he makes his routine rounds with patients, reviews the charts and provides the attention and focus to them in a usual fashion. Before finishing his last patient, he stops at the nurses' station and calls Sabrina.

"Hi Sabrina, I was thinking about you and decided to call."

"Hi Lorenz," she replies while smiling. "It's nice hearing your voice. I hope your day is going well. I'm with my aunt and sister so I can't talk long."

"Ok, I wanted to know if you were available tonight. I'd love to see you."

"Well, I have a few errands but tonight sound interesting enough. What do you say about 7? Will this work for you?"

"Seven it is, let's call if things change."

"Sure. See you then, your place."

"Bye lovely woman."

"Bye" and she turns to Simone and smiles. "That was Lorenz. He's ready to see me again and it hasn't been 24 hours."

"And did you expect anything different from him," asked Simone.

"No, nothing different, except that he's not my normal type.

"That's what gets you hurt. I'm glad you've changed your taste of men. Hopefully you'll not cry on my shoulder this time." Aunt Marge added.

"Oh Aunt Marge, you're so dramatic. I didn't cry on your shoulder. I asked for advice, and then I cried."

All three ladies began to laugh at the comment. As in older times, the young ladies sought advice and comfort from their favorite aunt. She understood the emotional challenges a young lady would go through. With no mother available, Aunt Marge was a great substitute and was hip enough for the times. She gave great insight to many things. And it seemed that her advice protected them from the harsh pains of relationships; that is, when they followed her advice.

Aunt Marge lifted her left hand and placed it on her forehead. "I'm feeling a little warm in here. Is the heat up today?"

"No Aunt Marge, the heat is off. The air conditioner is off; the weather is perfect as this is a weird summer's day. It's so nice out; one could mistake it for fall or spring. I suspect you not wanting to head outside for the porch, you weren't feeling very well," said Simone. "Are you feeling differently than before? You mean so much to us, that we wanted to make sure you were feeling better. After your soup, we'd hope you were up for a ride to a park or the mall. We know how you like to window shop. Do you think you're up to it?"

"I may want to enjoy the sunshine. It would make me feel better. I'd like that as I think of it."

"Good. Let's get your sweater just in case it's a little cool." Grabbing the sweater from a dresser drawer, Simone notices a top that reminded her of childhood. It was the lacy pink sweater that Aunt Marge wore on special occasions. It was the same sweater she wore to my graduation, in the pictures on Thanksgiving days at grandmother's house, and any event calling for a picture. I think it's the only sweater you'll find on any picture. She loves this sweater. I'll take this one and see if she wants it.

Moving to the front of the house, she holds the pink laced sweater in her right hand while walking through the hallway. Simone looks on the wall for pictures reflecting her aunt in the sweater. She stops for a moment and looks at one picture in particular. It's a picture of Aunt Marge and Uncle Arthur during a time when she seemed so happy and content. I remember the day they took this picture. As a matter of fact, my mother took the picture and she laughed so hard about it being professionally done. Just think, an eye from my mom being professional, no way. It is a nice picture and Uncle

Arthur is so handsome. I hope to find a loving man like him. He was awesome. Moving right along into the den, Simone calls out to Aunt Marge. "Will this sweater do?"

Aunt Marge turns, looks at the sweater and answers, "yes that one is nice. Are you two girls ready?"

"I think we are. I am not going to stay too long because of a scheduled shoot. But I will be along for a short period of time. I hope that doesn't bother you." answered Sabrina. No it doesn't bother me one bit. I know you're a professional lady, and you have to work. As a matter of fact, I'm proud you do what you do. Says much for today's woman; I wish we had opportunities you enjoy back in my day. Life for me would surely be different."

They grabbed their purses and headed to the car. Aunt Marge with her pink sweater didn't mention the fact that it was for dressier occasions. Unlike her normal focus, she never evaded to the point that enjoying the park in the afternoon would be successful. It's a normal comment from her. And she'd comment on things so often, it became expecting. Aunt Marge not making comments is an odd occurrence, especially since there were multiple opportunities.

Moving away from the den one slow step at a time, Aunt Marge went for the front door. Raising one arm, she allowed Simone to place the sweater over the left arm and quickly spread the rest of it over her back. In one full push, and still walking towards the door, Aunt Marge completed putting on the sweater and immediately raised her right had towards the front door. "Get my purse Sabrina, and come along dear" she shouted.

"Got it Aunt Marge, and I'm right behind the two of you," replied Sabrina.

"Let's not move too hasty and fall over the stairs Aunt Marge," Said Simone. "I think we can get to the park in enough time. I'd rather we get there safely than have an accident along the way."

"OK," replied Aunt Marge. "Which car are we taking?"

"I can't drive because I'll have to leave for a shoot from the park," answered Sabrina.

"That makes it your car Simone. Let's just get going. The sun will be down before long and you know I hate driving in the dark."

"Who said you were driving?" They chuckled together while settling in the car. Sabrina whipped her car right along the street behind Simone. Waiting for things to get moving, Sabrina turned on the radio at a popular hip-hop station. She started swaying to the music and immediately thought of Lorenz. "Oh, I'd love to get him dancing. The way that man moves, it's remarkable. I feel him now," she thinks. Simone finally settles in, places the key in the car's ignition, and starts it right up. She checks Aunt Marge once more to ensure her seatbelt is connected. She then turns on the radio and hears the song Sabrina is moving to. "Can't you turn it down a little baby?" asked Aunt Marge. "It's a little too loud for me and you know I'm not a fan of this suppose to be music."

"Not a problem. I don't mind listening to something else." Turning the radio to an oldies station she asks, "How about this station? Will it do?"

"Yes, child, that's fine."

Simone signals and ease into traffic. Sabrina follows so there are no cars in between them. Heading north, they observe life all around them. Multiple people about, the street vendors hustling, kids running on the side walk, and stores with customers heading in and out. The number of people out and about seems like droves. It's as if there was a parade and they either forgot about it or didn't care for the parade subject. "You know," says Simone, "I can remember this road being empty and never any traffic."

"Yep, things sure do change. I'm not saying things change to be an odd ball, but it's a way of life. We change. And sometimes it's not for the better."

"What is that suppose to mean?"

"Not that all changes are good. It's so different these days. Just something I noticed every day I get older; and supposedly wiser. You know the saying, wiser with age."

Snickering Simone replies, "Yes, wiser for sure but with age, come on Aunt Marge, you're no older than 50. How can you say wiser with age?"

"Child I wish I were 50. I'd have a new man in my life, go dancing all night, and have that man yelling early in the morning. I'd whip it on him."

"What?" exclaims Simone, "I don't think I've ever heard you talk that way."

"I am a woman you know. I may be old in age, but I can still think about those great days."

Pulling into the park's parking lot, Simone signals Sabrina to park next to her. And in swift motions, she places the car in park, un-hooks the seatbelts, and turns the car off. Jumping out of the car she smiles at Sabrina making a gesture, you're not going to believe what I heard.

Walking around to Aunt Marge's side of the car, she finds the passenger door open and one leg out with a foot on the ground. Immediately she grabs Aunt Marge's arm to assist her in getting out of the car. "I know this is slowing you down, but thank you for being so kind and patient with me. I love the park. Can you feel the fresh breeze?"

"Yes, I feel it. I love bringing you here. It's the same park you brought us to when Sabrina and I were kids." While closing the car door, Sabrina says "I remember when we came to the park; you were the only adult with us. I mean all of us. It had to be 13 kids with you. Today I look back and wonder how did you keep us in line and behaved so well?"

"It was easy those days. You all behaved so well. The fear in you was I'd tell your uncle or parents. The repercussions were devastating to you then. And besides, you all were so good. I had no problem with either of you. I loved you all so much, and you were all like my kids back then. Even when your folks would drop you off, you didn't even say good-bye to them and immediately started with me. I had all of you eating out of the palm of my hand. Literally," as she laughs.

They walk along a paved walkway and sat on a bench near the small lake. The trees were so big, full of leaves, green and colorful with bristling sounds as the winds gently touch each leaf. The sun was out but not causing great heat. The warmth of the day was that of spring or fall. Not common for a summer's day, and surely not a day to miss the outdoors. Aunt Marge sat on the bench and hummed an oldies song she recently heard on the radio. It was just like the days of Simone and Sabrina's child hood. "Old habits die hard," said Sabrina. "I remember that same song when we played kick ball over there."

"Yea, I remember. It's been sometime since we came to this park. We use to come here so much. Hey, let's look over near the pond where we use to play."

"OK"

"Aunt Marge, will you be ok for a minute or two?"

"I'm fine. You go ahead. I'm sure no one will bother me," answered Aunt Marge.

"We'll be right back" said Simone, as her and Sabrina walked away towards the old playing field. "Girl, something's up with Aunt Marge," she tells Sabrina. I don't think everything is fine in her mind."

"Yea, she's gotten old but I'd never think something is wrong. I guess things will be ok if she started to rest more often."

"No, I think there's more going on than what's showing. She talked about missing sex on the way here. Can you believe that? She never talked about her having sex. Even when we use to ask her everything our parents wouldn't answer."

"You know, that's right. She never mentioned her sex life to us. It was always," Simone and Sabrina answers in unison, "those fast girls got their dues, not my pretty nieces. But she'd answer our questions, no matter what we asked."

"She answered them all right. I remember when I thought babies were brought by a big bird and she showed me where a baby came from. It scared me to death just thinking a baby would get through that part of my body. A baby was so big and my vagina was so small. I asked her how and she told me that they'd stretch me so far that I wouldn't snap back to normal. I think I was 12 years old at the time."

"That would scare anyone." Simone laughs with her hand over her mouth.

They arrive to the pond and now see boats, ducks, and a concrete ramp; nothing like the solitude of years before. Immediately the girls turn back towards Aunt Marge, see her sitting there not moving; just sitting there in peace and harmony with the surrounding. Quickly the girls turn back to face the pond "Wow it's changed. I guess no one thought this would ever turn into to a boating pond. At least many kids are using it for miniature sail boats. At least it's not a super market parking lot."

"That's a great thing right?" asks Sabrina.

"I think so" said Simone. "Let's get back to Aunt Marge. We should be sitting with her before you leave."

"Yea, let's do that." They turn around and head back for the bench. Aunt Marge is sitting with no motion. She's sitting silently for the first time in days. She hasn't moved one muscle from the last time they looked around. No rocking or head moving. "Is she asleep you think?" asks Sabrina.

"No, I bet she's just meditating or something like that."

"Probably so, she hadn't' been out in the park for sometime now and enjoying the sound of the birds is probably helping her relax."

They arrive to bench with Aunt Marge and finally take a seat. "Aunt Marge" asks Sabrina, "Are you ok?"

"Mmm huh"

"Good. You know I'll have to leave in a few."

"Mmm huh"

"I'll let you know when the time comes. What are you doing?"

"Listening to someone calling my name."

"I don't hear anything," said Sabrina. "Neither do I" said Simone.

"Hush, I hear it loud and clear."

The girls then sat in silence as Aunt Marge closed her eyes and started snoring with her head leaning forward and her chin down towards her breast. "How can she sleep like that?" asks Sabrina.

"I don't know. But as long as she's content it doesn't matter. It's got to be comfortable for her."

Minutes pass and Sabrina looks at Simone to indicate her time is up if she wanted to make it to her next shoot. Standing up from the bench, she touches Aunt Marge to say good-bye and noticed no response. No body movement as before and no snoring. "Simone" she calls out. "Simone, do you think she's still asleep?" Simone looks for signs of breathing, notices there's a moist spot on the grass, and started to panic.

"Aunt Marge," she yells in a loud voice. "Aunt Marge wake up," she yells. No response or movement from their elderly aunt; nothing at all, no movement or breathing, and the moist spot isn't from rain or running water. Immediately Sabrina calls for an ambulance, while Simone grabs Aunt Marge's wrist and looks for a pulse."

"I found a pulse but it's weak."

"Try to wake her; I'll get the ambulance here."

"Aunt Marge, come on. Wake up. Please wake up." Nothing; no response or movement from Aunt Marge as Simone holds her close and trying to wake her. She doesn't respond but Simone can feel her faint breath.

"The ambulance will be here shortly. They said in five minutes," barks Sabrina.

"Good," replies Simone. "Come on Aunt Marge, wake up."

Faint siren sounds are now heard. Each moment goes by, the sound increases. "Good, that's the ambulance. It doesn't seem like it will ever get here."

"Three minutes, can you hear a siren? I don't understand why it's taking so long for them to arrive."

"Three minutes, seems like forever. Come on or it'll be an hour before they arrive. Come on!" pressures Simone.

In two minutes the ambulance arrives with the EMT specialist running to Aunt Marge's position. Immediately they place Aunt Marge on a gurney and look for vitals. The routine vital checks; blood pressure, heart beat, are going and the EMT started asking Simone questions. "What's her name?" he asks Simone.

"Marge" she replies.

"Ms. Marge, can you hear me?" He asks while raising her eye lid and flashing the light in her eye for a pupil response. No response from her, but her pupils barely move. Checking the vital signs, he realizes that there's little sign of life. Immediately he calls to his EMT partner. "Let's get her in the ambulance and head for East Medical Center. Everything's faint. I'll start an IV on the way."

"OK, let's go. Ready lift," the EMT specialist replies. They lift Marge onto the ambulance and calls for either of the girls to come along. "Which one of you is coming along?"

"Sabrina you go in the ambulance, I'll follow." Said Simone. "We'll come back for your car later"

"I have to call the shoot for a reschedule." Sabrina shouted.

"OK."

The EMTs move urgently. Without looking back, they did exactly as planned and headed to the hospital. Sabrina in the ambulance holding Aunt Marge's hand and dialing to cancel her photo shoot, she speaks to her photographer with a sense of fear. "I'm sorry the shoot can't happen today. I'm with my Aunt Marge on the way to the hospital. We'll have to reschedule. I'll call you later." Immediately ends the call.

Simone, driving in her vehicle, calls her office and exclaims following the ambulance to the hospital. She tells the director of her mishap. And was reminded that she wasn't to come in today, however if more time is required, please let the company know.

The ambulance maneuvers about traffic arriving at the hospital in minutes. Especially since traffic surprisingly kicked up; some kind of event happens, and as usual the city shows up in massive force. Pulling up to the dock, the ambulance doors open and a nurse is waiting for immediate situation report from the paramedics. The nurse grabs Sabrina by the hand to assist her exit and then moves her to the right of the vehicle. The paramedics are jumping with extreme caution to ease Aunt Marge down with the roller gurney and get her into the emergency room. Right through the double doors, there's multiple beds, people moaning, stations with harsh wounds and there were open spots with medical equipment in the ready. Doctors, nurses, and technicians were moving briskly about as if each patient was on their last leg. And it was up to them to keep them all alive and well.

Simone parked her car in the emergency lot, whisked away towards the hospital doors as if she's running the hundred yard dash. Nearly missing an oncoming car, she moves like the wind to reach Aunt Marge. Side stepping the counter, she blazes through the double doors of the emergency entrance and immediately looks for Sabrina. Moving from curtain to curtain, she glances quickly to see where her aunt landed. Running behind her is a clerk trying to stop her from entering deeper into the area.

"Miss, Miss," the clerk yells.

Simone, without turning shouts back, "I'm looking for my aunt and sister. They arrived just before I did in the ambulance outdoor."

"Miss, Miss," the clerk exclaims. "If you'd come back to the counter I can tell you where she is.."

Just as Simone stops, Sabrina calls out "Simone, over here." Simone stops and turns towards Sabrina, in two steps, she's next to Sabrina and Aunt Marge. The clerk stops and asks if either has time to check Aunt Marge in as soon as possible; both Sabrina and Simone turned and in unison answered "yes" and without a miss in heart beat, turned back to Aunt Marge. Sabrina saddens from fear and leaves for the waiting room.

Doctors were checking her and unnoticeably Lorenz started shouting out directions.

"Status on this patient," he asks the paramedic.

"Not sure exactly, her vitals are: low palpitation, sweaty skin, feverish, and low blood pressure. We arrived on the scene and her condition hasn't changed. It's your job to know why. We transported her here and kept her stable. Our job is done. Let's go partner."

"Thanks guys. I'll take it from here. Nurse let's get her into 24. Retake her vitals while I give her a once over." Lorenz starts the routine checks for indicators or symptoms. He scans her pupils, checks her heart beat, and breathing. He takes notes of her condition under Simone's observation. "Simone, right?" he asks. "Can you tell me what her day was like before coming here?"

"Sure, she had a bowl of soup, talked a little, we went to the park and she fell into a deep sleep. She fainted and we couldn't get her to respond. That's when we called the ambulance to bring her here."

"Did you notice if she took some type of medications?"

"No, nothing that I know about, other than the prescription she had from the last time being here."

"We don't have an idea what's causing her to be in this state. I'm going to review her record and see what type of meds she's on. She's stable for the time being." Lorenz turns away and heads for the nurses' desk. "Nurse, can you get me the records on Marge Blaine please. Call me when you have them." He walks away from the nurse's desk and heads to another emergency bed.

Simone places a call to Sabrina. "Hey, where on earth are you?"

Just as Sabrina walks through the emergency room doors, her cellular phone rings. "Hey," she answers. "I'm in the waiting room."

"Oh, ok. Aunt Marge is stable right now and Dr. Maynard is reviewing her medical record. He couldn't find anything immediate as an indicator to what's happening to her."

"Did you say Lorenz Maynard?"

"Yes, he's on call. I guess you aren't worried about Aunt Marge since you're asking about Lorenz."

"Yes I am worried about Aunt Marge. Just surprised to see Lorenz on duty; are you coming out? Or should I come in?"

"I'm heading out. Take a seat and I'll be right there."

Simone ends the call, snaps her cell phone back to carry shape, places it in her purse, and heads towards the waiting room. Immediately she notices Lorenz at a different bed where they are performing an emergency something. Blood spurting all over the bed area while nurses and Dr. Maynard makes an attempt to stop the bleeding. It was only for a moment that Simone looked, but it was long enough for a queasy feeling to fall over her. In a dash, she jumps through the double doors leading to the waiting room. "Sabrina," she exclaims "You're not going to believe what I just saw." And before saying anything, she caught herself not to announce her thoughts because of multiple people looking at her. She calms her voice down and says, "The usual thing and nothing more."

"I can only imagine." Said Sabrina. "Well, what's the verdict?"

"Nothing yet, the doctor has to review her record before doing something. He's got to know what's going on before he can do anything. He's in his prognosis and response phase. I'm sure he'll let us know something as soon as he finds out. Let's find a seat and wait for the doctor."

Minutes rolls by leading to 45 past the hour. No sign of a doctor coming out to explain. Sabrina walks to the nurses' counter and asks about her aunt. The nurse looks for someone, hesitates, places a pad down on the counter, turns around as if searching for someone, stands, and walks back to the ER section. Sabrina looks at Simone and shakes her head from side to side showing disgust with her facial expression. Sabrina stands at the counter waiting, minute after minute until 7 minutes pass. A nurse appears from the back and asks, "Can I help you?"

"No" Sabrina replies. "Another nurse is checking on my aunt. I'm waiting for an answer."

"You can have a seat and I'm sure she'll call you when she returns."

"Thanks but no thanks. I want to be here when she arrives."

Two minutes pass and the nurse returns to the counter. She looks at Sabrina and says, "The doctor will be here shortly."

"You can't tell me what's going on with my aunt?"

"No I can't. I was directed to tell you the doctor will be here shortly. Please have a seat."

Sabrina turns toward the seat and immediately the doors to the ER opens out. A doctor walks out for someone in the waiting room. This time it's a call for a Williams. Just the sound of the name being so close to Willingham is nerve wrecking. The people leave their seats heading to the doctor for an update. Within a few minutes the three people around the doctor begins to cry. One whaling loudly enough to send streaking pain down one's spine. "Oh, God no" in a loud cry. The three embraced each other and sits near the doors, the doctor walks back into the ER as if to continue his work. Sabrina and Simone observes the three people and tears begin to fall from their faces. Sympathy for them eludes from the people in the room. You can see the multiple faces focused on the three and no one moving towards them. Minutes later a different doctor walks out and calls for "Ms. Blaine." No responses to his call. The doctor repeats "Mr. or Ms. Blaine." Again, no response within a minute, the doctor returns through the doors looking at the chart. Sabrina jumps up to the nurses' counter and asks, "When am I going to find out the conditions on patient Marge Blaine"

"The doctor was just calling for Ms. Blaine"

"Oh my goodness, we were listening for Willingham. Please get that doctor back."

"I think I can manage. Have a seat and I'll get him back."

"Thank you," said Sabrina.

Within a minute the doctor returns to the doors and calls for Willingham. Both Sabrina and Simone walk over to hear the doctor's explanations.

"Ms. Willingham" the doctor calls.

"Yes," both Sabrina and Simone answers.

"There's good news about Ms. Blaine and of course there's troubling news. Ms. Blaine suffered a stroke and that's the bad news. The good news is that it wasn't bad enough to paralyze her. So, you'll have to watch her diet, help with the meds, and continue a daily regime of exercise to continue her muscle use. And from her chart, I noticed she was here before. I asked for a few more test to ensure there is nothing else on the horizon. Let's keep her here for two days."

"Oh, sure thing doctor, we'll have her back in two days." said Simone. "Is there an appointment set up for her?"

"No, Ms Willingham, I'd like to observe her for two days." said the doctor.

"Oh, she was just here for a few days with multiple tests. I think you can see her record and besides she'd like to be home." explained Simone.

"Well, I know the case well" answered Lorenz as he approached. "We need to test her to make sure of our diagnosis" as he smiles at Sabrina.

"Well, it's your call and I think it's a good idea since you know the history" replied Sabrina.

"We can't let her stay here" said Simone.

"We can" replied Sabrina. "Let's let the doctors be doctors. It'll be ok for two days."

"Good, then its settled." replied the ER doctor. "The nurse has the information. I'll pass it on to her primary provider. She will let you know the test schedule. I think it's the best thing to do. And you two can see her as soon as we're done here. She's being transferred to a room as we speak. I wish I can tell you what room, but I haven't the slightest. I'm sure the nurse has the room assignment."

"Thank you doctor" Simone and Sabrina said in unison. They immediately turned to the nurses' counter. "We're looking for Marge Blaine's room," said Simone

"Just a moment" the nurse replies and looks at the computer screen. "She's in room 671, 6th floor."

"Thanks."

Sabrina and Simone walks to the elevators pushed the up button and silently waited for the elevator's arrival. "Simone" says Sabrina.

"Yes," Simone sighs.

"What are we going to do to help Aunt Marge? Should we place her in a senior citizen home?"

"You know I hate doing that. And the reality is our schedules are hectic and there's no way we can support her day in and day out. Maybe we can get a live-in help."

"I don't know about the live in. I think a live-in is dangerous; unless it's a family member that wouldn't mind."

"You never know about family unless you ask. There's so much having her placed in a home or having someone come. We have to really look at this for a minute. We were lucky to be with her this time. Imagine if we'd visit and she was still at home with no one around and then her having a stroke. Would we be as lucky?"

"You have a point. I think we should put her in a home where there's 24 hour observation."

"She's going to hate that idea. You know how independent she likes to be. I bet she'd rather have a live in."

"But the live in is no guarantee for 24 hour observation."

"Neither is the home. But at least there's a greater chance someone is around to help if need be."

"Yes, you're right. We should look into it." The elevator arrives and doors open. The two ladies enter the elevator, Sabrina presses the 6th floor request button, and steps back to the center of the elevator.

"Hello Sabrina" a voice enters the air from the rear of the elevator. Sabrina turns and locks eyes with Lorenz.

"Oh, hi Lorenz, I didn't think I'd see you right now."

"Oh you're not here for me?"

"I wish it were for you. Not that I don't like seeing you, it's my aunt."

"Oh, it's nothing that you can't handle?"

"Mild stroke. She's had a mild stroke. I think it's a second time."

"The doctors have a plan for her. You must be heading for her room." The elevator stops at the 4th floor. "This is my stop. Please call me later. I'd love seeing you again." Lorenz steps out of the elevator and walks without turning around. Simone sees that he didn't turn around as the doors closed. "You blew that one didn't you?"

"Oh heck no. Didn't you hear him want to see me soon? He's going to; it's just at my leisure."

# Chapter 9

## *"Quality of Life"*

Elevator doors open on the 6th floor. The girls walk to room 671 and enters without knocking. There are six people in the double bed room, two nurses on each side of Aunt Marge. The other patient seemed very quiet. She isn't moving as if she is sound asleep. Nurses were doing the last IV prep, and comforting Aunt Marge the best way possible for the moment. Aunt Marge seemed nearly out of it, as her eyes were barely open. But it was an improvement since arriving hours ago.

Rodney jumps with excitement as he tells Dan of his wonderful date with Simone. "I'm telling you it was great. No better than great, it was awesome."

"Sure it was the best ever. It had to be, I've never seen you so energetic after a date."

"Oh, it's that noticeable?"

"No doubt, it's noticeable alright. Another step and I'll figure a way to package your energy and sell it as kinetic fuel for cars."

"No man, you don't understand. She was just amazing, beautiful, classy, and beautiful. Did I say beautiful?"

"Yes, I think you said it three times. That woman really has you doesn't she?"

"No, well, maybe, I guess so."

"Oh, she has you alright. Have you called her since the date?"

"No," replied Rodney. "I haven't called her yet. As a matter of fact, I'm waiting for her to call me."

"Now why on earth would you do that?"

"It's a classic way to ensure she had a wonderful time during the date. Plus it doesn't make me look to aggressive or desperate."

"If the date was so great, why would you think you're being aggressive?"

"It's just classy to wait."

"You're much better than that Rodney. You do your thing man, call the woman and talk to her about the next time you get together. It should be easy to get things set up for the next date. Not that you'd have to do more than the first. Setting your standards so high during the very first date was crazy, but it's done now. So what do you think would work for an encore?"

"OK, I'll call her. And let me think, it should be something simple and yet elegant.'

"Yes, elegant and simple."

"I got it, a picnic in the park on a Sunday afternoon."

"That sounds nice, but did your first date have a ride in the park?"

"Oh, yea, but it was a good experience. And if dining in the park seems a little much for a second date, then I'm just showing her I like wilderness."

"Ha, ha, ha, that's funny," laughs Dan. "Wilderness? Don't you mean nature?"

"So you get the picture."

"Man this woman has you out of mind and character."

"You know she is awesome, just awesome."


Rodney walks in the bedroom of his apartment, picks up his cell phone and starts to dial her number. He dials six of the seven digits, and just before pressing the last number, he looks in the mirror and sees his image with a great glow. Yes, glowing in the middle of the day and its all because of Simone. Wow! Man I look so different. It's a wonder I recognize myself. I haven't felt this happy since, a long time ago. Placing the phone back on the dresser, Rodney decides to get dressed first. He looks into the closet and selects a nice pair of black slacks, a light color blue shirt, and matching shoes and belt. He dressed as if heading out to the office or to meet a friend for coffee. Not too impressive but very neat, his clothes gave him the appearance of a neat person, with style, and class. He takes one last look in the mirror, nods with approval, and walks out to the living room of the apartment.

"You cleaned up quite well. If I have to say so," says Dan.

"Thanks man, I try to look nice when I have too."

"Did you call?"

"Snap, no I didn't. I started to but had a different thought. I'll surprise her with flowers and take her a picnic lunch. That way she'll think I'm spontaneous."

"Nice touch. He's back on track." Dan laughs.

Dan and Rodney leaves the apartment, they head for two different cars, waves at each other and drives off. Rodney calls Simone on his cellular phone. Three rings and no answer, Simone answers on the fourth ring.

"Hello"

"Hi Simone, its Rodney"

"Hi, I'm at the hospital. Can we talk later?"

"Hospital. What happened?"

"Something's wrong with my aunt. We were at the park and it seems as if all hell broke loose. Well not exactly all hell, but something unexpected."

"Is she doing ok?"

"Best to be expected at the moment, but not sure what the problem is."

"Are they running tests?"

"Yes and will run more tomorrow. Right now she's under observation for changes in condition. I know they'll find something this time."

"Let's hope so. I hope things get better. Are you doing ok?" asks Rodney.

"Yes, so far. I'm just worried about Aunt Marge. I want you to know how much fun I had on our date. I hope we get a chance to have another."

"That's what I called about. Start dating in an exclusive status. I'd like to take the chance on us without going through so much of the norm. I have a great feeling about you, us, and the future. I feel like nothing before and it's got to be because of you."

"Exclusive? I don't know about being exclusive so quickly. I hardly know you and how you are in multiple situations. I have to know how you'll respond to different places, things, and conditions."

"You mean, you're a woman who wants to see more of the person and not just looking to beat the ticking clock?"

"Why, shouldn't I be more aware of you as an entire package and not pass judgment from one date?"

Sighing, Rodney takes a deep breath and responds with doubt in his voice. "I hoped for a better response than take our time and build."

"Not your normal answer from a woman. Not too shocking is it?"

"No not shocking, just surprising."

"Surprises are good."

"Not this type of surprise. You see, multiple women dream of a day when a good guy comes into their lives and offer quality in a relationship. I understand your doubt in my character in some point. What I don't understand is our multiple encounters that show you how interested I am to take this relationship to a higher level. I thought you'd want us to move on."

"In my heart yes but in my mind its best to move slowly and see how we fit overall."

"Fit over all. I thought you knew this and it's why we started dating."

"Dating is it. Not moving in together and making plans for the future."

"Oh, I see, you think this is making plans for the future. As I said earlier, we would be exclusive. Are you seeing someone else?"

"No, no time for it. Between work and my aunt there isn't much time for anything else."

"Did you enjoy our first date?"

"Yes."

"How about the dinner at my place with your cousin, was I wrong to assume you were into me?"

"No, as a matter of fact, I'm quite glad you've shown interest. And of course I am interested in you. But I'm not ready for a commitment."

"Oh, very well, I see your point. Does this mean we can't go on any more dates?"

"Of course not, I'd love going on dates with you. Remember, I said let's build this relationship and not rush into it."

"Ok. Caution is the operative word to building. Well, I hope your aunt gets better. Call me when you can. I'd love to talk to you more."

"Is that it? You're ready to leave the conversation?"

"No, not really, but I thought you had something else going on that requires your attention."

"Yes I do, but you are my focus at the moment. I want us to do something soon."

"That would be great. But since you're busy, it has to be your call of when. I'll take care of the where and what."

"It's a deal. I'll call you soon."

"Talk to you then."

"Bye Rodney."

"Later, Simone."


Rodney ends the call, and in anguish snaps the cellular back to it storage state. "Man was I wrong or just too damn interested in this woman?" he asks himself. Arriving to his building complex, Rodney parks the car and heads up to his apartment. Walking into the family room of his apartment, he simply picks up the phone book with business and associate contacts. He flips pages looking for a name that strikes him with interest. Before he realizes what's happening to him, this name and number jumps from the page. "Oh man oh man, what a woman, and I pushed her away when I met Simone. Should I call or just sit for a moment"

"You should sit for a moment," Dan says while entering the apartment. .

"Man I didn't realize you were here. So you heard the conversation between Simone and me?"

"No, but I bet it was with Simone. I can only imagine your part, which isn't difficult to figure out with the look on your face. I bet she's being cautious. So don't do something foolish."

"Coming from you that's some serious advice."

"Yes, but remember that was before I heard how serious you are with Simone. I mean, serious enough to impress me that she's the one."

"Yeah, my thoughts exactly, she's the one."

"So be patient and let things work out. Focus on being there for her without being annoying."

"Annoying?"

"Come on Rodney, I've been with you as friends for years. Don't you know I understand you and how focus driven you can be with women?"

"It's not annoying to show your feelings to a woman on a daily basis."

"It is when they aren't open to it just yet."

"OK, no spontaneous gifts, visits, and multiple calls throughout the day with this one. I'll be patient as much as possible."

"Let's hold you to this. Oh, and give me the name and number of the woman you're about to call. I can use a date tonight."

"Yea, ah, no, you'll have to find your own. This is my stash for emergencies."

"Oh, you're going to do me this way. Just remember, when I get on the wagon of fun, there won't be much for me to share."

"When Simone comes around, I'll have a wagon of my own. I know it."

Sabrina walked to the cafeteria for a snack and a break from the room. Simone finished the call and attempts to contact Sabrina. She dials the number and waits for an answer. Again, the answering voice asks for a message. "Hey Sis, give me a call when you can or wake me if I'm asleep when you return. I think I may have pushed Rodney away too soon." After folding the cellular phone, Simone moves towards Aunt Marge, looks at her peaceful slumber, and allows a tear to fall down her face. "I sure wish you were available to talk right now Aunt Marge. I could use your views if I'm cold, or if I'm waiting for a prince charming that isn't coming. I could be pushing the prince charming away right now. I practically threw myself on him weeks ago at his apartment. I can't believe my fear or the want to be so careful. This could be the one for sure. Or, is it? I did have a wonderful time on our date. It was charming, romantic, and full of that special great feeling factor. It was too good to be true for a first date; no flaws and he was the gentlemen of men. Did it all scare me? Am I afraid of the quality he brings? I haven't had a man with so much to offer, the right touch per say. Is this what life has for me? Moving too fast for a sure thing to last; I practically told him to back off."

"Simone is that you," asked Aunt Marge. Quickly turning around to view Aunt Marge, Simone replies "yes ma'am, it's me. I'm here. How are you feeling?"

"Like a mule kicked me in my chest."

"Should I call a doctor? Is the pain unbearable?"

"It's really painful, but I don't want anything because I want to talk to you. I heard you talking about Rodney."

"Oh?" said Simone. "How did you know his name?"

"You called it out just loud enough for me to hear. I thought I was dreaming for a moment. You know how drugs can make you think but not respond."

"Aunt Marge, we shouldn't think about my deal with a man. We need to focus on you and how we can get you better."

"Oh hush young lady. I know what I want to do. I want you to listen to me." Simone sat in the chair next to Aunt Marge's bed. Giving her total attention, Simone gazed upon the elderly lady whom she adored in her life time. She attentively sat leaning forward in her chair, touching Aunt Marge on her arm, and without a word spoke to her through her eyes and ears. "I'm all yours Aunt Marge, tell me what's on your mind" in a tender voice.

"Child, you've done the things in life only many have dreamed to do. You deserve someone kind and intelligent. You can close doors that open wide and regret the time you have now and the gift presented to you. You don't know what God has for you and remember people come to you in light of what you think. It is a reason for someone to be so into you from little to nothing. Those relationships last a life time. Take your uncle and I for example. We dated for a short period of time and I knew he was my gift. I thought just as you and my mother said the exact same things to me as I'm telling you now. Take the gift of life being offered to you. Don't run away from it and make excuses with uncertainty. It's time for your quality of life. Go live it."

"Aunt Marge, that's the first time I heard of how you and Uncle Author started out. I had no idea you two dated for a short period before getting married."

"Yes, it was two dates and we walked down the isle. He was the best thing ever that came into my life. Look at the blessing his love brought me. That includes you and Sabrina. And don't forget the others I love so much. Go child, get your man and open your mind, spirit, and heart to him. He'll do right by you and be right for you. I'm getting tired and the pain is awful. Call the nurse for me baby."

"Yes Ma-am," Simone answers and runs out of the room for the nurse's station. "My aunt is in serious pain and she needs you right now," shouting with anxiety, "SHE'S IN PAIN DAMN IT. One of you had better move this instant." As her last word flashed out of her mouth, Simone returned to Aunt Marge's room and immediately took to her side. "I'm here for you Aunt Marge. Hang in there, the nurse will be her in a minute. I think one sent for the doctor."

"Thank you baby. I know this is hard on you, but its not as painful as losing your uncle. I can handle this baby. I can handle the pain."

Two nurses briskly walk into the room. Grabbing her chart, the nurses immediately give Aunt Marge a few pills and a shot the doctor ordered for any outburst of reported pain. In minutes the pain subsides and Aunt Marge returns to a relaxing state. Off to sleep in sound slumber she goes. Its moments like this that makes life seem like a battle. In Aunt Marge's mind, she dreams of days where there's laughter, fun filled days of love and affection from her loving husband. There were flowers in bloom, even when the days seem gloomy from a winter's storm. There was comfort in her home, when the kids would visit and show off their school accomplishments from the week before. There was her favorite dish she loved to cook, and cook, and cook. "My goodness, I'm missing all of the important things I use to have." Dozing back off into a deep sleep, Aunt Marge sees herself as a young woman walking on a sandy beach during summer. It was the same beach she loved to visit on the California coast. The beach where there's light colored sand, waves crashing against rocks, seclusion from the general public and of course a chance of romance. We are a romantic couple. "Come dear sweet man; walk with me on the beach next to the waves." Aunt Marge is dressed in a white sun dress she loved to wear over her bathing suit. She never gained weight to not dress so seductively in simple outfits. The wind blew her hair through the straw hat and the breeze made her laugh with the seagulls. Earlier in years she remembers the children attending middle school, how proud she was about all of her nieces and nephews graduating and moving to higher learning. "I attended each child's first day at college. Especially Michael, he was truly ecstatic about his first day. Michael had us running all over campus and even shared his first college meal. We teased him about that day for years. Don't you remember honey?"

"It seems like my years of living and those fond memories were fantastic. I enjoyed the exciting times of life, especially watching the children mature into lovely adults. Oh, and for them to have kids of their own, what a pleasant experience to share. Family makes a world of difference, and of course watching the next generation means the world. I'm so weak these days; I can't go to any of the kids' events. No baking for them, no college visits, no parks or playground, no picnics, and I can hardly stay focused on a movie or two from home. What kind of life am I living? Doesn't seem like the one I had, or not much to enjoy. I've lived well and done things most people only dream of doing. I've out lived my siblings, in-laws of my generation, and all of my friends. I don't know how much longer I have to hang on living this life. I just don't know. God, if you take me now, I'm sad only for not living as I did in the past. I'm happy because there is a greater life with my generation of friends, love, and family. Whatever you have in for me lord, I'll gladly go."

Still asleep, Aunt Marge mumbles unheard words to Simone. She would say the darndest things while sleeping under heavy sedation. "How could she utter anything is beyond me" said Simone. Aunt Marge seems pretty peaceful right now. I'd better call Sabrina. Dialing the phone with one hand, Simone looks out the window observing anything worth looking at. It seems like the sunset is beginning as the sky dims into darkness. Its night fall and the reflection of this long day, and the harsh reality of sickness, are coming to an end. One ring, two rings, three rings, fourth ring and Sabrina answers.

"Hey Sis."

"Hey, how are things?"

"I can't tell for sure. She's resting now. It doesn't seem like things are pretty bad for her at the moment, she looks comfortable. She's resting."

"That's good."

"When are you coming by?"

"On my way in now, I should be there within 20 minutes."

"Good. Can you bring a cappuccino, please?"

"What?"

"A cappuccino. It helps me sooth and settle my thoughts."

"I'll get one. I hope I find an open place this time of night."

"You will I'm sure."

"Increase that time to 30 minutes for the extra run."

"I'll see you when you get here."

"Keep the faith sis. Bye"

"See you soon, Bye."


"God, if you're listening, please get Sabrina here safe. Help Aunt Marge get better

# Chapter 10

## *She's The One For Sure*

"Dan she slammed me, rejected me, killed my ego from one phone call. I swore no woman would do this to me," said Rodney.

"Are you kidding? She didn't slam you; she probably meant you were moving too fast."

"No, she slammed the door in my face. I've never had a woman do this to me."

"It's true. As long as I've known you, rejection doesn't come your way too often. And besides, you don't get too excited over a woman who would think of rejecting you."

"Is this what rejection is like?"

"Ah, yep, sure is."

"Man is this crazy. I shouldn't let a woman make me feel so crappy. I've got to do something."

"Something like what?"

"Go to the hospital and see her tonight. She won't slam me down in person. I know it. I can get her to take a chance. Man, I've got to try. I won't be able to sleep or function if I don't."

"Rodney I've never seen you this worked up over a woman. Even before she creamed your ego and well heart for this matter, it's a first."

Rodney paced the floor thinking of what to do. Tears swelled up in his eyes, as each thought of not having Simone in his life, enters the forefront of his emotions. Rodney stops and looks into the dark of night through his apartment's bay window, he recalls other women in his life over the years. "None of my former girl friends are like Simone, they aren't comparable. Her features are so real, angelic, and her body is that of a Goddess. The woman is just fine, awesome, and truly compatible. I know this from one date." he thinks.

"Hey man, I'm heading out. You ok?" asked Dan.

"Yea, I'm ok," replied Rodney.

"Tell me what you did with Simone tomorrow. I know you're up to something. I know oh so well. Just remember, it isn't a conquest this time. It's real because I see it in you."

"Oh, you don't have to worry about me being stupid. I want this woman for the rest of my life. I know it."

"Good luck."

"Don't need it but thanks. It's fate. The rest of my life starts right here."

Rodney returns to pacing the floor, walking from one room to the other. Periodically he stops at the bay window and stares as if there is a message coming to him. Just like his childhood days when there was a letter on its way from a family member. He knew it would come and in anticipation he looked out the window for the mailman. Rodney turns back toward the front room of his apartment and then it hit him. An idea of a life time and it has to happen tonight. "If I can't get to her direct, I'll do it through her aunt. NO, that isn't a good idea, the woman is ill, not a good thought. How bad do you want this woman? Drastic measures call for drastic action."

Rodney rushed out of the apartment and headed to an all night convenience store. He jumps in his car and drives to the hospital, looking for an open convenience store in route. Seeing a gas station, convenient store opened, he turns in and parks his car at the front door. He enters the store and it's nearly empty except for the clerk and two other customers. The store has multiple items Rodney can choose for an impression. From candy, drinks, wine and beer, to day old flowers; all are items to present to Simone. Especially at a time where her spirit needs lifting, a small gift may do the trick. Rodney selected a couple of day old flowers. Two pink roses holding onto dear life; not quite wilted, but still holding their sweet smell. "These will do just fine," he thinks. Turning around from the refrigerated flowers, he checks for another item as a soft drink for himself. Looking intently to make the right drink selection he loses himself in thought and anxiety to see Simone. "Am I doing the right thing forcing myself in her life at a time like this? No class at all. I should just go home and wait it out."

Sabina pulls into a convenience store near the hospital and parks her car right in front of the door. Checking her purse for money, she makes sure she has enough for Simone's cappuccino and for her smoothie. "I've just enough without going to the ATM," she thinks. Walking into the store, she immediately head towards the coffee counter grabs a cup and starts the cappuccino. While it's pouring, she looks at the cups for the smoothie. Right in her line of sight is Rodney. Without stopping the start of her smoothie, she calls out, "Rodney, what are you doing here?"

"Sabrina, hey, I'm heading to the hospital to see your sister" answered Rodney.

"I'm heading there myself. She wanted me to pick up some cappuccino on the way."

"How's your aunt?"

"Not sure, Simone said she isn't doing too bad, but not well either. I guess she's in a middle state. You know how some people are when they've aged."

"No, I haven't a clue to that. I guess she's fighting to hang on and get better. You know, she sounds like a great lady."

"Oh, for sure she's the best."

They both walk towards the cashier to check out. Sabrina notices the roses Rodney has. "Oh, those are sweet. Are they for me?" Smiling as she knows the answer.

"Well, I can get you one, but these are for Simone. I wanted to bring a couple for your aunt but the selection is awful. Especially at this time of night, the last of good ones holding onto dear life. I didn't think your aunt would embrace dying flowers. Not good."

"Good point."

After paying the cashier, they both head to their cars. "I'll follow you on the way Sabrina. Don't tell Simone I'm coming ok. Please. I might change my mind about visiting this time of night."

"Oh, don't turn back. I'm sure she'd like to see you. Trust me on this."

"I can trust you on it. I just don't want to push my luck."

"Get in the car and let's go. Come along and don't let me down. I know she wants to see you."

"Ok, I'll follow you to the hospital. Wait for me so we can walk in together."

"Sure, no problem."

Sabrina and Rodney both enter their cars, one right after the other. Sabrina backs up first and pulls forward for the road. Rodney follows directly behind her. They both leave the convenience store with multiple things in mind. Sabrina, "I think Simone will love to have a companion with a strong shoulder." Rodney, "I hope Simone takes me in her mind and allow me to open her up to a wonderful life. If she doesn't, I' don't know what to do." Turning left at the next intersection, the hospital is there on their immediate right. Both drive into the parking lot. Sabrina finds a parking space close to the double doors and Rodney parks on the next row right immediately behind her.

"You found a nice space Sabrina," said Rodney.

"Like the lot is entirely full, how can I not find one?" responded Sabrina.

"That was obvious huh?"

"Are you nervous about something?"

"Yes I have to be honest. I want Simone to be happy I came tonight. I'm not so sure about this."

"Will you trust me? I know how much she likes you. I know she had a great time on your date. I know she needs someone like you in her life. Trust me on this."

"Ok, again, I'm trusting you."

They walk into the hospital through the double doors. Straight into the lobby, they see a security officer, nurse, and janitor talking in a group. The security officer scans them as they walk closer to the elevators. "Can I help you?" asked the officer.

"We are heading to the sixth floor. Going to see my Aunt, Marge Blaine in room 671" responded Sabrina.

"Please be careful with your step, I just waxed the floor" said the janitor.

"No problem" both Rodney and Sabrina replied.

Walking past the three people, Rodney and Sabrina took notice to as if they were being watched for family resemblance. No way can either of them ask to the relationship link. And without inquiry, they successfully pass the three just before entering the elevator. "I thought for sure one of those guys would ask us for proof of relationship." Said Rodney.

"No way, today the family nucleus isn't so structured; you'd think they could be family."

"Good point."

"What floor are we heading too? I want to get there before the flowers die."

"Sixth floor."

Rodney pushes the button for the sixth floor. The doors close and silence fell between them. "I hope Simone accepts these wilted flowers."

"She will. Stop worrying. I know my sister and how important you are to her."

"I'm important?"

"Sure, why do you think I told you to come along? I don't think she'd be nothing but excited to see you."

"I sure hope you're right on this."

"I am."

Arriving on the sixth floor, they exit the elevator as soon as the doors open. Sabrina exits first as courtesy and leads Rodney to the room. On the way, they pass the nurses' station and find no one at the counter. Without a second thought, they walk directly to the room. Just before entering, Sabrina tells Rodney, "You should wait out here. Let me get Simone to come out for a moment. You two can then go to the waiting room down the hall on the other side of the wing. It will give you some privacy. And it gives me time with Aunt Marge. You know, that quality just the two of us time. I need it."

"Ok, I'll wait until she comes out. Don't tell her about the flowers. I need the surprise effect in addition to me being here."

"Sure thing," replied Sabrina as she enters the room. Closing the door behind her, Simone immediately hugs Sabrina as if it's over for Aunt Marge. With a tear, she looks at Aunt Marge who is silently sleeping. "She hasn't moved since taking pain medication. That was just as you called earlier," said Simone.

"She looks peaceful. When will she get back to being herself?" Sabrina asked.

"I don't quite know. We had a real different conversation earlier. She over heard me talking to Rodney and as usual gave me her opinion." Simone said.

"Oh, Rodney is outside the door waiting to see you."

"I can't believe it. Out of all the times to visit, why couldn't he wait? Now is not good for me."

"Go easy on him sis. I told him you'd be glad to see him tonight. I thought for sure you wouldn't mind."

"He's a nice guy, but this is trifling. He could at least wait until Aunt Marge's condition is better. I don't like the idea of him thinking I should just fall into his arms. I don't like it."

"It wasn't quite my idea he comes, but I thought you'd be happy with it. He's really a sweet guy who adores you to death. Who else would come out here in the middle of the night trying to really show his feelings?"

"Impressive or not, I am not feeling it. He should just move on. It's like I'm not in the right state of mind to respond to this. I need him to leave. I should send you out to tell him I'm not interested anymore."

"What, not interested?"

"Exactly, not interested." Simone angrily replied.

"You should tell him yourself and be done with it if you feel so strongly against him. Don't lead him on; just tell him how you feel about his antics. I still think it's nice of him to be concerned about you and your feelings for Aunt Marge."

"Nice, but no thanks. I can find comfort from a dog and that would be better soothing. I'll tell him to leave and never call me ever again. I think he's trying to take advantage of me at a vulnerable state. How low classed?"

"Then you'd better tell him. I thought for sure you'd feel different. I encouraged him to come here tonight. I saw him while getting your cappuccino" said Sabrina.

"It's nothing like having to tell off a man in the middle of the night when your aunt is fighting for her life. Just so damn inconsiderate of him putting me in a state of mind to, ugh I'm so pissed. I am going out there right now."

"You better before you cool down and rethink how nice he is for being here."

"Come on Sabrina, you're pushing Rodney hard on me aren't you?"

"No, just reminding you about him being such a nice guy. Go, go and tell him what's on your mind. I'll be here with Aunt Marge. Go."

"I'm glad to lay into him."

Rodney, standing outside the room door heard Simone's last comment, "I'm glad to lay into him." Immediately Rodney turned to head for the waiting room where he now wished he stayed. Sabrina left him outside the door with the suggestion to take Simone to the waiting room "If I act as if I don't know about her disgust, I'd be better off. As a matter of fact, heck I'd better leave and let her just be. I can leave the flowers with the nurse and place a note on it." Without a second thought, Rodney went direct to the nurses' counter and looked for something to write with. "A sticky and a pen will do the trick" he thinks. He sees Simone walking out of the room heading in his direction. Rodney turns left and walks to the opposite side of the nurses' station. Doing his best to avoid Simone at the moment, he becomes stealth in his mind and ducks into a near office. Empty by chance and no one to ask if it were ok to be in there, he takes advantage of the concealment. Simone steps to the empty room where Rodney is supposed to be. "Not here. He should be glad he isn't here. I'm just in the mood to kick him away and without even starting. IF he's going to be so inconsiderate; I'm glad to see it now and not later. How fortunate am I?" Simone starts returning to Aunt Marge's room. A loud alarm goes off indicating a problem. Again, Aunt Marge isn't doing so well. Her heart is fabulous thinks Simone. "I couldn't live without her."

Sabrina runs out of the room trying not to be loud as others are trying to get some rest. She runs to the nurses' desk and looks for assistance. Simone, standing near the nurses' station sees Sabrina's look of disgust and runs without word back into Aunt Marge's room to check and see what's up. Sabrina walks behind the nurses' counter and looks into the immediate office, no one is around, she walks to the next office and finds Rodney, "Are you serious?" she comments on Rodney hiding from Simone. "Aunt Marge isn't breathing, have you seen a nurse or doctor?"

"Yes I have, as a matter of fact. There is one in this cot. I was just about to wake him."

"Excuse me. Hey doctor," she shouts while walking closer to the cot.

Lorenz rises from a deep sleep, he'd been there for 36 hours straight and it's the first time he'd gotten to get a little shut eye. As he wakes, he looks directly at Sabrina and asks, "When did you get here? I didn't expect to see you until Saturday night."

"Wake up, there's an emergency. My aunt isn't breathing any more. I didn't see her chest rise or fall, and her body seemed cold to my touch." Immediately without word, Lorenz rises and dashes out of the room. "What room?" he asks while briskly leaving the cot "What room Sabrina?"

"671, she's at the far end near the window." She replies running right behind.

Rodney decides to hang around just in case Simone wants a little support. He waits near the nurses' station. He intently listens for any information on how their aunt is responding to Lorenz.

Lorenz enters the room and immediately sees Simone leaning over Aunt Marge. Simone is crying, and Sabrina starts wailing in tears. Lorenz pulls Simone back while saying, "Let me tend to her. Move back so I can examine." Without responding, Simone grabs Sabrina and moves into the hall way.

"Sabrina, she's gone. I know it."

"No, let Lorenz see if it's true. I can't believe she's gone. I know she isn't, not yet."

"I didn't feel a heart beat and she's really cold."

"I know that, it's why I came out for help. I thought she was sleeping when I decided to check on her. When I felt how cold she is, it's when I ran to the nurses' station."

"You know she's gone."

A nurse came dashing by as the two girls huddled together in consolation. She ran right into Aunt Marge's room, responding as if it were a code red. The girls can hear Lorenz and the nurse calling out symptoms and instructions as if two well practiced partners were playing a routine sport. "Blow, 2-3-4-5, blow, 2-3-4-5, blow, 2-3-4-5-6-7 blow, and repeated for nearly three minutes. Nothing." Lorenz said. "We need to shock her heart." And the door flew open for two more nurses to enter the room. "Stand by- all clear" buzz goes the electrical shocker. Her heart didn't take it. "I guess it wasn't meant to be," said Lorenz.

While bigger tears are falling down Simone's face, Lorenz exits the room saying, "I'm sorry girls, she's gone. There is no heartbeat nor was she breathing. I tried to resuscitate her but she didn't respond. It was peaceful to go as she did. At least she had you with her during her last minutes. I'm sure she knew her time was up."

"Oh, no, no way, no way is she gone. I was just with her and I saw her breathe," said Sabrina.

Grabbing for Sabrina, Lorenz reaches to consol her with his embrace. The two of them stand together and Sabrina cries her heart out for the loss of her favorite aunt. Rodney observes Lorenz' move and looks for Simone. Simone walked back into Aunt Marge's hospital room to look at the items reminding her of the woman who meant so much to her. "I can't believe it," she says to herself. "I just can't believe it, my favorite aunt is gone."

"Hey Simone, are you ok?" asked Rodney.

"I thought you were gone."

"No, I hung around hoping to see you and have a talk. I never expected your aunt to pass on," said Rodney as he approached Simone in hopes of consoling her.

"No, who expects such a thing," replied Simone.

Within arms reach, Rodney steps closer with open arms and Simone immediately allows an embrace. Tears fall from her as she gets closer to Rodney. Crying on his shoulder, Rodney whispers, "She's in a much better place. Just think of her not having pain anymore. Nothing on this earth to interfere with her happiness, she's with you now and forever. Her love will never die, it's in your heart and memory. You have similar loving qualities of a great woman. She left you her legacy and dynamic character. She is in you Simone. You'll never be without her."

"But she didn't have to leave. Not yet."

"If not now, when? It was her time and she knew it."

"Still, it wasn't supposed to happen like this. I wanted to shower her with family love first. The family was getting together soon. It's still a plan but for a different reason now."

"Well, don't change your objective, just change the cause. You should celebrate her life."

"All the generations of children will want to be here for her." Simone speaks while still sobbing. "She was our matriarch."

"And you shall celebrate her life and love as a family. Don't worry about that at this moment; just find peace for yourself. I'm here for you."

Instantly Rodney's last four words struck a nerve. It was earlier anxiety where Simone headed to find him with a purpose. Anger struck and in a flash, Simone's body language and face reflected her emotion. Pushing away from Rodney, she moved across the room and in a flash her anger returned. "You are one dumb man. You must think I'm some desperate filly who needs a man for comforting. And you have the nerve to be here with some dead ass roses. What kind of man comes to a hospital and tries to get a woman on his good side? Do you think I'm so desperate of a woman or a fool of one?"

"Which question do you want me to answer first?"

"Oh a smart ass too; not only are you dumb, but a silly man at that."

"No, I came here to show you my love."

"Love? How dare you play on words like love and support?"

"Look Simone, do you want me to leave."

"Yes, but after I finish telling you a few things; hell, for that matter it's a waste of breath on you. Damn it, go, get away from me!"

"I'm gone. But call me if you ever decide this was a bad decision."

"Sure, I'll call, never."

Rodney leaves the room in angst. Mad as heck over Simone's out burst claiming him not to have any honest emotions for her. "Her loss damn it," he thinks. "I can have any woman on this side of Jordan. I got all emotional for a crazy lunatic. What kind of crap is this at a time where she needs support more than ever? Only a crazy woman would say such bull."

Outside the hospital room, Lorenz and Sabrina are still together. Lorenz, steps back as Rodney mumbles his thoughts. "Hey, is she ok?" he asks.

"The crazy woman is ok." Rodney replies.

"Crazy woman; I don't understand. What happened in there?"

"Simone is crazy, I tried to console her and she lashed out at me for being an opportunist."

"I'll go in there and talk to her," said Sabrina, as she walks in the room.

"No, don't go for me. Go for her and yourself. I think she needs someone but not me. Not now. Not ever."

"Don't give up on her just yet. It's a hard time; she's just lost her aunt." Said Lorenz.

"Give up? You can't give up on something you don't have. It was fun while it lasted. Hey doc, I'm heading home. I should have stayed there instead of coming here. I'd be much better off had I not come."

"Maybe a good point," Lorenz agrees, "but at least she knows you are serious for her and there if she needs you."

"Not any more. That boat sailed. See you around," said Rodney as he walks briskly to the elevators.

"Sure thing, I have faith on seeing you again."

# Chapter 11

## *Celebration of Life*

Family members were notified worldwide of Marge's death. Members started traveling from each coast of the United States, from the West coast of Africa, from Western Europe, Asia, and the far Pacific Rim. There were family members who Simone and Sabrina didn't know of nor recognized in thousands of pictures of Aunt Marge's photo albums she kept over the years of her life. "We didn't know Aunt Marge had so many relatives outside of us. I knew she was originally from the west coast, but my goodness, she didn't tell much about her up bringing," said Sabrina.

"She kept her past to herself. I can only imagine why," replied Simone.

"I'm sure we'll find out about her child hood from some of these people."

"What about the cousins we know? Have you called them?"

"Yes, I called them and that's how the word got out so fast. We have to get things together before many arrive. I'd hate for them criticize us for not having things in order."

"You're right about having things in order. She kept a folder of important papers in the bedroom closet. I'll get it," said Simone. Simone left the kitchen heading for the master bedroom. Stopping along the way, she admired a number of hall pictures. The hall way had pictures on each side and many of the pictures were of Aunt Marge accompanied with friends and family, and of course there is one portrait of her. The largest picture was of Aunt Marge and Uncle Arthur, embracing as ever in love. There's one with her and me, and another of Sabrina and Aunt Marge.

Separate but fair in attention; Aunt Marge was good at ensuring us she had no favorite between the two of us. I'll always admire that of her. No favorites. Immediately, Simone thought of one picture for the funeral program. "I'll suggest her portrait in the living room instead of any of these along the hallway." Arriving to the master bedroom, a single look around and one tear fell down her face. Things reminded Simone of her aunt, the brush, jewelry, the empty bed and the house coat she last saw her wear. "My goodness, will I ever stop crying" she thought. "The files; focus on the files."

Walking around the bedroom, she found a box at then end of the dresser next to the far wall. The square box was a two drawer cardboard file cabinet. One drawer has photos and the other marked important papers. "Aunt Marge was definitely organized." Simone opened the bottom drawer to find multiple folders with specific titles; insurance, household policies and repairs, legal documents, will, warranties, and others. Each folder held those documents most people throw in a drawer or keep in a brief case. Fortunate for her, the drawer was not locked, as some items were of value.

Simone took out the legal document folder and found multiple items of value. Stocks, bonds, and the house deed to name a few; "These documents are worth a pretty penny" she thought. The next folder she selected has the will. Another tear fell down her face, as she opened the folder and pulled out the folded document. Before reading it, she walked back to the kitchen so Sabrina can read the will as well. "Sabrina, I have it" Simone called out as she walked towards the kitchen.

"You do? Did you read it?" Sabrina answered.

"No, I thought we'd read it together."

"Good point. What else did you find in her folders?"

"Aunt Marge has stocks, bonds, and other valuable documents. She also has a bank deposit drawer."

"What? A bank deposit drawer is where most people keep valuable things. If her will was in the folder, then I wonder what's in the deposit drawer."

"I don't know because most of what I think of being as valuable is here in this folder."

"There's only one way to find out. Let's start with the will."

"Yes, lets."

Both Simone and Sabrina sat at the kitchen table next to each other. They both had one hand on each side of the folder where their view is equally on it. It was a scene from years ago as if the two were in preteen years and Aunt Marge sat across from them. Aunt Marge scheduled so many summer events that she presented the girls with flyers to better explain what they were going to do. The two young ladies read the flyers together exactly as they read the will.

"There's a letter in the folder. Should we read it first?" asked Simone.

"Sure, it might explain something not written on the will," replied Sabrina.

Simone opened the envelope and retrieved a letter. Unfolding the letter, a little piece of metal clattered to the table. It was a key. The letter read:

*Dear Simone & Sabrina,*

*If you are reading this, either I've passed on to a better place, or my mind is no longer sharp. Whichever the condition, please remember how important you girls are and how you two were the center of my life. Even though you never knew I had favorites, you girls were the ideal nieces. Please* believe me, it's hard having favorites, you two were easy to enjoy out of all the others.

Life gives special conditions all the time, and of those conditions you were the guiding light through it all. I love you as my own and always considered you as such. When your parents died, they entrusted me to support you through your trials and tribulations of life. I loved doing it. You two my girls, my daughters, my children; even though I loved your cousins too, you two were my sparkle. Please remember how much I love you and enjoyed you in my life.

You know, I never told you about my life. It isn't a secret, nor is it something I'm ashamed of. It just never came up. I realize over the years we've always focused on your immediate family and your uncle's side of the family. Since I didn't have children of my own, it was never a focus to tell you more of myself. It was never a time to tell you the history of my family and now is as a better time than ever.

My family was from beyond meager means, living a life style much greater than the one I settled for. No, I didn't leave for independence, and it was not to run away from that type of lifestyle, I honestly loved your uncle. My family roots started back from Ellis Island, mostly European as my grandfather was the true immigrant. Fortunately for him, he came here with a needed skill. A vision for business and a direction for market development, he created market research methods and commercials.

Yes, even in those days, there were commercials. Most were street merchants, talking about their items, so Grand father created a script and sold it to street merchants. This was before copy writing, so he changed it quite often for the typical product. His name became known throughout the city and to all merchants. He started placing advertisements in papers as they became popular. He grew to a marketing conglomerate.

My mother came into the world as the first American. She was beautiful. Long flowing hair and eyes of coal, her features were of Middle Eastern. Even though she was European by ancestry, she picked up all the genetics of the Mid East. She met my father, another marketing mogul. He too was of European decent and dark. Not quite the normal dark complexion of a Greek, but that of a Moroccan. He stood tall and lean, with a remarkable bone structure. Quite the handsome man if I have to say so.

I was the youngest of four children. My siblings were all well educated just as I but the standards of living we grew up to know did not make me who I am. When in school I ventured into the city and found a true love. I discovered a love of people. I opened myself to befriend any person within the city block. I ventured into to all sorts of areas. Most of them were forbidden to a person like me. Yet, I managed to get in there without a problem and was treated kind at every corner.

My new found love did not sit well with my family. I didn't do as planned according to my father. I went where my heart led me, and saw people as they were. NO color, race or ethnicity; just good people without accepting some misguided history. I explored on my own and found out who I am and what my true desires were. This is when I met your uncle. I knew then he was my love for life. I knew from his first hello, he was my heart and I his. Nothing could tell us differently, nor hold us back from being one in life.

My parents were quite upset with my decision to love a poor struggling man. Yes, your uncle was struggling in the world. He had grand ideas and a strong work ethic. He did all and everything with a focus to achieve in any business. And of course, you know of your uncle. He did what made him successful and achieved being the envy of so many. I'm quite proud of him and loved him for it. Though my parents didn't accept him from the beginning, he won their hearts later in years.

You should contact my lawyer, after you read this letter. He will guide you through the rest of my instructions. The will in the drawer is only partial in content. There is a reason you'll understand after your visit. And, be advised, there will be a large number of family coming if it is due to my passing. I know them, the word of my passing on will travel fast and they'll come from around the world. Believe me, they mean well and will do whatever it takes to support your decisions concerning me, so love them as you loved me.

Please remember that I love you with all my heart. Tell the rest of your cousins I loved them as well. Keep the faith as life continues to show you truth and love. Understand your journey and *please* listen faithfully to your heart. All in love will prevail as life trains you for greatness. Simone, you stay on your path to greatness. It's in your gene pool and be smart about your personal decisions. Sabrina, my rose pedals of the world; show them how lovely you are and stay focused on your gift. You have the chance to impact change and redefine beauty.

Without thought, you were my girls, my daughters of the world.

Love always,

Aunt Marge

Simone and Sabrina have tears in their eyes. The letter gave them a message of love and history. It made them reminisce to a time when she were still living and spoke while sitting in the den having coffee. It was a routine the three of them shared time and time again. The message was clear to visit the lawyer on the will. Not understanding why, the girls both allowed their imagination to run. Simone, "It has to be money or an endowment she left us." Sabrina thinking "It's a very important item of history that maybe her family left; the reason she didn't talk much about them is now something she wants us to know." Both girls sat silently for a moment before leaving the kitchen table. Sabrina stood first and said, "You know, this letter gives us a little explanation to her past. I wonder if there are many family members left."

"I bet there is. We have to find them. I think the answer is in the part with the lawyer," replied Simone.

"You're probably right. What about the will? Shouldn't we read it first?"

Without hesitation, Simone took out the will and unfolded the legal document to its full length. Sabrina returned to her seat after retrieving a glass of water. "Are you ready?" asked Simone.

"Yes, let's find out what she wants us to know."

Last Will and Testament. Being of sound body and mind when constructing this, all of my worldly possessions are to be distributed as such;

First bank account, I leave to Nephew Henry for his children's college trust fund.

This house, 608 Wilshire Ave, I leave to Niece Diane to solely possess.

All furnishings, left untaken by my nephews and nieces, may be sold and proceeds will be divided.

Additional properties and funds are under separate instructions at Berkley and Associates, PC 753 Holgorn Ave. 030-893-0213 (Attorney Philip Berkley III).

I request cremation and my ashes spread at sea during my farewell cruise. The funeral cruise is prepaid and prearranged. However, I leave the program development to Simone and Sabrina. Contact the Mosley Funeral Home and inform them of my death. They will know what to do. I leave additional coordination to your devise for the final touch. I'm confident you'll send me home with a nice farewell.

In addition to my wish, Sabrina and Simone are to equally share executor responsibilities of this will and testament.

Given full length of my testament on the 25<sup>th</sup> day of May, in the year of our Lord 2002...

"Yada, yada, yada, legal stuff," said Simone.

"I can't believe she didn't leave us anything around here." Sabrina said.

"Of course not, she saw us as independent, proud, and strong women. She told us that all the time."

"I'm just a little surprised at her not leaving the house to us."

"You know Aunt Marge, she wanted the most needy to have an opportunity of living a good life."

"What about the bank account. Are you on her account as joint owner?"

"No, but I'm sure we will both have access after probate. We have to see the lawyer."

"Why don't we call him and see if they are still around. I've never heard of this firm. Have you?"

"No, neither have I."


Simone picks up the phone and calls the number on the will. A receptionist answers, "Berkley and Associates, can I help you?"

"Yes, you may. May I speak to Phil Berkley the third please?"

"May I ask who's calling?"

"Simone Willingham, niece of Marge Blaine."

"I'm so sorry to hear of your loss. Mrs. Blaine was a great and loving lady. I'll patch you in right away."

Surprised to the response, Simone gazed at Sabrina in amazement. Covering the mouthpiece of the phone, she says "Wow" to Sabrina.

"Huh?"

"You should have heard the response when I told the receptionist it was for Aunt Marge."

"Ms. Willingham, this is Phil Berkley. I'm sorry for the loss of your aunt. What time will you like to come in and review the documents?"

"Thank you for the condolence. I, ah, we would like to come in tomorrow morning. Will this be ok?"

"How about 9:30. I'll have some coffee ready when you arrive. Do you like flavored cream with it? Your aunt sure did. She spoke highly of you two quite often. I finally get to meet you."

"9:30 is fine. Cream?" holding the mouth piece again, while asking Sabrina "What flavor cream do you want at the lawyer's office?"

"Cream flavor? I don't know; Amaretto." Sabrina said while shrugging her shoulders.

"Phil, I think we'd like Amaretto. We'll be there tomorrow morning."

Rodney is back in his apartment. Immediately he changed into his training clothes. He looks out the window to see if the weather will allow him to wear shorts and a t-shirt. Happy with his answer, Rodney leaves the apartment and starts running his route. "Three miles. A short run will do the trick and give me time to be in the office early." Rodney thinks. The normal things occur during the morning run. He lurks back and forth between cars as he crosses the street for the sidewalk. He tracks down a path near a dumpster, and circles at the park entrance. On the return, he passed the corner where he gave assistance to an elderly lady one morning. Another bend and I'm back in the apartment.

"Three miles in 23 minutes of running; I'm happy with this. It's not quite world speed, but it's good for me."

Returning inside the apartment, the answer machine is flashing. "I missed a call. I hope it isn't important." Pushing the play button, the answer machine rewinds the call and plays,

"Hey man, it's me. This is a reminder of our meeting, it's highly important for the future of the firm. Don't get side tracked with your thoughts of Simone today. I need you, we need you, and the entire firm needs you. Come with your best game today. Please. I'll see you at the office." Message ends.

"Talk about pressure. I must be driving my folks crazy with disgust. I don't know what to do with Simone. I want to give up, but she's the one. She is the one. Ok, later, think of her after this meeting. Think of what I can do to win her over. Come on brain, what should I do?"

Knock, knock, knock on the front door. "Hey, it's me coming in, don't shoot?"

"Hey Dan, if I had a gun I'd put myself out of this pain."

"What pain? You, running like a jack rabbit all the time?"

"No, Simone. Man I think I've lost her."

"Don't you have a big presentation this morning?"

"Sure, but that shouldn't stop me from thinking about her. I have the presentation under my belt. I know what to say and do. The job is easy; it's Simone I want to impress. She's the one dude. She is the one."

"Then think of her after the presentation. I'll help you set things up. But right now, it's got to be business. We have an hour to get downtown."

"I'll be ready in 20 minutes."

"Tick, tick, tick, times flying and you'd better get moving." Dan presses. "You've no time to mess around and look in the mirror. Skip that part and let's go."

Rodney replies from his room, "Heading in the shower now. I'll be out in a few minutes. I'll shave in the shower to save time."

"Too much information; just get moving," Dan says while turning on the news.

Rodney jumps from the shower, dries, and dashes nto the closet for his lucky suit. "Hey, Dan, can you call Berkley Associates and confirm us setting up the conference room in 30 minutes?"

"Sure. Do you have the number?"

"It's on the counter, on top of my brief case. It's the number on the cover of the brief."

"Got it. I'll make the call. You don't have much time. Get going."

"Right on it coach."

Dan makes the call from his cell phone. Dialing the number he calculates how long the drive will take to arrive with traffic. "Hello, Berkley Associates?"

A recording answers the phone call with a message, "Good morning, and thank you for calling Berkley Associates. I'm sorry but the office is currently closed. Our office hours are 8:30 am to 6:00 pm daily Monday through Friday. Please leave a message after the tone and a representative will contact you as soon as possible. Thank you again for calling Berkley Associates where the attorney is a family extension……beep."

Dan leaves the message, "Please call Rodney Witherspoon of Hillman and Kraft Marketing to confirm his early arrival to prepare your conference room for the 10:00 meeting. His cell number is 220-451-1223. Thanks and he's looking for your call."

Dan ends the call and shouts for Rodney "Hey, finished the call, left a message. Are you ready yet?"

"Almost there partner. I'll be out in a second."

"Times wasting, we have traffic to fight. We've got to get going. Hurry up."

Rodney finishes tying his tie, grabs his coat, and heads for the front room. "Ready dude; grab the briefcase and let's go."

"Are you driving or am I?"

"Your car is ready. Since you know the way best, you drive. I can review the presentation once more."

Both men exit the apartment and quickly walk to the car. Dan unlocks the door with his remote while walking down the side walk. Rodney checks his pockets for keys, wallet, and other items. He's happy to have everything with him. Finally entering the car, they both place seatbelts around them, 'click, click', and Dan start the engine and pulls off. "Hey did you forget anything?" asked Dan.

"Don't you think it's a little early?" asked Rodney.

"No, you forget, we have to take the interstate for the quickest route. And let's face it, during this time of morning it isn't so quick."

"You're right. I thought about taking the main street but that would be much slower. Oh, I didn't forget a thing."

"Why didn't you schedule them to come at our office?"

"The owner said he had a very important meeting with a client. Its one of his larger accounts."

"That makes sense. Did he say how long it would take?"

"About 30 minutes. He has time right after that and the next available opportunity to meet will be next quarter."

"A law firm is that busy. Wow!"

"Yes, that's why they want us to market them for growth while the tempo is high."

"Isn't it a weird time to look for growth when you're busy as ever."

"Actually it isn't. The timing is great. Think about it."

"I'll have to give that some thought," replied Dan.


Turning the car onto the interstate, traffic seems to be moving right along. Dan turns on the radio for a traffic report. "We have 40 minutes to get there."

"We'll make it. If traffic keeps moving like it is, there's time for a coffee stop." Said Rodney.

"Let's not get too out front yet. Traffic is slowing to a stand still."


Simone is ready and calling Sabrina. "Hey its time; we have 40 minutes to arrive at the lawyers. You know how they hate us being late."

"Yea, but it's a lot of time."

"No remember we have to get on the other side of town."

"I'm ready, just finished my coffee."

"Come on then. Grab that folder on the kitchen counter and bring it with you."

"Got it."

Simone and Sabrina heads out of Aunt Marge's house and jumps into Sabrina's car. They both click their seatbelts. Sabrina starts the car while Simone turns on the radio. She finds a channel giving the traffic report. "This is WKRK with the latest traffic. It seems like a snails pace for the interstate this morning. There is a stalled car at exit 282. Even though the car is on the side of the road, there's considerable rubber necking. If you're heading into town before mile market 282, take exit 288 and head North on Turnip. Turn East on Kinzie and hit the interstate just past the stalled vehicle."

Sabrina takes the announcer's advice. She pulls out into traffic and heads out of the neighborhood streets. At the major intersection she turns north and heads for downtown. Music blares from the radio as Simone looks out of the window. Not a word spoken from either of them as the car gets closer to a major intersection. Simone looks at the buildings and says, "You know, I've always wondered who owns those office buildings on this street. Did you ever notice they are always busy and full? I mean, the buildings are awesome in decoration as well as presentations. The entire two blocks accents the skyline of the city."

"Yes, I've wondered over the year. You never see space ads for these buildings. I guess the businesses own the building." Replied Sabrina.

"Maybe so; if the businesses didn't own them, could you imagine the revenue it brings per year?"

"It has to be quite a pretty penny."

Sabrina turns the car west to the next block to avoid the slow traffic. One block, she heads north again. "How are we doing on time?" asked Sabrina.

"Not bad. If you keep moving like this, we'll be there in five minutes or so. If not, I'll have to call the office and tell them we'll be a little late."

"I hope we find a parking space. You know how the city can get with parking."

"I thought the office has visitor's parking."

"It wasn't on the flyer and it's not common for that area."

"Isn't this a high power law firm?"

"Yes, but they probably didn't negotiate parking for customers. But you never know."

"We'll find out when we get there."

Rodney and Dan are two miles behind Simone and Sabrina on the interstate.

"Dan, take this exit," said Rodney.

"What?"

"Take this exit. I know another way to the office. I should have thought about it from the time we got on the interstate. It'll save us time out of this mess."

"Ok, which way after the exit?"

"Turn left. This will take us on Turnip. Once we get to Turnip, we'll turn north; right if you've forgotten which way is north."

"I know north. Just tell me which street."

"I'll remind you when we get to Turnip."

"Ok, good. I hope like hell you get us there within the next 15 minutes."

"If traffic keeps moving, we'll make it in 10."

"It seems to move quite well at the moment. We need to get there and set up before the meeting."

"Keep driving, we'll get there. Leave the navigation to me and just follow my directions. Here's Turnip, now turn left."

"I didn't expect Turnip to come so quickly."

"Remember, we aren't too far from the office buildings. Just keep moving if traffic allows."

"Right, I'll keep going with the flow."

Sabrina and Simone arrive at the office building. Sabrina maneuvers the car under the building to the parking garage. Finding a parking space, they exit the car and walk towards the elevators. Entering the elevator Sabrina asks, "What floor?"

"I think the 5th floor" answered Simone.

"Aren't you sure?"

"No, I didn't get the exact address. Why don't we go to the first floor and find the business listing?"

"Good idea."

Rodney and Dan finally arrive closer to the office building. Dan finds a parking space on the street right in front of the building. He places an old parking ticket on the window left in his glove box from days before. "This will keep new parking tickets off in case we take too much time. Can you remind me to check on the car after we set up?"

"No problem. Just remember we may take most of the morning and I'm not sure if your old ticket will do the trick."

"If it doesn't I'll call in an old favor. Besides, this account is worth every penny to win over."

"Then you're on your A-Game right?"

"A-Game, heck I'm on the top of the Pyramid."

"Oh, you're on the A-Game for sure, but you aren't funny; its time to get in there and set up the conference room. We can save the jokes for after the presentation."

"Man, you have to kill my motivation by being so serious. OK, it's on. Let's go."

Dan and Rodney take the equipment and handouts out of the back seat of the car. "Do we have everything?" asked Rodney.

"Sure. I checked your apartment before leaving and the office last night. We have everything as planned," replied Dan.

"Great" Rodney answered as he approached the door. Holding the door for Dan, and looking back at his approach, Rodney barely missed Sabrina and Simone entering the elevators.

"OK, we are nearly there. I'm kind of nervous Simone."

"Why would you be nervous? I'm sure whatever Aunt Marge left us will be fine. I never expected anything anyway. I would love for her to be here now and we didn't have to go through this."

"Yes, you're right. Having her here is better. But I'm curious to know what or why did we have to come here."

"You know the why Sabrina, it's the what we're after."

The elevator arrives at the 12th floor. The door opens immediately in front of the office entrance. Large letters on the glass door "Berkley Associates" in gold print with black edging. There is a receptionist behind an oak quarter moon like desk. Behind her is a beautiful picture of a sunrise over the ocean, as if you were standing on a beach with white sand, green palm trees, and scattered brush, and two hammocks under the shade of the trees. The receptionist was a nice young man. "Not quite what I expected," thought Sabrina. Simone leads the way into the office and speaks to the receptionist. "Hi, we are …"

.."The Willingham sisters" said the receptionist. "Please come this way, Mr. Berkley is expecting you. Can I get you anything to drink while you wait in the office?"

"Oh, no thank you" replied Simone

"Sure, a cup of coffee will do for me. Black if you don't mind."

"No, not at all" the receptionist replies as he leads them to the first office on the right. "Please take a seat and

I'll be right back with your coffee." The receptionist leaves without closing the office door all the way.

"What an office" says Sabrina, "Quality decorating."

"Yes, my kind of office. One day I'll have such a place."

"You know, Aunt Marge always thought you'd have one."

"I remember her always saying so."

Phil Berkley arrives in the office "Good morning ladies. I hope you didn't have a bad journey coming here so early."

"No, we didn't" replied Simone.

"I want to give my condolences again. I'm sorry about your aunt passing so unexpectedly."

"Thank you" replied Simone and Sabrina.

"Well, its time we get to business. I want you both to be quite comfortable as I read the rest of your aunt's will."

The receptionist returns with the coffee for Sabrina. "Thank you" she says to the receptionist.

"That will be all" said Phil. The receptionist leaves. "Ladies, the last will and testament of your aunt includes a large peace of history. Let me tell you this story before moving on to the document. Our families have done business for nearly 75 years. Yes, 75 years. Your great uncle and my father were partners in the early 19th century. Our family ties go back to billionaires of the early century."

"Billionaires?" asked Sabrina

"Yes billionaires!" answered Phil. "It's no secret and I'm surprised you didn't know of your family history."

"Well, Aunt Marge had no children and we never knew of her family history or any of her relatives other than those of our father," said Sabrina.

"This I know. She considered you two as her own. Though she may not have shown it, but you were her two girls. Anyway, her family was quite well off for years. Until her father's death, many didn't know of her existence. Her father left her over twenty five million dollars in assets, and two companies with an average annual revenue of two hundred million."

A knock on the door and without hesitation for a reply, Rodney opens the door and takes a step in. His head was faced down on the equipment he carried. Simone immediately stands from her chair and turns around in angst. Upon recognizing Rodney, she immediately says, "I can not believe you."

"Excuse me gentlemen" says Phil.

"Oh, wrong turn I'm sorry. Hello Sir, not a good first impression."

"Not to worry, many people mistake the double doors for the conference room. It's down the hall on the left."

"Oh no, he's not here for the conference room. He's here being nosey and infringing on my privacy." Simone says. "I didn't want to ever see you again, can't you understand."

"Forgive my intrusion. I had no idea you would be here Simone. I have a presentation with Mr. Berkley in a half hour. Again, I'm so sorry for the intrusion Mr. Berkley." Rodney replied.

"No problem. Since you reminded me about the presentation, please move on, we have to finish here." Said Phil.

"Sure thing sir; again my apologies."

"And you honestly think I'm buying that excuse" frowned Simone. "You just automatically end up here at the same office, on the morning we learn of my aunt's will. And you expect me to think of it as a coincidence? You must be out of your mind if you think you're going to get away with this intrusion."

"No Simone, it is totally a coincidence" Rodney speaks out. "Totally a coincidence; Mr. Berkley and I have a meeting, a business meeting in now 25 minutes. If you'll excuse me I have to set up." Rodney moves outside the door and walks away into the hall.

"Oh, we aren't over, and I mean I'm not through with your sneaky and whimsical ass."

"Please, take your seat" said Phil, "he's telling the truth. We have a business meeting and I have to keep my schedule. Please allow me to finish your background."

"Oh sure" said Sabrina. "Sit Simone."

Simone takes her seat and intently listens to Phil. "Where was I, oh yes, the companies includes two buildings. Yes office buildings. My office manages the businesses as a long term agreement with your aunt. We've kept her as a silent partner for years. With the revenue we make as a team, it's something I'd like to continue. But before I throw my business pitch, its time I read the will."

Phil reaches on the center of the desk, picks up two documents and passes each one to the girls. "Please follow with me as I guide you through Marge's last will and testament. Since we're pressed for time, allow me to direct you to the third paragraph.

'Leaving to Simone Willingham and Sabrina Willingham to share and share alike, the sixty percent of controlling stocks in both companies. I leave ownership in the Wrangler buildings on Turnip with operational control of the management organization, which is currently run by the Berkley firm. All assets mentioned are for each to share in one hundred percent of the decisions. Neither one of you can dispose of their assets unless it is to one of the other, or an immediate family descendent.'

"You mean Aunt Marge was a Wrangler?" asked Sabrina.

"No, not a Wrangler, but a Riesman."

"The billionaire Riesman family?"

"That's the family. As I said before, your aunt was the love child of Riesman and the only one to inherit both companies independent of the general family. The secret came out after his illness and there was a fight for the property. When your aunt married your uncle, she had no idea of her father, other than he was a nice man who always brought good presents. Her mother later told her of her father's position in the world just before she married your uncle. The family blew a fuse when she married such a struggling man. But the love of your aunt made the family understand and especially got Mr. Riesman to accept him. Now fair warning for you, there are a number of Riesman descendents willing to challenge this will. Especially since you aren't of direct blood, and your connection to your aunt is through marriage."

"So this is how so many people are traveling here from around the world and they knew of Aunt Marge's death long before the news?" asked Simone.

"Exactly correct Simone. I've been notified by multiple lawyers and law firms to make a deal for the control of stock and those buildings. My loyalty lies with Marge's wish. You had a wonderful aunt whom I admired with all my heart. She was like a big sister to me, a sister that was much better than my own. She never asked for anything or didn't create a hardship on the family or firm. And, she was the best partner, business partner, a man could ever ask for."

"And that's why you wanted to maintain your management perspective on the property and companies?" asked Sabrina.

"As a matter of fact, yes, I'd like the firm to continue with the current agreement. It's working so well and of course there are equal benefits to the agreement. You get to receive rewards and profits, as I do, and you get to be a silent partner. Remember, your aunt never flashed her assets to the public and lived a quiet life."

"We were very close to Aunt Marge, and we had no idea."

"Exactly correct, and she did use her assets quite smartly. As in your scholarship to college" Phil looks at Simone. "She was the main contributor to your personal scholarship. Sabrina, she was the one who helped you get well from your illness when you were very young. I doubt you remember."

"I remember her being in the hospital all the time. I had no idea."

"And, she helped the family quite a bit. Those cookies to every kid in school and being able to help in a moments notice; I'm surprised you all never took advantage. Especially you two girls. She loved you two so much, because you brought her so much as if you were her own. She talked about you all the time." Phil stands and walks around the desk heading for the door. "I hate to run, but I'm now three minutes late for my business meeting. Please forgive me. I need your answers for my proposal as soon as possible. Oh, by the way, she wanted to be buried at sea."

"At sea?" asked Sabrina

"Yes, at sea. I need a guest list of 300 people for a commercial cruise line. Her life will be the theme and I think it's appropriate as we celebrate such a great woman. It's the last paragraph in her will." Phil leaves the office headed to the conference room.

"A cruise, that's our aunt going out with style" said Simone.

# Chapter 12

## *It's Business*

"Can you believe that woman?" asked Rodney.

"Boy, she has it out for you. There is no way you can ever get next to her. It's not in the future my friend." replied Dan.

"I don't care, she's the one and I know it. I'll have to think of another way."

"Well, you do that some other time. Right now we need your best game forward. This account means a lot to the firm."

"I know its business first. It's always how it plays out. Business first."

"Did you place the handouts at every chair?"

"Only if you plugged the laptop and projector into the outlet."

"I guess we're done. Let's test the program."

The laptop booted up, the projector warmed as Rodney, and Dan looked on. They intently reviewed the power point slide show, added a few notes, allowed it to play on the large screen, and rehearsed answers to questions. All is set for the presentation and equipment checks out.

Dan walks out of the conference room in search of a coffee maker. Rodney stands near large window over looking the city. "How can she think such a thing?" thought Rodney about the recent incident. "How can she accuse me of infringing on her privacy and following her? She has to be traumatized with the death of her aunt. I've done nothing but make an attempt to show her my emotions."

"Right. Now can you get this out of your mind and let's focus on the meeting?"

"Yea, sure can. Business first! I have to remember business first."

"Good, because it's nearly time. Let's stand by the door and welcome everyone as they enter."

Moving into positions by the door, standing side by side, Rodney and Dan stand firm and presentable to the entering staff. "Good morning" they say in unison as each member arrives. Without hesitation, each member takes a seat at the conference table. Some start fanning through the handout, others look at individual folders or schedulers as they review or adjust their day.

"We're waiting for one more person" says Peter, an executive with the firm. "Phil will be right with us."

"Sure thing, we can wait as long as needed." Replied Dan.

Within the minute, Phil enters the conference room and takes position at the head of the table. "Are we ready?" Phil enquires.

"Yes we are sir," Rodney replies. "First, allow me to introduce us. This is Dan our lead designer for the firm. I am Rodney a lead Marketing Executive. We are here to present our company and win your business for your next marketing campaign. Please feel free to stop me at anytime for questions during my presentation of the firm."

On the cue, Dan starts the laptop presentation, three 20 second films of business and product commercials. The films run in sequence, one right after the other, without introduction. The film completes and Rodney runs right into the presentation. "As you just watched, the firm has major clients, creates dynamic customer reactions, and introduces products and services with quality. Our approach is creating material that meets the demands of both the company and the consumer. We have a niche in creativity, which brings your ideas to life. In your handout, you'll see a number of our clients, ranging from the top 500 to the lower 12 for any type of product or service. We pride ourselves with the opportunity to produce results in any market. This makes us extremely competitive and competent to capture the ideas and prestige you wish to present and attract the customer base to increase your business."

The laptop slide show begins with page two of the handout. "We create your campaign with your partnership" said Dan. "We jointly brainstorm as an extension of your staff, study the market base you focus, and create test pilots for immediate feedback as we develop a winning strategy and marketing brand."

"How do you ensure the right person is part of our team?" asked one executive.

"We send our best and brightest, whom we've recruited from top-notch schools around the country. We also place those with products and business interest as a match, so the motivation is there. We pride ourselves with a group of consultants who are savvy in multiple areas of business, so one can assist you in your market as well as helping you capture or expand your opportunity," answered Rodney.

"How long does a campaign take to develop?"

"With the partnership and objectives of your firm, it's up to the time scale of your efforts. Depending on the feedback we receive from the market, on average it takes three to six months; sometimes sooner if the decisions are made fast." responded Dan.

The conference continued smoothly and lasted longer than scheduled. The interest of the firm increased the time because the staff asked in depth questions; which is a great sign for winning the project and contract. Rodney and Dan are packing their items to return to the firm. Phil stands by and observes the teamwork the two are performing. "I'd think you two were sales men if I didn't know better."

"Phil, we are in a sense. We just take pride in our firm. We love our work," answered Rodney

"Oh, that's quite obvious. I'm glad my staff liked your presentations. It's going to be an easy decision for us. We have to talk numbers. Can you get back to me with more specific cost and not these generic numbers in the handout?"

"Not a problem. I will need to meet with you and get a more specific idea of the campaign you'd like to launch. I know we can do this as soon as you're available."

"How about this evening over dinner?"

"Dinner meeting sounds interesting. I can have everything in order by then."

"Good, my secretary will call you with the detail."

Standing closer to Phil, Rodney reaches his right hand out to Phil for a hand shake. "I'll be there and thank you for the opportunity to present our firm to your organization."

"You're welcome." Phil replies as he releases Rodney's hand and exits the conference room.

"We did it. I have the numbers in my head now so it's going to be a nice dinner. Have any plans?" asked Rodney.

"No, but I don't think I'll need to attend. You can do this for us. I have faith in you. But, where on earth will we find consultants you described?"

"Let's not talk about that here, I have a plan. I have a really good plan."

"I hope so."


Sabrina and Simone arrived back at Aunt Marge's house. Entering the living room, there are a number of new flower arrangements, cards, and two people sitting on the couch. Solemnly looking, the two gentle men stand as Simone enters the room. "Good afternoon ladies," the tall handsome man speaks.

"Good afternoon" Simone replies. "What can I do for you, and who let you in the home?"

"One of your relatives allowed us to wait here for you. Sorry to frighten you as we mean no harm. We are here to help you with your aunt's cruise line funeral request."

"We just found out about it ourselves, how did you know?"

"We received the call from the law firm. And since all things are planned, our first set of instructions is to inform you. Please allow us to show you what your aunt had in mind."

"Ok. Can you let us get something to drink first? Would you gentle men like a drink? Coffee, tea, or alcohol?"

"Coffee will be fine thank you."

"Sure thing, Sabrina and I will be right back."

The gentle men retake their seats and starts opening a book of pictures. Sabrina and Simone enter the kitchen and begin brewing coffee. Sabrina grabs the coffee pot and fills it with water. Simone grabs the filter and grounds for the coffee. Like clock work, the two put things together and grab four cups. Simone grabs the tray to carry the cups to the living room. Sabrina places the sugar dish and creamer on the tray. They both stand in the kitchen looking at each other. Minutes pass by as silence is finally broken. "How are we going to handle this?" asked Sabrina.

"I'm not sure just yet. Let's see what these guys are talking about first before we start going independent."

"Yes, let's hear them out. Are you ready with the coffee?"

"I'm pouring cups now. You want to get the crump cakes from the refrigerator?"

"No, let's just go with the coffee."

The girls leave the kitchen and head to the living room. Again, as they enter the living room, the two gentlemen stand. "Can we help you?"

"No thanks, it's not a problem. Cream and sugar are on the tray."

"Thank you," the guys say in unison. Now can we get to the plan? I'd like to start with your aunt's decoration idea.

She wanted us to grab her youth photos and create a pattern of her development on the main deck. We plan to decorate the passageways with her pictures. She also wanted one large portrait of herself in the center of the main deck area, where everyone on board is reminded why they're aboard. Take a look at the ship's layout and tell me where you'd like to place those portraits and what years."

"I have an idea" said Sabrina.

"You're the creative one between us, so go right ahead," replied Simone.

"Well, your aunt made a number of decisions early. So you don't have to be too creative, just the little things we ask will be sufficient."

"Good. This makes it easy to take care of the family invitations. They have to know when and where.'

"We have the announcements ready for print. All we need from you is which one you'd like us to send. She limited it to these two and asked you to pick one. We will need an updated list. She had three hundred in mind, to attend the funeral cruise."

"Three hundred?"

"Yes, three hundred; she included her family members who she suspected that will still be around, especially her father's children."

"We learned of them this morning. I guess we can give you an updated list from the people we know." Said Simone.

"The firm has a list of her siblings. You can invite fifty others as you see fit. The fifty can be in thirty cabins. Just let us know how you want to arrange the cabin assignment. The others are all taken care of."

"We'll have your list in a couple days. I need to call a few people."

"No problem. Remember to call us if you need assistance. We want to leave the dock on Thursday evening and return Sunday morning. This way only one work day is missed by all. I'm sure the family will like the ceremony.

Oh, we'll need your input for that as well. She set up a simple program, however allowed room for you to add an event or speaker. Let us know the modifications by tomorrow evening. This way the printing schedule will be completed on time."

"Again, no problem, we'll have everything done by Wednesday afternoon. The list of people will be available, and the program information will be there by tomorrow. I have to call everyone today as soon as we're done here. What time should all be at the pier for boarding?"

"The schedule says all aboard between 12-2pm. We leave dock at 4pm sharp."

"Great."

"What about the body and other arrangements?"

"All done, she wanted to be cremated and the ashes thrown over the ocean while underway. It's all in the program."

"Wow, Aunt Marge thought of everything. This makes it easy for us sis." said Sabrina.

"She did, and I think a little too well. We have other things to discuss too. Like what to do with, well' we'll wait until the time comes to discuss business."

"Yes we will."

The gentle men stood up and extended their right hands to the girls. They shook hands together, "Again our condolences for your loss," said the gentle men.

"Thank you and you'll hear from us soon. Oh, what number can we reach you?"

"It's on the card and call us as soon as you need or get those things completed."

"Sure thing" replied Simone.

The gentle men left the house. Simone and Sabrina sat for a spell, in silence while looking at Aunt Marge's arrangements. "Wow," Simone breaks silence, "she thought of everything."

"Yes, she did," answered Sabrina.

"First we have to get everyone on the ship. Let's start calling some of our people. We can get them to email their list to the ship's purser."

"That's a faster way to get the lists updated. Hopefully, enough will show to fill the thirty cabins"

"I'm sure they will. It's a cruise too. Why wouldn't they?"

"Going home with a bang, Aunt Marge does it again."

"As usual"

Sabrina starts calling Aunt Marge's friends and all the relatives she knows. Sabrina calls Rodney, and unfortunately, no answer. She leaves a message, "Rodney its Sabrina. You know, Sabrina Willingham. I want to apologize for Simone's behavior today at the office. She jumps to conclusion a lot these days. It's not because of you, its losing our aunt that's driving her out of her wits end. And I apologize for the misunderstanding at the hospital. Please forgive me. I thought my sister would be ecstatic to see you. Actually, I still think she would. So, I'm asking, or inviting you to Aunt Marge's funeral cruise. I'll send you an invitation for two. Talk to Diane about it. She knows the details. Please consider coming."

Sabrina then calls Lorenz to give him details for the funeral cruise. "Lorenz please plan on being there. I need you and it will be a great experience."

"A great experience? I've never heard of someone having a funeral cruise. It's definitely a unique experience." said Lorenz.

"Does this mean you're coming?"

"I'll have to reorganize a few things, but for you I'll be there."

"Great, if something comes up don't hesitate to tell me. I'm counting on you being by my side the entire cruise."

"I'll be there. It's for my girl right?"

"Your girl? I'm considered your girl! Then you'd best be there for sure giving your girl that needed support."

"My girl, I'll be there."

"I like being your girl" Sabrina sniggles. "Bye my man."

"Talk to you soon."


Sabrina and Lorenz end the telephone call. Sabrina then continues to call her list of relatives and neighbors. She contacts most of them and as planned for the family reunion, she tells everyone about adding a song from the family on the funeral program. Without a doubt and quick to accompany the suggestion, all family members have agreed to sing. No one suggested a particular song, but they agreed.

Simone calls Phil's office for an update to invitations going out to Aunt Marge's siblings and their family. She comments on being informed of who they are and how they are related. She insisted on meeting each and every one of them. As well, she wanted to know if Phil would speak at the funeral. Unfortunately, the secretary was there and took a message for Phil.

Dan steps out of the car after parking in front of the office. "It was awesome. We did a great job. I know we landed that account."

"Sure we landed the account. Did you have any doubt that we wouldn't?" replied Rodney.

"No. Well, there was a little doubt. It's because you haven't been on your game lately. You have Simone in your head and motivation to be with her."

"Yes I do, actually I really have her in mind. But it never stops me from being in business or performing."

"Oh really, I beg to differ. Aren't you forgetting who's been with you for years now? I can recall a Tiffany who took your heart, and you lost three accounts."

"That was my younger infatuated experience."

"So what makes this time so different?"

"I know from within, for sure because it's an emotion and desire I've never experienced. Simone Willingham, a dream girl of dreams."

"You have it bad, really bad."

"How long do you think this is going to last?"

"Forever Dan. Forever."

"I hope so. I've never seen you so intent on being with one woman. Just think, you haven't been with her intimately yet. Isn't that the motivation? You know, taking the challenge to get her in bed."

"Nothing like it at all. I'm really in deep with this woman. No Joke!!"

"I believe you, really I do. It's hard seeing you so different. Yet, I know you're quite serious. More serious now than a man can realize."

"Serious, I am dead serious. I really have to get her in my world, and I'll do whatever it takes to win her love."

"Your chance is coming. I can feel it for sure. Just because you normally get what you want."

"That's not quite how it happens, but I'll believe it."

"Let's get on to the office and get the troopers ready for this new contract."

The two guys entered the building and went straight into the office. Not a word spoken as they met the receptionist, glanced at the message list on the counter, smiled, and in unison stepped down the hall way to their perspective office. No one ran into their office or called for the results of the presentation.

Simone left a message for Phil with the receptionist. "Please call me when you get a chance. Since you knew Aunt Marge so well, I'd like you to speak at her funeral. As well, you know the family members I haven't an idea who they are. Please call as soon as you can. Thanks and I hope to hear your answer." She then ends the call and places the phone on the receiver. "I hope he calls and says yes to my request. It should be easy for him to introduce me to my extended family. As well it's nice to know he has interest in the companies we recently inherited," she thinks.

Sabrina leaves the den and moves into the kitchen. She grabs a glass from the cupboard, reaches for the closest wine bottle, and places it on the counter. She then retrieves the corkscrew from one of many kitchen drawers. She screws in the corkscrew on the wine bottle and with a pull pops the cork. Immediately she pours herself a glass of wine, takes a sip and calls for Simone. "I opened a bottle of wine, would you like a glass?" she asks.

"Sure, I need one" Simone responds while walking into the kitchen.

"It's been an exciting day, but more weird than anything else. I can't say how weird, but our newly acquired wealth hasn't sunk in yet."

"I know right. It's a lot to swallow, especially at a time like this."

"I know Aunt Marge coordinated her own funeral. How amazing is that? It's as if she knew something was going to happen."

"She knew. We all know about ourselves, it's just a matter of time. Aunt Marge was the type of woman who took initiative."

"Can you believe her being a love child? How amazing is that?"

"Especially a love child from a wealthy man; now that's the amazing part."

"Equally amazing is the amount she left us. I can't get over it."

"We might as well get over it because it's like we're here and so is her wish."

"It's all over, still thinking about it. But we have to get the funeral over first. What should we do?"

"Let's get the rest of the family notified. I know the lawyer sent the notice to the family members we don't know, but the members we know, we can contact them."

"It's time we start the call out."

"Diane knows. I called her right after contacting Lorenz."

"Good. Did she call anyone else?"

"I don't know, but I called Rodney too."

"No you didn't!"

"Yes, Simone, I did. The guy is crazy about you and he's doing everything he can to get next to you. Even taking chances that I thought was so sweet."

"What? You mean stupid. And I can't believe you invited him to the hospital. That was really bad sis, really bad."

"Maybe to you, but not to me; I thought it was really sweet and with him being so concerned about Aunt Marge and you, showed me how serious he is for you. Who else would take a chance from true love?"

"Love. How dare you say he loves me? You don't know he loves me and I know he's after our inheritance."

"How the hell did he know of our inheritance? How do you figure he found out?"

"He was at the lawyer's office wasn't he?"

"And we didn't know until Phil read the will. How can you be so idiotic about this guy? Are you that afraid of loving someone?" asked Sabrina.

"Love? You use that word so freely. No I am not afraid and it's not likely he's interested that way."

"He's coming to the funeral so you'd better be ready to see him. And this time don't freak out, just let him show his condolences."

"You kill me with this crazy inconsiderate act. I'll deal with it, but don't act as if it's a gift to me. I'll just deal with him being there."

"You do that, now we have others to invite" Sabrina says while pouring another glass of wine. "You want a refill?"

"No, I want to walk next door and invite Mr. Slocum to the funeral cruise."

"I'll call the others," said Sabrina.


Simone left the house and headed next door. Taking each step with caution Simone thinks, "How am I going to tell Mr. Slocum about Aunt Marge's death? Should I just give an invite to him and why am I worried about it. He and Aunt Marge have been neighbors for years. I'm sure he'll come and be honored to say a few things on the cruise." Arriving at the house and stepping closer to the door, it opened without her knocking.

"Hi Simone, I'm so sorry for your loss. I know you'll do the right thing with your Aunt Marge's funeral. When is it by the way?" said Mr. Slocum

"Oh, thank you for the condolences. I came to invite you to her memorial cruise."

"A memorial cruise? I know your aunt planned this one. It was her style for sure. I know it had to be her."

"You knew my aunt quite well."

"Yes, she mentioned something like that years ago. I thought she was just kidding about her dream final cruise. We laughed about it and I'll be darn if she didn't do it for sure. After your uncle died, she said her time will go out with a bang. And my gosh, she's actually done it."

"I know she'd love you attending. So will you come? It's on Thursday."

"I wouldn't miss it for the world."

"Would you be kind and say a few things about her?"

"Well of course. She was the greatest neighbor ever." He steps out of the door and gives Simone a document size envelope. "And this is for you kids. I tried to give this to her years ago and she wouldn't have any reason to take it. I want you kids to have it."

Simone takes the envelope and opens it. "Oooh my, I can't accept this."

"Sure you can. Its payment for her assistance years ago; let me tell you about the time I went through challenges in life. My wife was deathly ill and your Aunt gave us her last penny to help me stay afloat. I got behind on my mortgage and other bills for seven months. I tried to get loans and assistance from every program. Unfortunately I made too much money to qualify for any public assistance. I decided to stop working and focus on my wife during her illness. The job benefits were exhausted, and I had no one to turn too. My home mortgage only had a year left and just before going into foreclosure, your aunt paid it in full. I'm sure it was her last penny, especially since she was on a fixed income. I know your uncle left her with the home, but every day living, I'm sure she watched every penny. I tried to give this back to her for years and she wouldn't take it. Now, I feel better repaying my debt to her family. It's the least I can do. I know, it's a little more than what she paid, but since she didn't accept it, I put the amount in mutual funds and it matured. So, every penny is your family's money. Every penny and I have no regrets."

"Sir, the check is more than I'm sure she'd accept. You should keep this and enjoy your retirement."

"You sound just like your aunt, so kind, but no. This is for you. I have my funds and I'm doing well. My retirement is fine. I made sure to never go through that hardship again. So, thank you but no thanks."

"If that's the case, I'll add this to the family's account for future distribution."

"You do that and I'll be at the memorial cruise. Just let me know my time to speak at her memorial."

"Sure sir, Have a wonderful day."

"Thanks, you do the same. I'll see you there."

Simone walks back to Aunt Marge's home in disbelief. "Another cashier's check for nearly two hundred thousand dollars; something else to share with the family. And a greater level of respect for Aunt Marge. You think you know someone and it's nothing like you think at all. She was awesome." As Simone enters Aunt Marge's home, she walks directly to Sabrina who stands in the kitchen on the phone. Looking at her in direct eye contact, she hands Sabrina the envelope. "Look at this" she says. Sabrina takes the envelope and reaches in to pull out the paper content. "Oh my goodness!" she exclaims. "I can't believe this."

"I know right. I can't believe it either. I don't know what to say about it, but it's for Aunt Marge."

"She gave that amount to him?"

"No it was much smaller. He banked the amount in mutual funds and never gave it to her. He tried but she never accepted it. He wants us to have it."

"No, you can't take this much money from an old man."

"I tried to return it but, he insisted we keep it. It's ours."

"More money to add."

"Yes, it is. I think we should distribute this amount to the next generation for college."

"I think we should add it to the scholarship funds. That way it's for everyone and not divided or loses any of its earning power."

"That's a great idea. Did you call everyone?"

"Done, I've gotten in touch with the key members. I'm sure they will pass word to the rest. You know how they communicate with everyone."

"Good, then its up to us to get things ready for Thursday."

"Let's do it."


Rodney enters the apartment with intentions of just relaxing after a long day. He heads to the kitchen and pulls a glass from the cabinet. He also pulls a bottle of whiskey from the shelf, heads to the refrigerator, and retrieves ice and soda.

After mixing a cocktail, he heads for his favorite spot on the couch. "It's been a long day. Even though the presentation hit the spot, the office group responded with action. My mind is still on Simone and winning her over, it's good but finally over. My long day is over and mind tiring at the least" he thinks. Sitting in silence and listening to whatever sounds the apartment makes, he hears a beep from the answering machine. "I recall jumping to the sound of the answering machine with haste in hearing who's called. Now, it's different. My motivation to hear the message is nothing like before. There was a time it was the first thing to do. Now, I'll get to it sometime in the future." Additional sounds are coming apparent. Water running in an adjacent apartment, cars roaming by on the near street, humming sounds from the ceiling fan, and air flowing in the central air conditioning vents have a hum to them. All these sounds are relaxing and soothing.

He takes another sip from his drink, looks around the room, and remembers his time line to do other things. "I'll start my chores after finishing my drink and after a change of clothes," thinking to himself. After his last sip of the cocktail, he returns the glass to the kitchen. He then pushes the play button on his answering machine. "Rodney, this is Sabrina. "Rodney its Sabrina, you know, Sabrina Willingham. I want to apologize for Simone's behavior today at the office. She jumps to conclusion a lot these days. It's not because of you, its losing our aunt that's driving her out of her wits end. And I apologize for the misunderstanding at the hospital. Please forgive me. I thought my sister would be ecstatic to see you. Actually, I still think she would. So, I'm asking, or inviting you to Aunt Marge's funeral cruise. I'll send you an invitation for two. Talk to Diane about it; she knows the details. Please consider coming."

Rodney ends he message and calls Diane for the rest of the instructions. "It's Thursday and two additional nights;

the ship leaves the doc at 4:00 pm. boarding starts at noon. Please come, I'd love seeing you there, and of course Simone wants you there. Even if she doesn't realize it, she needs you. So, call me with confirmation. Oh, don't forget you can bring one guess if you like. You have a cabin for two. Call me if you need further directions." Diane instructs. Immediately Rodney calls Dan. "Hey, what are you doing Thursday to Sunday?"

"Working I guess. Why do you ask?" replied Dan.

"We've been invited to Simone's Aunt Marge's memorial cruise."

"A cruise? This is new to me."

"And new to me as well, but it's my chance to see Simone once again. Even if she doesn't want me now, she'll remember me supporting her through seeing me on the cruise. I can bring a guest. Are you interested?"

"When is it again?"

"Thursday through Saturday, leaving at 4pm Thursday evening. I didn't get the details of where it's headed, however it would be a great experience. And you know cruises, there's going to be single women. You'll love the experience. Oh, its no cost to us and the cabin is reserved for two."

"Maybe I shouldn't go, the chances you'd have with Simone may be blown."

"No, not even a thought of being with her thoroughly as such; but it would be a nice situation to face. I know it's not likely to happen. But are you coming or not. I need you there to support me and have fun. What do you say partner?"

"For you huh? Well, I'm there partner. I guess it'll be a different experience."

"Great, I'll call Sabrina and let her know we both are coming."

"Let me know the rest of the details later. I've got to go. Call me later."

"Will do."

# Chapter 13

## *"The Celebration"*

Many family members and friends are showing up to the cruise ship. Groups of people are roaming while fruit drinks are served to anyone who'd like one. The fruit drinks are many Aunt Marge enjoyed during her life. The ship's decoration is themed of the many phases of Aunt Marge's life. From her early childhood to the age of her death, each deck has something unique reminding passengers of the reason they're aboard. Pictures of her life with many of the passengers are mounted near each elevator. They were much like the ship's map giving direction. Everything on the ship touched or interfaced in Aunt Marge's life.

In the dining rooms, the menus are full of Aunt Marge's favorites. Her best chicken recipe is one of the items on the main menu. And the greatest cookies ever made are on the dessert list. Though there were a variety of items to consume, many were a reminder of the sweetest woman that ever lived.

Table decorations didn't miss a step in the theme of things. Aunt Marge's floral arrangements, reflected in the many pictures she took, are all throughout the dining rooms. Her favorite colors help accent the waiter's uniform. Her classical music she once enjoyed filled the room. Not to over do it, these items were a part of the cruise and not the only thing offered.

Cabins are all assigned and the decks have family and friends situated in eras of interaction. Amazing to all, she coordinated the bunch quite well. It was as if her expertise was that of an event planner. Aunt Marge knew exactly how she wanted to leave this earth. At least, she knew how to put the family and friends in a pleasant situation.

Rodney and Dan arrive at the pier. They both climb out of their cars grab their luggage, and head for the boarding ramp. In stride they walk pulling the rolling bags and without saying a word, hastily maneuver up the gangplank. "Hey is this going to be something else or what?" said Dan.

"I think its going to be quite interesting myself" answered Rodney.

"You know, things will be quite fine during the cruise. You'll find Simone and spend some time selling yourself all over again.'

"Not so sure about that. I think she'll be a little busy with the family."

"If you thought so, why did you come along? She wants you here."

"Have you forgotten? She didn't invite me. Her sister did."

"Oh, that's right; I forgot who gave you the invite."

Arriving to their staterooms, they notice the cabin door slightly opened across from theirs. Cabin Sierra 78 has jazz music blaring from its television, water running from the head, and the window shades open allowing the natural light to shine through. No sign of the occupant just yet, the guys turn to their door 77 open it and step in. Looking around, they quickly decide who is where and place their things accordingly. In no time, they hear an announcement over the ship's PA system. "Welcome Aboard the Princess Enchantment. Thank you from the family and friends of Marge Blaine for attending the most amazing memorial cruise ever taken. As you settle into your state room, you'll find the memorial schedule and guest list. The guide also provides instructions in dining, safety, and additional information for an enjoyable three days. Do not be afraid of using the staff for your assistance. As a reminder, the family would like you to remember, there's no cost to anything you wish to do aboard the ship. So enjoy as much as you like and make it the best memorial experience in your life. Again, I wish you an enjoyable cruise."

Settling in to their staterooms, both Rodney and Dan decide to tour of the ship. "Let's head to the main deck and see who's on board," suggests Dan.

"Yes, let's do just that. I wonder if the crew is serving drinks. I could use one right about now," answers Rodney. "Let me get cleaned up a little before heading out. It'll only take a minute. You never know who you might run into."

"You're hoping to run into Simone. I can understand. Take your time. Get it right. I may get lucky with a cousin."

Simone and Sabrina are in their cabin when they hear taps on the door. "Hello, just a minute" answers Sabrina, as she walks to the door. She looks through the peephole and can't seem to make out the guest. She opens the door, and steps aside to look at either side of the passageway. Still, no one is standing near. "I guess it was the wrong cabin," she says to Simone.

"Oh really, look again." Sabrina looks.

"Hi Sweetheart," says Lorenz.

Sabrina embraces Lorenz with kisses and hugs of pure happiness. "I am so glad to see you. I knew you'd make it."

"I am a man of my word; at least I try really hard to be."

"Let me show you to your cabin," replied Sabrina. "Simone, feel like exploring the ship?"

"Will I be a third wheel?"

"No, not at all," said Lorenz. "Please come along, it could be fun once I drop my bags and we will hit the main deck."

"I know you two hadn't had time together, so why don't I take a rain check on the tour thing?"

"No way sis, come on. Lorenz and I have many moments coming during the cruise."

"Are you sure? I hate being a third wheel."

"You shouldn't be alone now. Come on let's get moving. We have things to do when we get back to the cabin."

"Ok" she answers while walking towards the passageway. Sabrina grabs Lorenz' hand and leads him down the passageway. Simone follows, step after step as if walking in the footprints of a bigger brother. "You know, I still can't believe we're here for Aunt Marge" she tells Sabrina.

"Neither do I; it would be a great trip if it were for a different reason. I'm sure Aunt Marge wanted us to enjoy this as much as any other cruise."

"Yea, I think so, and let's not keep this as a memorial cruise. Let's make the best of it. Why not? It's paid for" she says while giggling.

Dan and Rodney leave their cabin just as Mr. Slocum, Marge's life long neighbor, bumps into them.

"Hello young man, it's nice seeing you here.

Lorenz, Sabrina, and Simone ride the elevator down two decks heading to cabin Sierra 47. They exit the elevator and head right for the cabin. They pass the first cabin number on the higher end. Walking towards Lorenz' cabin, they come across Rodney, Dan, and Mr. Slocum. "If it weren't for you, we'd probably been here sooner."

"What's that sir?" asked Dan.

"Yes, you found Marge on the street remember?" as he pointed to Rodney.

"I did what?" replied Rodney.

"I can't be mistaken; it was you who knocked on my door to get an ambulance. I remember it quite well. And you stayed on her side until it arrived. I may be old and forgetful, but one thing I don't forget is a face. Plus, such a grave event as saving a life is one you don't let go. You saved her life. If it weren't for you, I wouldn't have found her for hours. Which the EMT said, it was good that you called us in time."

"I saved her life? I remember seeing an elderly woman on the street and not moving. I stopped to give assistance. She didn't seem to respond to my questions so I knocked on your door. I stayed with her until...I remember now."

"Yes you did. I'm glad you were there." Looking to his right there's Simone, standing in awe. "Simone, have you met Rodney?"

With a tear in her eye and struck from the new information, she held her hand to her mouth and without saying a word, ran back towards her cabin.

"What's wrong with her?" asked Mr. Slocum.

"Star struck" answered Sabrina.

"I'd say he's a star. A good guy too."

"You know Mr. Slocum; I told her the same thing. It's why I invited him to the celebration."

"Glad you did. I'll see you around Rodney, Sabrina, and young men," referring to Dan and Lorenz. He then turned towards the exit and moseyed along the way.

"See you soon sir" replied Rodney.

Sabrina, holding Lorenz' arm, says "Rodney you should go to Simone. She'd really understand your sincerity now. "

"I don't think it's a good idea," Replied Rodney.

"Why not?" asked Dan.

"It's not a good thing. Just think, you hate someone, blame them for harassing you, and now you find out he isn't such a bad guy. It's confusing for me, yet alone for her."

'I see your point" said Lorenz. "Think of it like this, you've been there through it all, shown your effort and persistence, and now the opportunity to make it come true is here. Why not take advantage of the opportunity? It's in your favor."

"You're a marketing guy; you know the saying, 'Get it while it's hot'" said Dan. "Besides, she's your dream girl. You've admitted it many times over."

"Ok, ok. I'll head to her cabin. Meet you on the deck later?"

"Yea we'll be there" replied Dan.

"Right after we, Sabrina winks at Lorenz, catch up on lost time."

"I'll catch you on the deck. It's no telling what time we'll see these two."

Rodney knock's on Simone's cabin door. Waiting for an answer he thinks," I'll tell her I didn't know. I'm sorry for not knowing it was your aunt. The connection never dawned on me. No, that's not it. How about...."

"Oh its you." Simone opens the door and answers.

"Yes it is. I'm sorry for not telling you about finding your aunt."

"You would forget something like that. You'll do anything to get next to me. And it's a big thing that you saved my aunt earlier in the year."

"You know, I can't believe you." Rodney says while entering the cabin. "I didn't know the lady was your aunt. How could I? I was running and saw a woman on the street all curled up. I thought she might have fallen, and needed some help. I had no idea it was your aunt. I had no idea."

"Oh, the hero excuse; you had no idea. It seems like you're all over my turf, in my life, nearly every corner. Its killing me seeing you so much when I don't want to."

"Ok Simone, that's it. I am crazy about you, willing to do anything in the world for you. I've dreamed of you being my woman. My focus centered on you and how to win you over. It's like a challenge that's crazy with passion. Now I see it's my fantasy and no chance of it becoming a reality. I've never had a woman so hard to crack. And I ask myself all the time why am I fighting so hard to be with you? Why is it you I want so much? My dreams are filled with you. Yet, every move I make, every comment reaching for you creates an opportunity for you to push me farther away from you."

"Push you away? You mean skillfully challenge you to believe there's no chance for us."

"No skill, just rude and harsh. I think I've gotten my fill and want no more." Rodney turns to exit the cabin. Just before leaving the cabin, he turns back to Simone, "you know, a man with admiration and affection for one woman can only take so much rejection. I've done nothing but show who and what I am. I see now, it wasn't enough."

"Enough it was. Close the door behind you on your way out."

Rodney leaves and gently closes the cabin door. He shakes his head from side to side and walks towards the first hatch leading to the outside deck. "Man, was I stupid for wanting her so much?" Pushing the door open, a strong breeze hits him and a tear falls. He leans on the protective deck siding and stares into the water. "And I can't believe I'm nearly broken up for a woman I never had. How can it be? Is it love that I have for her or is it the lost of a fantasy? Which ever it is, I can't believe the pain it's causing.

Simone turns to the portal and stares at the ocean and sky wondering of Rodney's words. "You know, there is no way he knew the woman was Aunt Marge. Why am I so ignorant to believe he didn't know? Why am I so afraid of him? He's right. I've never had a man do nearly as much for me. The romantic evening we shared was awesome, having dinner together at his place was fun, and his bringing flowers to the hospital so late at night were very thoughtful. And I push him away from me. Why?" Simone turns around to leave the cabin still pondering her thought. "I better rethink this. A man with so many qualities doesn't come often. And he's interested in me without really knowing who I am. At every opportunity, he's shown true qualities of a good man.

He's thoughtful, helpful, a civic contributor, and quite responsible in business. Oh, and he's handsome." She walks to the nearest exit to the upper deck. Opening the door she immediately sees Rodney by the rail. "Rodney" she calls,

Rodney turns to Simone and says "Oh, I can't take anymore" and walks toward the ship's aft.

"No, Rodney, don't leave. I need to share something with you."

"Sorry, I can't stay" he says as he continues to walk.

"Hey, I'm not going to run behind you."

In a faint voice, he answers, "As if you'd ever" and continues building distance between them.


"I am so glad you're here" said Sabrina. "I want this time together to be very special, even under these circumstances."

"Special in deed" Lorenz replies as he takes Sabrina in his arms. He gently kiss her on her neck, tracks upwards to her lips, kissing each inch. They fall into a deep kiss and embrace right next to the bunk. Falling on the bed, the two scramble to get undressed. Without any hesitation and like an orchestrated ballet, they find themselves intertwined in passion. "It's been too long since I've last had you" Lorenz said.

"Oh, don't think we'll do that again."

"I need you, as I've never needed anyone in my life. I need you."

"I need you too Lorenz. I can't live a day without having you in my life. I dream of you, reach for you, and desire you at every moment of the day."

"Baby, is this love?"

"Yes, its love." She answers. They both stop moving as they lay on their sides facing each other. Lorenz stops breathing for a moment and Sabrina stares deeply into his eyes. And without any signal they both whisper "I Love You." In their eyes, a moment of time froze and there was silence. Lorenz' left eye welled into a tear and Simone's right eye let one teardrop fall down her face. They held that moment together and embraced with greater strength. They held each other so tight their bodies breathed in unison, their strokes were electric and they both cringed from pure physical pleasure. They both held each other as if it were for dear life. Not letting go for nothing or anyone, Lorenz broke silence just as he looked deeply into her window of affection "I really love you."

"You know babe, it's a new day for us."

"Yes, a new start and direction in life."

"I can't believe it. I am so glad we shared this moment, and it's truly one day I'll never forget."

"Neither will I. It's the first time I've told a woman I love you."

"Oh Lorenz, you can't be serious. I don't mind being the second or third woman as long as you mean it."

"No Sabrina, you are the first and only. I'd like to keep it that way. Not saying it's the future, but I breathe better when I'm near you. I rise to the sky and soar with the birds at every thought of you. Each moment I'm thinking of you. And my heart pounds fast in the sight of you."

"I see, it's slightly different for me. My heart doesn't pound as fast, but my mind wonders to our future. Our pregnancy, our apartment, our struggle; I see our future and it's vivid. I've never looked so deep in my soul to the meaning of my dreams. Each dream has you involved, living next to me, and there. Lorenz, I've never dreamed of a man so exact and involved with me. I love you."

"Hello my lady, my princess, my queen. Welcome to the castle of my heart."

"Hello fine sir, my prince, my king. I love being in your castle."

Dan finds Rodney walking on the ship's sun deck. "Rodney" he calls.

"Yea" he responds as he walks along the deck and barely turns toward Dan.

"No way, I can't believe she turned you down again." Dan walks to catch up with Rodney.

"That she did."

"How bad did she do it?"

"She will always be my dream girl. It's just not in her book. As a matter of fact, it's becoming my book alone all the time. I've got to let it go. Man, I've got too."

"Then let's make the best of the rest of this cruise. We'll start over and get back to my best friend who lived for himself."

"Sounds like a good idea."

Family and friends are heading to the ship's main theater for Aunt Marge's memorial service. Her favorite songs are playing and multiple flowers, wreaths, and pictures spread across the stage. The podium is center stage, prepared with notes for each speaker. Programs spread across the theater for each person present. People settle in and the program begins.

Simone steps to the podium, and welcomes everyone to the service. "Thank you for coming to Aunt Marge's memorial service. She was a dynamic woman, sister, friend, cousin, and neighbor. Her life graced us with truth, happiness, energy, and most of all, love. She gave us the type of love biblically described and truly practiced in definition. She provided us with an awesome taste of quality in living. She gave us more of herself than any of us can ever imagine. I, for one, received so much of her, that I find myself understanding her as I know myself. Everyone here received her life's influence and today we celebrate her life." Simone steps away from the podium and leaves the stage.

A young gentle man steps on the stage and sings a wonderful ballad, solemn in delivery and very melodic in verse. It was a favorite song of Marge in her youth. Not religious in nature, but surely a song of emotions. "I am a nephew of Marge Blaine. She was my greatest support in music, and because of her I launched a career in entertainment. I'll always thank her for doing so. There is no greater love for someone, than providing encouragement to achieve your dream. She encouraged me through it all." He steps down from the stage.

Mr. Slocum approached the stage and pulled a card from his pocket; notes for his speech most suspect. He places them in the middle of the podium and clears his voice. "Mrs. Marge Blaine gave her best for all and everyone. If you remember her, you'll know she contributed above and beyond whatever the expectation. I mean, she gave her all without ever expecting a return. I am her neighbor and friend for over 27 years. I am a recipient of her definition of quality of life. My family and I are a part of her, an extension of your family, and I in fact, I feel like a brother who's lost his sister. We shared laughter and tears over the years, my kids call her Aunt Marge, and the grand children addressed her as their special Great Aunt. I say farewell to a lovely woman, one of love, a sweet woman we cherished. Farewell to you Marge, my sister. I know you're flying with angels."

Simone approached the podium as Mr. Slocum stepped off the stage. "We decided to keep the program short and sweet. You know Aunt Marge would have made sure we didn't fuss over her. So, in kind, we're going to do exactly that. Everything here on the cruise is a theme of Aunt Marge. She coordinated everything, even the program you hold in your hand. She wanted us to celebrate her life, and I for one intend to do so. In the spirit of Aunt Marge, we'd like you to indulge yourself in every aspect of this cruise. Yes, we'll miss Aunt Marge, yet she'll be with us forever." Simone steps down from the stage. The ship's band plays music while the curtains open and the lights dim. A large portrait of Aunt Marge appears as a stage backing. Dancers appear on stage in multiple costumes. All costumes are placed in different eras of Aunt Marge's life. Every song of an era plays, a couple reflects Aunt Marge's favorite dance.

A gentle man appears at the moment of the last dance. He moves to the center stage and stand with a microphone in his hand. Automatically he starts with a joke of childhood and the changes Aunt Marge made with all the kids. From their first blanket to the cookies sent to college campuses. And at every joke, the theater roared with laughter. For five minutes, the comedian told situational jokes from Aunt Marge's life. For each minute, there were roars of laughter.

When the comedian ended his session, another saxophonist took center stage. It was Aunt Marge's favorite instrument. The woman played a lovely piece of music, Aunt Marge's favorite for sure.

The next event was another dance; a creative dance from Aunt Marge's favorite theatrical play. The dance was awesome and very entertaining.

Last event and surprising to everyone was a message from Aunt Marge herself. "This isn't my last will and testament, or the reading of life instructions. It is my farewell to you. To my family, friends, neighbors, and associates and everyone here, I give you a gift. My greatest gift to anyone and everyone is the gift of love. Please don't sit and memorialize me as a person passing on. Think of me as a distant friend without the means to call. You know the limitations of technology. No phone available and you know letters are slower than a snails pace. Think of it as, whatever means on this earth, isn't available, but I will be there. Yes, I'll be there for you.

I brought you here on this cruise to understand its continuing life that counts. You have to live and let live, reach for the fun in your heart. You have to take what I gave you and go for your dream. Stop trying to compete with society's standard of living and enjoy life. You only live once.

Last, because I want to keep this short, remember I love you. I love you all and will be here for you. So, in light of the situation, I will share with you one thing. I leave multiple funds to assist you when needed. There are tight stipulations you'll have to meet, but it's for you. Use it wisely and without being foolish. For more information, see my lawyer's firm and specific standards and direction are in place to help. And for my last gift, you should receive envelopes in your cabin. It's a surprise.

Remember, this is my gift to you so I expect you to enjoy the rest of the cruise. I sure loved cruises. It's my farewell so stop crying and raise your glass for a toast." Waiters passed out chalets of grape cider. "To my family, friends, and acquaintances, I loved you all and please love each other for life. Your best years are yet to come. Share your knowledge, your will, and your skill. Now drink up and enjoy my gift to you." The tape ends.

Simone, in tears, walks on the stage while the band softly plays. "Let's follow Aunt Marge's advice. Enjoy our cruise gift. Everything is on your schedule in the cabin. I'll have her ashes on the top deck to release into the wind. Sabrina and I will do this at sunrise tomorrow morning."

The theater empties of its patrons. Sabrina and Lorenz sits at a table booth and chat in surprise. "You ok baby?" Lorenz asks.

"Yes, I'm ok. Wasn't she awesome?"

"Yes, she was awesome."

"I really miss her. I'd love to tell her about us. She'd be excited about our new found love. Its all because I'm the last she thought would be so deep with emotions; especially over a man."

"No, she wouldn't be excited about it, she'd tell you its about time."

Sabrina punches Lorenz and says, "Sure she would" and laughs.

Simone returns to her cabin in tears. She stands on the cabin's balcony and looks out to the horizon. Tears fall harder and internally she tells Aunt Marge, "Farewell my second mother, best friend, and mentor. I'll never forget you. And thanks for a new future." She then sits on a chair and watches the sun set. In a few moments darkness approached

# Chapter 14

## *A New Beginning*

Lorenz returns to the cabin to study before returning to the hospital. Automatically, he assumes there's much left for him to finish the internship. He enters the cabin, grabs a book and sits on the balcony over looking the ocean. After reading a few hours, Sabrina enters the cabin and calls out "Lorenz, are you here?"

"Yes, I am on the balcony."

"With all the things to do on this boat; you come here and read."

"It's an important thing in my preparation. You know, I'm not finished with my internship just yet. As soon as I feel comfortable with the program, I'll slow down."

"I know baby, but it's our time together. We haven't much time so why not make the best of it? I have multiple shoots next week and it's my turn to glow with our love."

"Yes, you're right. I only wanted to catch up and review a few things before returning to the hospital. As well, I thought you'd like to enjoy catching up with your family."

Sabrina grabbing Lorenz' arm and pulling him up to her in the cabin saying, "That's nice of you to think of me, but you're important to me too. I don't want our time to waste when there's opportunity to get closer." Embracing Lorenz with a long luscious kiss, she pushes him on the bed for a full embrace.

Pier side, the ship docks and sets for debarking. The announcement over the intercom instructs passengers with debarkation events. Deck after deck, the announcer directs the passengers off the ship and onto the pier. Simone and

Sabrina grab their suitcases and head to the debarkation hatch. They exit the ship and walk to the parking lot. Not saying a word to each other along the way, they silently discussed the recent events. One look at Sabrina and Simone knows of her new found emotions for Lorenz. Sabrina, understanding Simone's disgust, stays clear of conversation about Rodney. Both ladies continue to load the car upon arrival and sit in the driver and passenger seats. Sabrina, driving the car, starts the engine while Simone stares into space towards the open parking lot. "Are you ok?" asked Sabrina.

"Yes, I'm ok" answered Simone.

"Good. We're starting a new life and it starts now."

"I realize this is a new beginning for us. New found wealth, a career decision to make, we have to develop a plan to continue Aunt Marge's work, and no time for a man."

"No time for a man?"

"No time at all for Rodney. I've decided to focus on our new beginning."

Sabrina drives out of the parking lot into traffic. She stops at the traffic light before heading towards home. Pausing in her thought to ease Rodney in as a subject of conversation, she considers a way to respond. "You mean, you didn't open the door to Rodney when he went to the cabin to talk to you?"

"I opened the door and heard him out. I'm not ready for anything with him. He may be a good guy and all, but it's not a good time for me."

"So, if it isn't now, when is it a good time?"

"I can't answer that right now. I haven't an idea."

"You mean to tell me, you didn't give a quality man like Rodney a chance?"

"Sabrina, giving Rodney a chance isn't important. I think we have a lot to do in the near future. We have a heavy plate with what Aunt Marge left us."

"Sure, we have a large plate of change, but support is important. Especially from a smart intelligent, man like

Rodney. Did you ever think he'd be of assistance to you or us for that matter?"

"No, he'd be a nuisance. I'm sure of it and that's why I decided to focus on us and our inheritance for the time being. A man can come at a later time in my life. Right now isn't it or he isn't the right one."

"Your decision sounds final. I guess he's out and money is in. I never thought you'd push a quality guy away when he presented himself to you."

"I didn't see him as quality, and besides, we have other things to achieve now.

"I agree, we have other things to achieve, but I have Lorenz and he's part of my new objectives in life."

"Enjoy him while you can."

"What's that suppose to mean?"

"Just what I said; enjoy him while you can."

"That is so discouraging and I can't believe you aren't happy for me."

"Oh, I'm happy for you, just not sure he's there for you and not our inherited wealth."

"You know what Simone, he has no idea about what Aunt Marge left us and I'm in love with him."

"In love with him, are you sure?"

"Yes I'm sure. Have you ever heard me claim loving someone before?"

"Well, maybe when you were younger. You know, the teenage phase we all go through. But all in all, no I haven't."

"Then you know I'm really into Lorenz. He's it, I'm telling you. I had no idea this feeling would be so great and it came unexpected. It was a sneak attack on my heart. When he told me...."

"Told you? You mean he told you first?"

"Yes, he told me in the most romantic way. It was awesome and the connection is out of this world."

"Oh, wow. My little sister is really in love. I just thought you were on your usual fling and having fun. This time you actually fell in love."

"And you rejected the same offer of affection. That man loves you and he did all the right things. I can't believe you rejected Rodney."

"That's my business. It's my objective to love who I see fit and at a time that's best for me. Never is it a time to love someone to please you nor him for that matter. I choose and he isn't the one."

"You want my opinion?"

"Not really, but you're going to tell me anyway."

"You're passing up a wonderful man and they are hard to come by. You know, we aren't getting younger and the pool of great available guys is slimming. I honestly think he's one that got away."

"I appreciate your opinion, but he's not one that got away. As a matter of fact, he was thrown to the wolves for all I care."

Silence grew heavily in the car. Both Sabrina and Simone decided not to say anything more on the matter. They both focused on internal thoughts as Sabrina drove to their perspective homes.

Lorenz arrives at his apartment from a cab. He exits the cab, grabs his gear and heads to the apartment building. "Hey Lorenz" Robin exclaimed. Not seeing anyone in his direct sight, he looks around on the street for whoever called. "Hey" Lorenz answers.

"I haven't seen you for a few days. I know your shifts didn't change or did they?"

"No shift changes. I took a couple days off and went to a funeral. I mean a memorial service." Lorenz responds as he recognizes the voice.

"Oh really? I'm sorry some one passed away. Was it a relative of yours?" asked Robin as she looks out of her apartment window. Lorenz replies as he looks towards Robin. "No relative, it was my girl friend Sabrina's aunt."

"Oh, your girl friend; I hope all went well. I'll catch you later."

"Yes, maybe later."

Lorenz continues upstairs to his apartment and opens the door. Robin walks after him as he enters and hands him a postal envelope. "Before I forget, this came for you earlier this week. I called the hospital to get it too you, but no one would help me find you."

"Thanks, I appreciate you signing for the letter."

"Oh, no problem. Should we open it?"

"I will after I settle in. I need to put these things away first. Thanks again for holding and delivering the letter" he says while escorting Robin out of the apartment.

"Will you let me know what it is? She says as she turns toward Lorenz. "Remember if it weren't for me, you'd not have the letter."

"I will. And thanks again. I appreciate it. I'll call you later right after I open it." Lorenz then closes the apartment door and places the letter on the coffee table. Robin returns to her apartment and continually wonders what's in the letter.

Lorenz finally settles in from the cruise. He grabs a drink from the refrigerator, sits on the couch, and gets the letter. "It's from the hospital. I wonder why the hospital administration is sending me a letter." Lorenz opens the letter and begins to read the content. "Oh my, I passed all exams and this is my official notice of completing my internship. I thought I had two more surgeries to perform. My last two months is for preparing for a job someplace in the world. I've got to talk to Sabrina. She should have input to us and our next move. I can't leave her behind. I'd better call her." He picks up the phone and dials her number. Just as the phone rings, there's a knock on the apartment door.

He answers with the phone at his ear. "Hey, Robin, what's up?"

"Have you opened the letter?"

Lorenz holds his hand up towards Robin signaling give me a minute. Sabrina's answering machine picks up "....Leave me a message." The message ends with a beep. "Hey, give me a call when you can. I have great news and need to talk to you. I love you." Lorenz hangs the phone.

"Love you?" Robin asks. "You mean you're in love with that model woman? Are you sure its love?"

"Oh, its love, no doubt Robin. It's love all the way. I've never felt like this before, and you know, my type of women doesn't beat my door down. It's a gift and I'd like to cherish my gift while I can. And she's an angel, a lovely one at that."

"All this time, you never recognized me as a woman of caliber."

"Recognized you? Oh, you're a gold mine and a lovely person. I never thought of you in that manner. Was I suppose too?"

"Damn right you were supposed too. I am a quality woman and cared for you in ways you'd never know. I've wanted you to be with me from the time you started your internship. What's that, three years ago?"

"I never knew. I'm sorry about that. Its just I never focused on women until Sabrina. And I hadn't planned on seeing her then either. It just happened and I'm glad it has"

"Thanks a lot Lorenz. You break my heart without knowing it. What a man you are." Robin turns in tears and runs across the hall to her apartment.

Lorenz stands at the apartment door for a moment as he watches Robin slam her door shut. "Wow, I knew she was kind of interested but, not my type. Why didn't I tell her years ago instead of being nice? Man, I blew that one." Lorenz thinks. "Oh well, I didn't lead her on either." Lorenz closes his door and starts looking at multiple hospitals throughout the country. "I know there's someplace I can land a position on a staff or practice. There's one for me out there somewhere. I wonder where Sabrina would like to go. I know she's able to go anyplace with me."

Sabrina arrives at her place and settles in for the evening. She picks up her phone and dials her access number to retrieve messages. "You have three messages. To hear your messages....Your first message is: Sabrina, your next scheduled shoot is Friday morning at the Waycross building. Be there at 9:00 am. Call me if you have questions." "It's the agent, he never leaves his name; as if I need it," she thinks." Next message the answer machine announces. "Hey, where have you been? You know I can never get my fix of being with you. I'm crazy about you. Why haven't you called me? It's been months now, is there something you want to share with me? Call me." It was James, her long time beau of excitement. He travels all over the world and is her main focus when he's back in the states...Next message. "Hey, give me a call when you can. I have great news and need to talk to you. I love you." Sabrina's heart flutters at the sound of Lorenz' voice; she immediately dials his number. Lorenz answers. "Hello."

"You called. What is it? It sounded urgent."

"Well, its exciting news. I'm finished."

"Finished what?"

"School silly."

"Were you that close? I thought you had another year."

"No, this was my last year. I thought I had two more procedures to perform. My last was before the memorial cruise. I got my confirmation letter today."

"That's great news. Congratulations Doctor."

"Well, it calls for a celebration. And it calls for us to think of our future."

"Yes. I'm heading over to your place as soon as we hang up."

"I'll be waiting."

Sabrina drops everything, grabs her purse, and heads for the car. She drives over to Lorenz' apartment and arrives in twenty minutes flat. She walks up to Lorenz' apartment and knocks on the door. "Who is it?" Lorenz asks.

"Hey it's me." Sabrina answers.

Robin opens her door and immediately yells "You're the one; the bitch who took my man!!"

"Excuse me?"

Lorenz opens the door and exclaims the same. "What in the world are you talking about Robin?"

"You know, its true Lorenz. She stole you from me."

"How can you say such a thing when there's nothing between us?" said Lorenz

"You better get this woman out of our business Lorenz. You know, I don't play with my emotions and will not allow you to do it either."

"She isn't a girl friend of mine. She is my neighbor, I swear."

"Sure you do Lorenz, tell her of the time and many of nights over the past three years you spent at my place. Tell her how I helped you study for your exams. Tell her."

"All those things are true. She fails to mention we were always friends and neighbors. It never went anywhere. I swear Sabrina, when I told you I love you, it's from my heart and no games. Think about it, you've never questioned me before, why start now?"

"Robin" said Sabrina, "You're quite delusional. Lorenz and I are serious now, so whatever you thought you had, isn't anymore. There, he's my heart now and I'm ensuring it stays that way."

Crying, Robin returns back into her apartment, after shouting "You bastard!!"

"So, where were we?" asked Lorenz

"You were going to talk about your letter and finishing school. What's next?"

"We have to decide what cities to submit my resume. You know, I can either stay here or move to another part of the world. I don't want to make that decision on my own. Especially since I see our future together, it's a decision we need to make."

"Really, you want my input to your career?"

"I want your input to our future. I'm not going any place far from you. I love you and I really mean I love you." Lorenz kisses Sabrina.

Simone elects to review all of those documents, deeds, and letters from the lawyer's office. She drafts a list of items to achieve for her transition. Immediately she starts planning how to achieve each item on the list. From establishing a new business to maintaining those programs, Aunt Marge managed. She looked at her own wants in life. The list of things she created while sitting on the balcony over looking the ocean. Not one item on her list included having a relationship, though she'd like one, but not at the moment. "If I only had someone to bounce my ideas off of" she thought. "My ideas seem right in line with a solid future, a comfortable one, and sharing it....well, it'll have to be shared with Sabrina."

Lorenz returns to the hospital for his scheduled shift. "Hey, Doctor Lorenz" said the nurse.

"Hi Nurse, how are you?"

"I'm great. We missed you. I hear you're finished here. Are you ready to move on?"

"No, not really; I didn't expect to finish so soon."

"Soon? Don't you realize you've been here for three years plus?"

"I have but it zoomed by so quickly."

"It's because you were so focused. I hear the hospital director wants to chat with you."

"Oh, is it something I failed to do?"

"It's nothing of the sort. As if you'd fail anything. Anyway, you should run up to his office when you get a chance. He's asked about you once this morning."

"Thanks and I'll catch up with him sometime this morning. I'd like to catch up with my patients first."

"As usual, welcome back."

"Thanks again and I'll chat with you soon" as Lorenz walks down the hall, he waves and holds one thumb up towards the ceiling. The morning moves into afternoon in no time. Lorenz finishes his time on the job by focusing on each patient. No variations with the current patients, he sits patiently with each one so there's a full understanding of each. Can you believe no one inquired to my getting engaged?" he says to his last patient.

"Congratulations. When's the wedding?"

"Wedding" Lorenz replies. "What wedding?"

"Didn't you say you were just engaged?"

"No, I didn't say I am engaged, I meant I'm thinking of asking Sabrina to marry me."

"Oh. I misunderstood. I assumed you asked and she accepted."

"No I haven't asked her just yet"

"Then why not? Let me tell you something while I can. Once you find someone special and your life seems better, you have to embrace the change. If you don't embrace the change and not capitalize on the opportunity, your life loses. Yes, you lose on a gift greater than you can imagine. If its love, as I see it is, then go and make the world a better place. You have to do it soon before it changes. Once you capture love, it gets better and better over time. Go tell the young woman how you feel and ask her. Hesitate no more; your life depends on it."

"I see. Did you get married?"

"Yes, but not at the moment I should have. I allowed conditions to change before asking. If I hadn't hesitated, the love you have now would be the same love you enjoy in later years. Don't let your beginning get away from you. You need the spark as a reminder for hard times to come."

"Yes, yes, you're right. I have to act now. Thanks. Oh, before I leave, can I get you anything? You have the right amount of painkillers, you're on track to recovery, and your tests were all negative. Is there anything I can do to help you feel better?"

"Yes, call my wife in I've something to tell her."

"Sure, no problem; and thanks for the advice." Lorenz leaves the patient's room and signals the patient's wife over. She approaches; Lorenz stops her and says, "The wise man wants to see you. He's doing great so take good care of him" and leaves the woman to her husband.

Sabrina telephones Simone after her morning shoot. Simone answers "Hello."

"Hi Simone, I have lots to tell you. Are you busy?"

"No, not really, I'm reviewing a list of things I want to get done. It's a good thing you called."

"Yes, it's a great thing I called."

"Great? You're excited about something. What is it? Did you get a magazine cover deal? Did you land another a major account? What is it?"

"I think Lorenz is going to ask me to marry him."

"There you go, fantasy world colliding with reality. What makes you think he's going to ask you?" inquired Simone.

"Why do you have to criticize my thoughts? Why?"

"I'm not criticizing your thoughts. I'm a realist and Lorenz isn't ready for marriage. Where'd you think he can get the time for you during his internship?"

"He finished. He's graduating soon and asked me to help him select a city to live. He wants me to go with him."

"And you think that's a marriage proposal?"

"I think it's a step in the right direction. I see myself going with him. Either as his wife or not, I'm going. Knowing Lorenz, he's going to ask. I can feel it."

"Then I wish it comes true for you. Don't set yourself up for disappointment. You know how men can disappoint you."

'There you go again. Why Simone? Why do you always find a negative point in my life and situation?"

"I'm not being negative; it's a protection for your heart. Expect the worse and if chance you're right, then all is well. But if you're wrong, don't expect the pain to leave so quickly."

"Is that what happened to you and Rodney? Did he hurt you before he got a chance to show you love?"

"No, nothing got in our way, it was my decision. He wasn't right for me."

"I think he is. And a matter of fact, he's the best guy who's ever shown you the right type of interest."

"He's got you fooled. Whatever he did to impress you, didn't work on me."

"He's authentically a good guy. One day you'll understand."

"One day I just might." Simone replies disconnecting the call.

# Chapter 15

## *Three Years Returning*

Rodney wakes early morning for his routine run. Heading out of his apartment, his neighbor stops and pauses with a morning greeting, "Good Morning" he said while walking past.

"Good morning." Rodney replies.

The neighborhood changed over the years. The vacant lot near the old apartments is now a major condominium complex. Fortunately, Rodney purchased the penthouse condo years ago. The marketing firm he started flew into profits within the first year. The new firm is amazingly profitable due to the multiple new accounts it won throughout the state. The best thing is he didn't leave the neighborhood he loved so much. Practically all the friends and relatives are close by. The minimal life style change landed him into a superb comfort zone; perfect for bouncing back after a heart disappointment.

Stepping on the sidewalk, Rodney performs his routine stretch and prepares for his morning run. Heading on his short track, he takes off with a strong pace. "I've got lots to do today" he thinks while running south on the main street. Just as before, the street livens with people and activities as the morning evolves.

More cars are moving along the main street as he turns right at the next block down near Aunt Marge's old home. As in every morning in the last two years, and like clock work, Rodney makes his run in 40 minutes. His route leads back to his home where he finishes his workout and prepares for the business day ahead. His suits are immaculate, stylish, and tailored, projecting a true executive. He thinks while dressing, "A quick drive to the office in my sports car, I'll stop at the coffee shop on the way up to the 12$^{th}$ floor, and a good day ahead. Without a doubt it's going to be a wonderful day."

Dan calls Rodney's cell phone with an urgent message from a client. Rodney answers the call "This is Rodney."

"It's the MaxMin account. The CEO didn't quite like the results of our test market. He thinks the numbers are too low as a result of our marketing strategy. He wants to talk to you this morning or he'll cancel our contract."

"Don't worry. Get Mark to catch the recent numbers for PitPot and Elab Men for a comparison graph. Meet me at the office and get Mr. Johnson to schedule a meeting at MaxMin this afternoon. We'll win his confidence back in no time.

"Ok, will do."

"What are you doing in town? I thought you were meeting a new client."

"I met him last night and it looks great. I can't see a reason why he'll not contract with us for his next campaign."

"Great. I'll see you at the office."

Rodney goes to his sports car and starts the engine. Right away he smiles. "Life is good" he thinks, "Life is real good." Driving to the office, Rodney passes the park he and Simone went to during their date. A big band was practicing musical numbers they listened to and it brought a good memory. Rodney pulled out of traffic, parked the car and stepped onto the park's grass. He spotted a bench and took a seat. Listening to the music, he allowed himself to day dream and reminisces to a time of pure enjoyment with a woman he totally admired. "She was so lovely and full of life. I missed out on a wonderful woman. Even though she didn't want anything to do with me, I still think she was the one. I see her smile, hear her laughter, and feel her in my arms as we dance. I can actually smell her perfume, and remember her touch on my arm when we walked to the carriage. Oh she was lovely in every way. I hate things didn't workout; life goes on." I have to write her:

Funny thing this morning; dreaming of you was a blast from the past.

Unexpected thoughts of you were deep in my conscious. The vivid view of you wearing this awesome blue, shoulder cut dress, which is revealing yet covering. As awesome as you normally are whenever you present yourself. Your eyes were sparkling, matching the natural glow, and your smile was amazingly bright, so awesome, and soft. What a beautiful sight.

It's as if my dream was a reflection of past, or deja vu as it encompassed me seeing you. At a time when things are not great between us, I dream of you with the dandiest view. A vision of beauty for sure and sweating desire beads my skin, and I feel the moisture the moment I wake. It's you out of no where, guilty as I may be, still thinking of the life you lead. Why? It's a question given some thought to answer. Yet, my answer remains the same. You can fight it as much as you can. But the reality is love. No other reason can explain.

No, this isn't a note to draw you in, neither is it an attempt to change your thought. It is just a simple paragraph sharing my dream of your beauty. Its how each thought of you makes me smile deep inside. It's how you bring warmth with a beat of my heart. Its how the pure vision of you in my mind, is the same in life. Oh, you're such a beautiful soul.

When I analyze my dream and search for its meaning, the answer comes clear as night. Not quite without doubt do I look beyond the imagination of sight. Yet in an attempt to see without the light, the vision of you is such delight. Open eyes and muscle strain, squint really hard causing eyes to pain. And still the darkness breathes beauty of sight, a vision of you in midst of night.

Sweating, breathing, calm and awe, a vision of your sweetness so true. Awake and eyes dilated, adjusted to night but still I see your beauty in sight. Only if a ghost appeared, or a picture on the wall stood still. A blink of eyes report the same to the brain, it's you in my mind a desire to see. Then sadness fills the air and my vision of you disappears. I remember the madness I brought to one's heart and weakness I contend to hold. The other side of sadness and its something I do control.

Celebrated yet, though sadness clings, as I view the moment of happier things; my message of love and missing you, came through the vision of seeing the beauty in you. Even in the darkest night, and still the glow of a lovely sight. My beauty in blue a love to see, a dress one wore, just for me.

Twenty minutes pass and Rodney snaps out of his day dream. He looks at his watch, stands, and returns to his car. Rodney gets back to his earlier plan, arriving at the office thirty minutes late. He snaps into super executive role and has business rolling to his usual pace. After the second meeting, he sets a path to catch up on the lost half hour from this morning. He calls for a brief update from key organization members. One by one they bring him up to speed on sales, marketing, and projects. By noon, he's one step ahead of his agenda. Rodney is back to himself and the day becomes another business success.

It's nearly 6:00 pm and the majority of Rodney's staff has left for the day. Rodney, sits in for additional reviews of client contracts. His normal routine, spending arduous hours ensuring the next campaign is greater than the one before. He sweeps every project with a fine toothcomb, being detailed in his review. He takes notes on each project for tomorrow's briefing and also to satisfy customer expectations. As well, he lists each client's chance of opportunities for new business. A skill he picked up over the years in marketing organizations. Time moves into early evening and his day finally comes to an end. Rodney finds himself set to leave the office and notices the traffic jam on the main street. He decides to take a stroll down the street, as he did many times before, instead of fighting traffic. At the end of two blocks, he finds himself at the art gallery he often visited. A walk through always gave him solitude and peace from the remarkable paintings. "Each painting was a story" he always thought.

Simone steps lively at the exercise tape playing on her television. The flat screen television has three uniquely sculptured people performing various exercises according to a tape. She followed their exercise routine religiously and used it as an additional workout to her physical trainer visits. "I love the way exercising makes me feel" she thinks while moving in rhythm to the music. Simone stops at the end of the tape and heads for her shower. She steps into her bathroom, an elaborate section of the house where multiple amenities make up her favorite room. Yes, the mansion has magnificent bathrooms with her master being the favorite amongst four. This bathroom had a steam room and an individual shower. It also provides access to a large wardrobe closet. As she enters the bathroom, she can't help but step on clothes and towels left behind by her husband.

"Stefan is such a spoiled slob" she thinks. "Why can't he put the towels and his dirty clothes in the hamper like normal people?" She throws those items in the hamper and strips. Simone jumps in the shower.

Stefan walks into the kitchen and grabs a cup for coffee. He moves over to the coffee pot and dislikes the odor of the fresh pot. He places the cup down and heads upstairs to chat with Simone. "Good morning darling." Stefan says.

"Hi" Simone says with a smile and moves closer to Stefan.

"The cook made regular coffee this morning. He knows I hate regular coffee. I'm heading down to the coffee shop on the strip and get me a cup. Would you like anything?"

"What type of coffee did the cook make?"

"I told you, regular beans. It didn't seem to have a flavor to its odor."

"No, you go right ahead and get your coffee. I'm going to enjoy what's down stairs."

"You do that. Don't say I didn't warn you when the taste is horrible."

"Warning is heeded but thanks anyway." Simone reaches out to kiss Stefan, but he turns and leaves the room without looking back. "Typical" she thinks to herself.

Simone finds a matching outfit from her wardrobe; gets dressed and heads for the kitchen. She has breakfast consisting of bacon, eggs, coffee and juice. She finds her PDA in her office and reviews her schedule of events, notes, emails, and documents. She starts her day making multiple calls to business clients and partners. She has her hand into various types of businesses, like marketing, insurance, and property management. All of these business contracts and partnerships were made years earlier after receiving the inheritance. Simone followed her check list from years ago.

Three hours into the day and no sign of Stefan. "Boys will be boys" she thinks.

Simone closes her office door and heads for a drive to the beach. The chauffer pulls the large luxury car to the front, steps out and opens the door for her entry. Simone looks up to the sky, sees the sun shining bright, and feels the warmth on her face. She then decides to take a convertible and sends the limo away. She walks to the garage, jumps in her favorite convertible and drives onto the main street from her home. The top down, wind blowing, warmth, blue skies and sunshine all supports her decision to drive the convertible. "Beautiful, just beautiful" she exclaims.

Driving down the main street on her way to the beach, Simone passes her husband's car parked at a coffee shop. "At least he's socializing with the locals. He's truly a people person and I'm sure they're getting a kick out of him. He's such a cad. I'll stop after my time at the beach if I see he's still there." The next block she's at the beach parking entrance, Simone turns into the parking lot, replaces the car top for storage and security, and exits onto the parking lot. She immediately grabs her bag and heads for the sand, walking closer to the water line. She finds a spot in the sand where there's direct sunshine, few people, and a view to die for. She sets herself up for a few hours of sunshine and solitude while the waves crash along the shore. Enjoying the view, she falls into deep thought of life and its changes from years ago. "I'd never have anything of this life if it weren't for you Aunt Marge. I'm sad you're not with me to enjoy this, but thankful for this change; and what a change."

Simone's cell phone rings, breaking her thought. She answers, "Yes, this is Simone"

"Hi Simone, it's your lawyer Phil, How are you?"

"Oh, Phil, I'm fine. I'm out here at the beach and the weather is awesome. It's such a beautiful day."

"I have news for you, some good and some bad. Which do you want first?"

"I'll take the good news."

"Ok, ninety percent of our commercial real estate is full of tenants. This is a change over the last year where sixty percent was the norm. I don't know what's happened but whatever it is, we're happy. The profit for the properties will exceed projections by twenty percent at a minimum. You're making more money this quarter than I reported earlier. And this is the great news. Are you ready for the bad news?"

"After hearing that, how can any news be bad?"

"Well, there's a hostile attempt to invade the business. There is one stipulation Aunt Marge left in her will that we didn't take into account. I didn't mention it because it wasn't a threat. Now, it's a threat from the city and you need to look into it. I have all the information leading to eminent domain for one of your major building properties."

"Eminent domain; is this where the government buys property?"

"Yes, it's from the city where they take a property for the good of the city or community."

"What property are they interested in?"

"The shelter your Aunt Marge started years ago. It's in the middle of the city and practically runs itself. Aunt Marge funded the effort for the past twenty years. The want the building and the operation shut down."

"Who wants the operation shut down?"

"The city leadership and a major developer want to revitalize the area with new amenities."

"I set up a meeting with them on the fourth. Can you make it? I think your presence will make a world of difference."

"I'll get back to you on this within the hour. I'll get Sabrina to join us."

"That's a great idea. The two of you with a solid front will make a difference. As well, the money you give the city will also challenge the developer. It's a political move but the developer stands to make a heck of a lot of money on the project. Let me know as soon as you can if you'd make it or not. I can reschedule for a later time but the risk is they'll move without us sooner than later."

"I'll get back to you soon. Talk to you later."

Simone disconnects the call. Immediately she dials Sabrina. Watching the ocean waves crash against the shore, she waits for the rings. "I wonder what country she's in now."

"Hey Simone, funny you're calling. I was going to call you tonight. What's up?

"Hey, where are you?"

"We're in Paris. Its beautiful and we're enjoying every part of it."

"Oh, when are you heading back to the States?"

"We weren't planning to right away. We were thinking of heading to the coast of Spain for a romantic week and then do a shoot in Prague. Why do you ask? Are you planning to visit with us? We'd love having you two along."

"No, the offer is nice, but not this time. I'm calling about Aunt Marge's shelter and helping the homeless program."

"She started what? I thought we knew everything about her work. Where is this program and what is it?"

"It's back in our home town; she started the program over twenty years ago. It includes an old warehouse she transformed into a boarding house. She supported the program with funding and little assistance from contributors. She did it practically alone from what I understand."

"Is it in trouble or something?"

"Yes, it's in trouble and needs our help. There's a developer pushing the city government to execute a take over of the property. The powers to be want to develop a civic center and shopping mall in the location. The city thinks it will enhance interest for downtown. Fortunately for us, they haven't made much of an effort to purchase the building, however I heard from our lawyer, it's not come to

257

table yet. We have to be there when they present the need for eminent domain. When can you come back?"

"I guess if it's that important we can be back in a few days. I'll have to change a flight and coordinate with my agents. How long will it takes us to discuss this with the contractor?"

"Phil has a meeting schedule in a few days. I can coordinate with him to make sure we're present and influence an alternate solution. I'd hate for Aunt Marge's work to end."

"Yes, I'd hate for that to happen as well. I know she'd fight to help the homeless to the very end."

"Then plan on being home in two days. I'll meet you at the airport and we'll stay at a suite near downtown."

"Ok, Simone, we'll be there."

"Good. And tell James hello."

"You do the same with Stefan."

The girls disconnect the call on Sabrina's last comment. Immediately Simone heads back to her car after picking up her things from the beach sand. She stands and looks out into the beach for a last glance of the beauty it offers. "I'll be back in a few days" she tells the ocean and sand.  In her car, she pulls into traffic reversing the route taken from her home. Along the way and near the coffee shop, she searches for Stefan's car. With no car in sight, she heads directly home without stopping as earlier planned. Within minutes, she arrives at her home and immediately parks her car in the garage. There, she realizes Stefan returned home with a few guests. There are two additional cars in the driveway. When Simone entered the house, she notices the back sliding door is open and the butler has a tray of drinks in his hand. The butler is walking around the pool where there are five ladies and three men lounging and swimming. Stefan is in the pool near one lady, deep in conversation while the others are lounging in chairs. Simone steps through the doors and approach Stefan. "Hi darling" she says. Abruptly and surprised, Stefan turns away from his guest and responds.

"Hi, Simone, these are my guest from the coffee shop. Everyone say hello to my wife Simone."

"Hi Simone" they speak in unison.

"Hello everyone, are you enjoying yourselves?"

"Yes" responds one gentle man on the lounge chair. The others nod indicating affirmation.

Simone whispers "Stefan we need to talk."

"What now? Can't you see I'm entertaining?"

"Excuse me young lady, can you give us a moment?" Simone says to the woman next to Stefan.

"Sure" she replies as she moves away.

"Stefan, don't be an ass, I'm not complaining about your guest. This is business. We have to meet my lawyers back home. Sabrina and James will meet us there in two days. I'll tell you the rest after your guest leaves."

"I'd prefer not going and just enjoy my home. Your home isn't my home. My guest and I can have a wonderful two days while you're there."

"I'd not like to think as much. It's a serious reason to pull me back there. I wouldn't ask if it were something I can do alone."

"You can do this alone. Simone look around, you've accomplished all of this without me. I'm sure you can do whatever it is there without me."

"That isn't the point. We are in this together aren't we?"

"Yes, we're in this together, but whatever it is back there, you're in it alone. I'm not going." Stefan moves toward his guest and directs Simone away.

"You're an ass." Simone shouts.


Two days pass, Simone's plane lands as scheduled at the city's airport. Just as the plane doors open, she grabs her things and heads to pick up her luggage. She maneuvers throughout the airport and finds her limousine driver.

Picking up her luggage, she turns and looks for Sabrina. "Her flight is supposed to land the same time as mine. I wonder if she's late." Simone thinks.

"Hey" Sabrina shouts loudly.

"Hey Sabrina, how long have you been here?"

"Oh, a few minutes; long enough to get a cappuccino. And they're nothing like in the old country."

"Glad to see you. Where's James?"

"He decided not to come. You know, it's..."

"Business" Simone finishes the sentence. "Yes, Stefan said the exact same thing. So we're here alone without our guys. What a shame."

"Not in my eyes, its quality sister time and we'll take advantage." Sabrina smiles and moves towards the luggage.

"Is this all your luggage?" asked Sabrina while pointing at five suitcases.

"Yes, they are all mine. Where's yours?"

"It's on my arm. I've learned to travel light. I thought you'd travel light coming here too."

"You never know what you may need and who you'll run into."

"Yes, I guess. You never know. Do you have someone in mind?"

"No. Not really."

"Sure sister, not really" Sabrina giggles.

"Let's go driver." Simone directs to the driver and nods her head to Sabrina.

The girls walk to the waiting limousine, enter and leave the luggage for the driver to place in the trunk. The driver takes them to a luxury hotel downtown. Upon arriving to the hotel, bell hops jump to service as the limousine stops. Simone and Sabrina walks to the counter, "Reservations for Willingham" Simone says to the desk clerk. Immediately the manager arrives at the counter and interrupts the clerk. "Did I hear Willingham?"

"Yes you did" replied Sabrina.

"Welcome" he says with a smile. "We have the Star suite penthouse floor. The entire floor is at your disposal."

"That's great." Sabrina smiles in reply. "Yes, my flight was quite long and I'm ready to relax."

"As you wish" the manager says while he calls the bell hop. "Take the Willinghams to their room; the Star Suite."

"Please follow me" the bellhop directs.

The ladies immediately follow the bell hop to the elevators. The entourage shadows the ladies in a different elevator. Sabrina, Simone, and the bell hop arrive on the 27th floor and walk directly to the suite. "Ladies" the bell hop says while holding the door open. Simone and Sabrina enter and drop their coats. The bell hop directs the following entourage to place the luggage just inside the door of the suite. "Ms. Willingham, where would you like your luggage" asked the bellhop.

"Leave it there, we'll get it" replied Sabrina.

"Sure thing madam. And the key?"

"Oh, you can leave it on the table by the door."

"Thank you ladies." The bell hop leaves the room after following directions.

Sabrina moves outside of the second bedroom and retrieves her luggage. She rolls her bag into the room while looking around for the phone. She grabs the phone on the way to the bedroom and dials zero. "Front desk, connect me to a Paris, France Operator please." Waiting for the connection, she begins to complete the clothing distribution as if it's her new home. "Connect me to 8984747" Sabrina tells the operator. "Hello, James?"

"No, James is indisposed can I take a message?"

"Indisposed? Tell him Sabrina is on the phone."

"No, James is indisposed at the moment. I can take a message for him, if you'd like to leave one."

"Who are you?"

"I'm his secretary. Who are you and what's your business with him?"

"I'm his wife. Did you not know of his marriage to this beautiful model?"

"Excuse me, you're the third woman today saying you're his wife. Sorry, you'll have to call back when he's available. Or, as I've told the others, you can have him call you."

In a heated response, "You tell that ass to call his wife Sabrina! He has my number." Sabrina ends the call.

"What were you yelling about?" asked Simone

"Oh, some bimbo's playing a game with me about James. Same jealousy move to get my husband because he's a hot man."

"You have to fight the dogs too?"

"Yes, I'm afraid so. I never thought it would be so tiring but I love him and he's fun. I can't see myself living without him in my life."

"I never thought you'd go with him after his disregard for keeping in touch. He didn't talk to you for months on end. You surprised me. But you know, love is awesome and feels great when you have it?"

"We girls tend to forgive but not forget. He's mine anyway and it's going to stay that way for a long time."

"I feel the same about Stefan. He can be a pain in the rear, but he's one catch of a man."

"Aren't you going to call him?"

"No, I'll wait until he calls me. I don't have to check up on him."

"Check up on him? That didn't sound to comforting. Is he enjoying life too much without you?"

"Well, if you must know, he's living the life for sure. He hardly does anything with me except big events. Then he's on his own mostly. I can say one thing; he's a fantastic lover in bed. Without him, life is just a bore."

"You know it's nothing like we were years ago. My how we've changed; do you think is because of this money?"

"We haven't changed. We've evolved into living the quality life Aunt Marge spoke of before she died."

"Oh, you know, if Aunt Marge were alive, we'd have different men in our lives." Sabrina smirks.

"Yes" Simone sighs, "we would for sure. What ever happened to Lorenz the love of your life back then?"

"Last I heard, he went to South America to practice medicine. It was right after our break up. I didn't want the white picket fence type life or live the trapped doctor's wife role. I realized it after he was offered positions in Milwaukee, and Minot."

"You didn't want to live in those cities?"

"No, not at all, it would have been difficult to retain the business. So I offered to take him to Paris, or Madrid where he can put his training to use. There I can stay in the business. I thought it was a compromise."

"I guess he didn't want it."

"No, he actually said he'd love to go."

"Ok, you're confusing me. He said he'd go and then you two didn't go. Why?"

"He came to Paris right after my shoot. I got there first for a few days and ran into James. Before I knew it, James and I were waking together the next three days."

"Oh, you're bad."

"No, I'm good." The girls laughed. "James showed me the way to live again and not think too much of tomorrow. I am not the type to take on the pains of others. Lorenz is a man of people and I'm not quite dedicated to helping others."

"You've come to grips with yourself in that manner. Again, we are not Aunt Marge."

"No we aren't."

"And because of her, we're back in this town. You know why we're here?"

"Yes, I know. So what are we going to do?"

"At first I thought we'd let the city buy it and be done with it. But, the shelter is a good program and a great write off for the business organization."

"I think we should sell it and give the money to a different organization. We'd get the same write off wouldn't we?" asked Sabrina.

"No, not quite the same but close" replied Simone. "We'll talk more about it in the morning with the lawyer. Meanwhile let's go see some of the town. We can at least go down town."

"Why not, I'm all for it. I'm sure there's a nice restaurant around."

"Yes, I'm famished."

"Good, let's go."

# Chapter 16

## *Meeting Once Again*

Rodney enters the art store as if a magnet pulled him in. He immediately walks to another painting of embracing silhouettes reflected by moon light. Strolling around the multiple paintings, he stops at a picture in the park, reminding him of his first date with Simone. "Damn, I can't stop thinking about her for some reason. It's been months since I had her on my mind. If I don't control my thoughts of her, I'll never get her out of my mind or out of my heart." Moments past and still he finds himself pondering the painting.

Simone and Sabrina leave the restaurant and decide to stroll down the street. They whole-heartedly laugh at the traffic complainers. "Those poor guys fighting traffic and caught in the rat race. Aren't you glad we don't have to do that anymore?" asked Simone.

"Yes, and my goodness, its gotten worse over the years. At least we didn't have to sit in one spot for longer than a few minutes before moving a few feet. These cars haven't moved for the last three blocks," responded Sabrina.

"No, they haven't moved at all. I'm glad we decided to walk instead of using a cab."

"Good decision Simone."

"Hey, here's that old art store I use to visit to dodge traffic. Let's look around.'

"Ok, we might as well; it's like another 12 blocks back to the hotel."

"We can use the breather. Who's in a hurry anyway?"

"Not us." Sabrina replies giggling.

Simone and Sabrina walk through the art store and look at multiple paintings. Just shy of Rodney, Simone turns with her back to Rodney as she passes him. As usual these days, Simone hardly pays attention to others who are not in her direct view. Her attention is exact on her interest. "Hey" Sabrina whispers, "Isn't that Rodney you just passed?"

"Rodney who?" Simone replies.

"Oh, you've forgotten the man who fell for you after countless meetings?"

"Rodney. The same man who chased me for months and the man who supposedly saved Aunt Marge?"

"Supposedly actually happened and yes, one and the same Rodney."

Rodney heard his name whispered about. Not actually thinking it's about him, he moves on to the next isle of paintings. Looking intently at posters, he's certain of a voice amongst the two women. Immediately it dawns on him it's Sabrina. "No it can't be her. She doesn't live in the city anymore and it's not logical she'd return since her sister moved away as well." Without continued thought, Rodney placed focus back on the posters.

"Well aren't you going to talk to him?"

"Why should I talk to him? He was not the man for me and you know it."

"Who are you trying to fool? You fought your emotions for him like fighting a war of terror. I'm not saying you have to open a door to him, just say hello and catch up. Is that so hard to do?"

"If we ran into Lorenz, would you talk to him?"

"Without a doubt and intently so. Especially after my last phone call to James, I sometimes wonder if I made the right decision."

"Ok, if we pass him again, I'll break the ice."

"Pass by? You are a Willingham woman, beautiful, powerful, and smart. Why be nonchalant? Go be direct and impressive as you are. I'm sure he'll respond to just the sight of you. Just stop him and be silent; works every time."

"You sound like you're still in the game."

Sabrina laughs. "No, I'm not but I still have skills"

Rodney turns at the end of the isle as if he's heading towards the exit. Simone quickly maneuvers to intercept him without running and being so obvious. The rapid clip clap of her heels shatters the silence of the store. "Rodney" she calls. Rodney stops, turns, and look at the well dressed woman coming his direction. "Yes" he replies.

"Remember me, Simone Willingham." Simone says while reaching her right hand forward.

"How can I forget such a beautiful woman? Of course I remember you" Rodney says to her in return, and thinks to himself "It's the same woman I fight to forget."

"How nice seeing you."

"Is it really you Simone?"

"Of course it is. I think of you all the time."

"I wonder how you think of me these days."

"I've kept up with your career and you starting the firm. I'm waiting for you to take it public so I can purchase stock. You're such a good investment."

"Oh, really, I'm surprised you think of me in such a manner. How are you?"

"Oh, I'm quite happy and content. Life continually treats me well."

Sabrina walks up and nudges Simone. "Hi Rodney" she says.

"Hello Ms Sabrina, my dear friend and ally."

"Ally?" asked Simone

"Yes, ally" answered Rodney. "She was in my corner all the time. Too bad we didn't win."

"Oh, yes I remember; how nice of you two to team against me?"

"It was nothing of the sort. I thought Rodney was the best guy for you" replies Sabrina.

"And so did I." said Rodney "I'm still the best, but situations change."

"Are you married now?" asked Sabrina

"No, that situation hadn't changed. Still single, and focused on my firm. How about you? Are you married...ah either of you?"

"Yes, two years and counting" answered Simone.

"Well, as it seems now, I am."

"What's that suppose to mean?" asked Rodney.

"It means I'm married but mad at my husband at the moment." Sabrina smirks.

"Oh, I hope it turns around for you. I'm sure Lorenz would be happier when you're happy."

"I thought I told you my husband's name is James."

"Wow, I must not have paid attention or did I miss something. You aren't married to Lorenz?"

"No, not Lorenz, James; Lorenz is in South America working for a medical assistance non-profit organization. You know, help the children or something."

"My goodness, what happened to you two? If anyone had gotten together, I thought for sure it would have been you and Lorenz."

"Long story, but let's just say, my heart opened to a wonderful guy. One from my past and I love him dearly."

"Ok. So what's your story Simone? As cold as you were to me, what made you decide to get married?"

"Cold to you, nonsense; I wasn't ready. After aunt Marge died, the inheritance, and the game you played, I didn't think we were a good match."

"What about the date and the intense flirting between us. Was that my imagination or something real between the two of us?"

"Your imagination."

"No way, you were interested too. Don't pretend you weren't and I know it because I know you." Sabrina

268

comments. "As a matter of fact, he was in your mind long before Aunt Marge passed on. Why don't you admit it?"

"It's ok, water under the bridge. I'm glad you moved on."

"Actually, there are times when I think of you and what if I made the decision to get deeply involved. I still think of a time that could become a reality." Sabrina steps away and provides an avenue for them to search those emotions. "You go sis, and let him know you're still crazy about him" she thinks to herself.

"Simone, I think of you too. Much more than I care to admit, but reality sinks in from the pain you left me holding. I've never fought to have a woman accept me with open arms. I hadn't shown anyone as much nor fell for anyone as hard as I've done for you."

"I never asked you to Rodney. I never encouraged you to do those things for me. I expected the normal guy."

"I am a normal guy. I think you deserve royal treatment. A man should give you total affection and attention as you truly deserve. I thought for sure you'd accept honest and sincere love, since you deserve such and now I'd hope you're receiving the things you desire most in your life."

"I do, think you weren't so normal. As a matter of fact, you seemed to scare me with the attention and focus. I've never had anyone show me so much, nor pour their hearts out over the small time we interacted. Stefan does for me quite well and I know it's a challenge to get all the things from him, but he does well."

"Stefan is a lucky man. Where is he? Didn't he come along?"

"No, he's home. He had other things to do."

"Business must keep him pretty busy."

"No, he doesn't work per se; he has his own way of enjoying life."

"What does he do if he doesn't work?"

"Oh, he makes me happy."

"If his time was available to come, why didn't you bring him? Has he been here before?"

"No, he isn't interested in my history. Not much of a history buff."

"Has he met Sabrina?"

"Yes" answered Sabrina, as she walks back to their location in the Art store.

"You've met Stefan I assume."

"Well, yes and no. I've talked to him over the phone, but we've never met."

"Sounds like a hell of a guy. Well, Simone it seems I've taken up enough of your time. I hope you enjoy your visit. I should leave before I ask too many other questions"

"You shouldn't go on my part. You should go out for a drink with us."

"No thanks. One drink and I'll have to ask you to marry me."

"That wouldn't be so bad" answered Simone.

"Are you asking or are you trying to tell me something?"

"Neither, I'm realizing after seeing you again its time for change." Rodney moves closer to Simone, reaches out and embraces her as a long lost love. Holding her close he whispers "I'm still in love with you. I've never stopped loving you or given up on the dream of having you in my life. Many times I tried to release you. And many times my dreams of you grew stronger. You are my dream."

Simone, shocked at his whisper, she breaks the embrace, looks into his eyes and smiles. "I can't believe you. After all this time you come up with a line. As if you'd sweep me off into the blue. I can't believe you."

"What?"

"I can't believe you. You're trying the same old smooth act you present to every woman. Why can't you be who you are?"

"As if I'm not being who I am. Its crazy you're the only woman I reach out to and yet the one and only who holds my heart. How dare you accuse me of dealing with multiple women when you never gave me a chance?"

"I gave you a chance years ago. You had to be the good guy in everyone's eyes. Too bad you weren't the good guy in my eyes. It's too bad you didn't understand my needs or desires in a man."

"Now I'm a mind reader and I'm confused."

"Confused? How can you be confused as if I didn't show you and tell you over and over again?"

"Oh, you showed me interest, just like today; you tell me if this isn't confusing."

"You aren't paying attention to me. You never did."

"Pay attention. I nearly worshiped the ground you walked on and you don't think I paid attention." Rodney walks away from Simone. He has a beaded path for the store's exit. "You're a lunatic and this makes it easier to move on and heal from something so idiotic. I should have never opened my heart to you. Never!"

"Good bye foolish man."

"What the heck are you doing?" asked Sabrina.

Rodney leaves the building and walks to his car. "Damn it she does it again. I can't believe I empower her to hurt me. Such a selfish woman; she can kiss my...no need to get vulgar. Just let her insensitive and screwed outlook drive her to Stefan. Heck, I don't know why she's my heart anyway especially since there are so many available women in the world. I guess good guys finish last when it comes to the heart."

Sabrina sways her head from side to side in disgust. "You are confusing. I agree with Rodney. Honestly does Stefan show you anything Rodney has shown you over the years?"

"No, but he's not the type to do so."

"Then why do you put up with the disrespect and harsh treatment?"

"You wouldn't understand."

"I understand. Believe me, there are times I wish Lorenz was in my life. Take today for instance, I don't think Lorenz would have a woman answer the phone and ignore me as his wife. Oh, I understand."

"Probably so, but I need a challenge, with my guy. If he gives me everything, treats me with the utmost respect and admiration he's a weak man. I have no room or need for a weak man"

"Weak?, he's successful in many areas and a self made millionaire. And you call him weak. If anyone saw him as weak or unexciting, it would be me. Why on earth...? It doesn't matter."

"I understand you and your taste Sabrina, but you don't understand me. I have to have a challenge."

"I know you aren't going to like what I say, but Rodney is better for you than Stefan could ever be. Why are you pretending to believe differently?"

"Because Stefan is my challenge and I can change him over time."

"You've lost it sis and as bad as I'd like to say it, you're right. You have to have a challenge to keep you on your toes."

"There you go Sabrina. Now you understand my view of things. Good guys finish last in my book."

Printed in the United States
153514LV00001B/50/P